Treachery
in TERREBONNE PARISH

DOREY WHITTAKER

Treachery in Terrebonne Parish
A Mike Majors Mystery
Copyright © 2020 by Dorey Whittaker

Doreysbooks@Outlook.com
DoreyWhittakerbooks.com

Published 2020
KDP Publishing, Seattle, Washington

ISBN: 978-1-7351754-0-9
Kindle/Ebook ISBN: 978-1-7351754-1-6

Dedication

I N TODAY'S complicated world, everyone cries for justice, but few come alongside the weak and offer to help those who need it the most—those living on the lowest rung of the social ladder. This novel is dedicated to those few who have stepped up to the plate and dedicated their lives to help those who cannot pay for their services or who cannot enrich themselves by fame for having done so.

To all the Mike Majors of this world who believe in our system of justice, but see its flaws and work within the system to fix it. These humanitarians are not born, they are grown out of experience and developed out of their responses to those experiences. This story is dedicated to just such a man.

Acknowledgments

ALTHOUGH I have dedicated one or more of my other novels to several of these individuals, their value to my writing merits another acknowledgment. Writing is a lonely world comprised of hours upon hours of research, plot-line development, character backstories that will never reach the finished page, but those hours of development enrich the character's mannerisms, making these characters fully fleshed out as they arrive on the scene. Although this is solitary work, there are sparkling moments when a scene comes together so brilliantly you have to share it with someone before you dare continue. Having a few kind, patient, and faithful people who believe in your work is wonderful; however, having these people also be honest with you is priceless. This acknowledgment goes to my patient husband, Bruce, who has endured many a four-in-the-morning writing blitz because he understands that I must write when inspired. He has also endured repeated readings while I struggle to downsize a scene to only its essentials. Bruce is the person my readers can thank for being spared reading the endless rabbit trails that have been cut from this story.

I most gratefully thank my pre-publish reader society: Carol Temple, Fern Sutton, Mary Jo Mills, Ruthalee Wright, Mary Jane Murray, Nonie Stoecklein, and Jim Terpening. Thank you for all your patience, for faithfully reading each chapter and giving me your feedback. Thank you for loving my characters almost as much as I do.

And a grateful acknowledgment to Linda, my editor, for her creation of yet another beautiful cover and layout of the interior.

Table of Contents

Remembering How
It All Came About

TERREBONNE PARISH is the last place I would have chosen as my third do-over; but do-overs, especially ones as huge as mine, are seldom chosen; they seem to be divinely appointed. At least that is what my Tilly used to say. But before I tell you about Terrebonne Parish, I guess you need to know a little about me so you can appreciate exactly how huge my "do-overs" really were.

My name is Mike Majors, and I am a sixty-two-year-old man who feels it is more important to tell you that I am recently widowed rather than brag that I am a retired, decorated, thirty-year veteran detective of the Miami Police Department. Why is it more important to me? Because my thirty-nine years with my sweet Tilly made me a better man than any award I was ever given. I had not felt the need to call a "do-over" for many years, but this story I'm about to share required three of the biggest "do-overs" of my life, and they all happened to me because of my Tilly. And since I am between cases right now, I decided I had better write down the full particulars before important details escape my memory. As I write this story, I decided to make it a fictional novel—not because it is a work of fiction, but because I always listen to those who are smarter and more educated than I am. My brilliant lawyer, Char, suggested that I write this book as a work of fiction, so I am not sued for using names and telling the truth as I see it. There is the truth, and there is what you can prove in a court of law. The real truth does not make what you cannot prove untrue—just not verifiable. I will leave that battle to the lawyers of the world and instead write what I know to be true.

The year is now 2020, and I am taking advantage of the nationwide shutdown to write this story because people like my Tilly, Char, Jewel, Mike and Clara Brown, Dwight, and Dr. Harvey deserve to have the unvarnished truth told. I have four cases on hold because of the Covid-19 pandemic, so rather than get frustrated at my inability to pursue their cases, I decided to share how I happened into this line of work. But to appreciate my journey getting to this point, I need to start at the beginning.

To give you some background, I was the third son of Douglas and Virginia Majors of Pittsburgh, Pennsylvania, born just two years after he returned from WWII. My middle brother was born nine months after his return, and I came eleven months later.

If you grew up in the nineteen-forties or fifties and you were fortunate enough to have been born a boy, you probably played neighborhood sports without adult supervision, so you likely know all about "do-overs." Do-overs had specific unwritten rules, and no one went over them before starting a street game because everyone knew what they were. Calling a do-over was admitting you had failed to do your best. You are not challenging someone else for having failed you—you acknowledge you could have done better and are asking for another chance. In my neighborhood, Chuck Gooseman was the only one who was never allowed to call a do-over because Chuck was the best player at everything. Do-overs were how we tried to even the playing field. They were our way of extending grace to the younger boys so they would willingly fill the outfield positions in order to field a whole squad. No one made fun when someone called a do-over, but at the same time, none of the younger boys took advantage of our generosity. Looking back, I think those days with my pals was the purest form of camaraderie, blending mercy with mockery. Peer pressure was needed to help the momma's boys from falling into tears when they struck out, or when they scraped the skin off the palm of their hands as they tried to slide into base on the hot Pittsburg asphalt.

Thomas "Tooie" Moran had the hardest time holding back the tears when he got hurt. He was the smallest member of our team and had an overly protective mother. Tooie's dad had come back from the war a broken man and had left the family when Tooie was a baby. He walked like he had two left feet and wore glasses, but Tooie was the last person ever to call a do-over; he was just happy to be part of the team. His intrepid spirit impressed all of us.

I think our camaraderie developed out of a real need for fairness. Most of us boys never got a do-over at home. Most of our dads had gone to war right out of high school. The ones who made it back joined the steel mills and took no guff from anyone—especially their own boys. While most of the country was experiencing the booming '50s, Pittsburgh steelworkers were struggling to keep a roof over their heads and food on the table. We all knew our dads were unhappy, and most of us took our turn showing up a few times with a nasty bruise or a black eye because our dads came home in a bad mood and took out their displeasure on us. We all knew that no one would ask what happened because we knew what had happened. We gave each other permission to ignore the obvious, and while we played street ball, everything was normal. We never spoke about important matters, but I am relatively sure that I was not the only one who grew up in a house devoid of do-overs.

My father worked in the steel mills, and my mother was a part-time Avon Lady when she wasn't busy keeping house, cooking three meals a day, and trying to keep my two older brothers and me out of trouble. But Mother's biggest job was playing interference for us boys when Dad came home in a foul temper, which was most of the time. Dad was what you would call "old school." He believed his job was to be the provider, and he took that job very seriously. My dad was a hard worker in a hard industry, and he resented the fact that my mother needed to be an Avon Lady in order to keep us boys in shoes, let alone all the extras three growing boys required.

Like most of the dads in my neighborhood, my dad had been drafted into the Army right after high school. Pearl Harbor had happened during Dad's senior year, and three boys from our neighborhood had died that Sunday morning. Except for the brilliant valedictorian of his class and two boys who had had polio, all the other boys of his class knew they would be going to war. Two days after graduation, Dad married his high school sweetheart because he knew his notice was coming very soon, and when it came, he left his bride expecting their first child. Dad didn't even meet my brother, Doug, until he was three years old. Dad came home at the end of the war and went right into the steel mill because that was what he was supposed to do. He never talked about the war, and he never looked for better jobs. He and my mother had two more babies practically back to back, and life went on. We knew he loved us, but he hated his life, and sometimes his violent temper got the best of him. This was the norm in our neighborhood.

But as much as the fathers on Maple Avenue hated their lives, on every March 21, June 7, September 16, and December 7, all of our dads disappeared for the afternoon and came home hammered those nights. We never discussed the reasons why, but we all knew they had spent an hour standing at their classmate's grave in silence before going to their favorite bar. There they pretended to be seventeen again and began a night of drinking to chase away the demons that refused to leave. I'm not sure how old I was when I finally knew what was going on or who had told me, but every boy in my neighborhood knew not to mess up on those days or the days before or after, for fear of all those demons being unleashed on one of us.

Whenever Mother would buy us new shoes from her earnings, she would say, "Go out back and scuff them up a bit, so they won't look so new." It wasn't that Dad didn't want us to have new shoes; it was the fact that no matter how hard he worked at a job he hated; he simply could not make enough money to keep his boys in shoes. Seeing us wearing a new pair of shoes would become a lightning rod for one of his tirades.

My oldest brother, Doug, being five and six years our senior, followed Dad into the steel mill right out of high school. He got married, started a family, and mirrored our father in every way. My brother, Charlie, and I were determined to live a different life. Charlie graduated in 1964, and in those days, the sons of steelworkers didn't consider college an option—at least not in our dad's house. Without a college deferment, Charlie knew he had to do something if he wanted to avoid Vietnam. I knew that Charlie was not built for war, but who is? All that summer Charlie spent waiting for his draft notice to arrive, but I cannot ever remember having a conversation with my brother about how he felt. You just didn't go there in our family.

I began my senior year in high school rather oblivious to anyone else. I was elected class president and was excited to share this news with my family when the floor of our world fell out from under us. I had gone upstairs to change out of my school clothes, and on my bed, I found a note Charlie had written to the family. The note started,

By the time you read this, I will be safely over the border into Canada. I received my draft notice last week and knew if I didn't want to spend Christmas in a rice paddy with a gun in my hand, I needed to get into Canada before any of you knew what I was doing.

Charlie wasn't the only draft dodger heading for Canada, but he was the first and the last of my dad's boys who would dare do such a disgraceful act. I knew that Charlie's actions had just sealed my fate, and my dad would make sure of that. My mother was both heartbroken and happy—heartbroken because she knew Charlie would have to stay in Canada for many years if not forever. She also knew that my dad would never agree to go visit his cowardly son. Per my father's orders, Charlie was now dead to us, but knowing that Charlie would be safe brought Mother great comfort. On the other hand, her youngest son would not be so fortunate. The day I turned eighteen, my father walked me into the recruiting office downtown and said, "You are not waiting to be drafted, boy. You will volunteer for service."

A few short months later I was in Da Nang, seeing things that change who you are. Serving my country helped me better understand my dad, although that understanding did not improve our relationship. However, having some grasp of what he had experienced solidified my resolve not to be like him. I clearly remember the day I was standing in the middle of Da Nang, when I resolved that if I survived Vietnam, I would live a different kind of life. I had joined the Marines in June of 1965 and was released from duty in June of 1969.

I was not home two days before I knew I needed to make some huge changes in my life. The steel mills were not for me. My high-school sweetheart had faithfully waited for me, and I did not want one more day to pass without making her my bride. Having both grown up in Pittsburgh and because City Hall had suspended the three-day waiting period for wartime marriages, I picked up Matilda at exactly nine o'clock, and we headed to City Hall, applied for our marriage certificate, went down to the lab for our blood tests, and waited the required six hours for the lab results. While we waited, we bought a local paper and checked out the want ads and the available rentals. The summer of '69 was hard on everyone. The general mood was depressing, the economy was struggling, the attitudes toward returning vets was quite negative, and Tilly and I had no idea what we wanted to do with our lives. We had no positive direction, only a long list of what we did not want. After six hours of studying the want ads, we decided that the biggest thing we did not want was to continue living in Pittsburgh.

At four o'clock, we stood before a judge whose name I cannot even remember, and I took the first truly important step of my whole life—I made Tilly my wife. Only her older brother, Joseph, was there with us. Tilly's mother, recently widowed, dared not ask for time off even to attend her daughter's wedding. I used some of my muster pay to treat my new wife to a three-day honeymoon in the Catskills of southeastern New York. On the second evening there, we were joined at the table by a young couple from Miami, Florida, who were visiting his parents for their annual family vacation. They were a good ten years our senior, and he was doing well. By the end of that evening, Tilly and I had decided we were moving to Miami. We did not know what we would do there, but at least we had a destination that did not include Pittsburgh or my parents.

Tilly and I packed and headed to Florida in the summer of '69. I had simply seen too much in Vietnam to return home and pick up my old life. I needed some distance from my overly opinionated parents. I wanted a new life—one that Tilly and I could create without outside pressures. Thanks to Tilly's influence, I never got into drugs or alcohol—a downfall for many a vet.

We settled into our first apartment in Miami in July of '69. Tilly and I had moved south without any idea of what I wanted to do with my life until I saw *In the Heat of the Night,* a movie that had been out for several years, but I had not seen it until the local theater booked it for a second showing. I went to the theater three nights in a row. "They call me Mr. Tibbs," rang in my ears for days. I had been reared to think like Police Chief Bill Gillespie, but Vietnam had changed me. I had been surrounded by black soldiers who soon became my friends. Color disappears when your life is on the line, and they are watching your back. I came home a different person from the boy who had left. Some good, some bad.

In the movie, African American Philadelphia police detective Virgil Tibbs (played by Sidney Poitier) was arrested on suspicion of murder by Bill Gillespie (played by Rod Steiger), the racist police chief of tiny Sparta, Mississippi. After Tibbs proved not only his own innocence but that of another man, he joined forces with Gillespie to track down the real killer. Their investigation took them through every social strata of the town with Tibbs making enemies as well as unlikely friends as he searched for the truth.

I was hooked! I knew I wanted to track down killers and be a Virgil Tibbs, so I used my GI bill to enroll in night school. While I worked all day to support my family and attended college every night to earn my degree, Tilly kept busy on the home front rearing our two boys with little help and guidance from me. I graduated, secured my dream job, and the long hours away from home continued.

I rationalized the long hours were so I could be a good provider, and in the era in which I was reared, being a good provider was the measure of a man. Tilly made sure my boys respected me; they just didn't know me. In my era, I had also been reared to believe that respect was love. Boy, was I wrong! But to understand exactly how wrong I was, I should tell you a little about me so you can understand why so many men who grew up in the 1950s still struggle with this attitude.

I grew up being taught that "real men don't cry," and they definitely don't share their feelings. We were expected to find something we were good at doing and do that something day in and day out for the rest of our lives. Back then, there was never talk about self-fulfillment; the instruction was simply, "Go out and find a job, boy! Pay the bills and be the father."

I had been the third son of a World War II veteran, and try as I might, I cannot recall ever hearing a story about my father's war experience. My singular memory involves a John Wayne movie, *The Sands of Iwo Jima* that aired in 1961. My dad was what was called a "working stiff" in the steel mills of Pennsylvania where I was reared, and back then, we never went to the movie theaters. My dad was a huge John Wayne fan, and the big events for our family revolved around Wayne's movies reaching the small screen. I was fourteen years old in 1961 when our family gathered for an early dinner so we could relax in our living room and watch the first Sunday night run of The Sands of Iwo Jima. Even on our black-and-white television, Dad could hardly wait to watch that John Wayne movie.

Being a steelworker, my father had hands like a vise. I grew up thinking he could bend steel with his bare hands, but that night while watching that movie, I saw my dad cry for the very first time. He hadn't cried when his mother died or when my older brother was killed in a freak car crash because "big, strong men don't cry," right? I'd like to find the idiot who started that lie and teach him a thing or two...but I digress. That night I caught a glimpse into my father's private hell as he watched that movie. My mother must have understood my dad's pain because even though it was a hot August night in PA, she was sitting right next to Dad on the sofa, clutching his hand tightly.

I remember feeling embarrassed—not that my father was crying, but that I was witnessing a moment so personal and private between my parents. I remember thinking that incident felt even more intimate than the night I accidentally walked in on them making love. I was fourteen and had no idea what my dad had experienced during the war, and I knew he would never tell me—not even five years later when I was sent to Vietnam. *Why are men so afraid to talk about it?*

Even after I returned home, my dad and I never had an honest talk about our mutual experiences. My conclusion was that if men are not supposed to cry, then stay far away from topics that require the shedding of a few tears. So, what did I do after Vietnam? I did the same thing my dad did. I went out, got a job, took care of my family, and kept everything bottled up and private; I just refused to do that in Pittsburgh—anywhere near my father.

2

A Pup Learns His Lesson

F OR BETTER or worse, I chose a career that was well-suited by this compartmentalized thinking. A good detective cannot become emotional over the gruesome scene of a young girl's life ending in such horror. "Address the evidence rather than the victim and walk around the blood-spattered room to study the pattern of the spray rather than focusing on the fact that the lives of some parents somewhere will be forever altered" became my mantra. My job was to find the person who would wantonly take another's life. My job was to collect enough evidence to put this person away for life, so another child would not have to experience this same horror. But in order to perform my mantra workday after workday, I had to master two irrefutable rules:

▶ Manage your emotions.

▶ Never bring it home with you.

Every *pup* had to learn and apply these first two rules. *Pups* were what we called first season homicide detectives. Every one of us had

---

been a pup, and we knew the importance of these two rules, and the lessons that fed into them had resulted in the longevity of our career. We all understood the initiative and drive of young pups—their eagerness to show off their stuff and to prove themselves as tough, ready and capable. We also understood the uniqueness of our chosen career, and pups who did not follow these rules did not survive.

I was a pup back in 1976. At twenty-nine years of age, I had survived Vietnam, had a wife and two children, had completed college, and felt like I knew everything. I was like every other pup, but I was fortunate enough to have a patient mentor by the name of Charlie Spamoda, who was nearing retirement. I realized that Charlie knew his business, but being a pup, some lessons begged to be experienced, and my patient mentor knew when to quit instructing, to step back and to let the lesson itself do the teaching.

I had been on the team for about three months and was feeling quite full of myself. You know the feeling, right? We had solved several *clean kills,* and I was beginning to strut around as only a pup can do. One afternoon a call came in around three with the code word *Vicks!* I had been told what that particular code word meant, but a strutting pup seldom believes these warnings are meant for him.

In Miami, *Vicks* is code for "a bloody mess"—a *smelly,* bloody mess. Civilians and pups have no idea what a bloody mess smells like; no words are adequate enough to describe it, so Charlie was going to let me experience the smell. Charlie had me drive to the site, and we pulled up to the aqua-green house with yellow crime-scene tape stretched everywhere. Before getting out of the car, Charlie opened the glove box, pulled out his cobalt-blue jar of Vicks, scooped out a fairly large amount and packed both of his nostrils before offering me the jar.

Seeing the slimy mess on Charlie's face, I passed—as every foolish pup does the first time.

I strutted up to the officer manning the front door as if I were in charge and asked, "So what do we have in there, officer?"

My second clue should have been the fact that this seasoned officer did not return my gaze; instead, he kept his eyes averted as he handed me blue booties and replied, "The body is in the back bedroom on the right. M.E. is already there. He wants everyone to wear booties."

My arrogance continued as I slipped on the booties and headed to the back. Like I said, nothing prepares you for the smell. I was not in the room for more than thirty seconds before the open-faced roast-beef sandwich I'd savored for lunch started turning over in my stomach. A sudden dump of stomach acids began to mix with the rich, flavorful cup of Colombian coffee I had enjoyed with the sandwich, and I felt like a nuclear bomb was exploding inside of me. For one or two minutes I pretended I was fine as I pulled out my notepad and tried to focus on the crime scene.

This is definitely not a clean kill. I had been warned never to personalize the victim, but this poor child—this baby girl—appeared no older than my own Joseph, and she had been eviscerated. Even with my limited exposure, I could tell that some of the work had been done pre-mortem, and my stomach began to flutter. I had been taught that becoming emotionally invested in the actual crime scene was deadly to an investigation but doing that and staying human was beyond my understanding.

My head began to swirl as I imagined the horrors this poor child had endured before death had mercifully ended her pain. They say animals can smell fear...*is that what I am smelling?* Intellectually, I knew to expect a certain raw odor from massive blood loss, but this stomach-turning foulness was worse than anything I could have imagined. *Am I smelling the residue of this child's fear? Did some sick sadistic psychopath actually enjoy creating this smell?*

I knew I was breaking all the rules, but I felt powerless to stop the ramblings of my mind. *I never want to become so cold-hearted and unfeeling that I can walk around a scene like this and simply do my job; it would make me just as sick as the unsub who did this.* Without any warning, "Mount Vesuvius" began to erupt.

Charlie wisely made sure he was not standing between me and the exit. As I flew past him, he just handed me a barf bag and smiled. I did not quite make it all the way outside before losing everything. I tried to keep the contents of my stomach in the barf bag so I would not contaminate the crime scene, but when you feel like you have emptied everything you have ever eaten and still wish you could empty more and it would not be enough, you have learned your lesson. *Never again will I turn down the offer of Vicks!*

As I sheepishly walked back inside, Charlie handed me his bottle of Vicks, which I gratefully accepted. Then he directed me toward my next lesson. "Mike, I need you to focus on the evidence, blood spatter, position of the body—anything that might give us a clue about who did this and when."

I felt paralyzed and asked, "How old is she?"

Now we did need to know this as well as who she was in order to locate her parents, but Charlie knew my question was evidence that I had done what most pups do: I had fixated on the girl—not on the murder scene.

"Mike," Charlie bellowed with considerably little patience, "I need your eyes to be focused here. You cannot help this girl, but you can help her family by taking control of your thoughts and emotions. If you can't do that, then you need to think about another profession."

I learned that in order to do this job, you must compartmentalize your emotions. You must learn to control the urge to toss your cookies or you will find yourself transferred to another department. Pups are allowed one such outburst and then you either learn to push that churning mass of liquid in your stomach so far down that it can't possibly make its way back up or you are gone. Every seasoned homicide detective knows from experience that you have about two hours before that acid-filled lump you pushed down hits your large intestine and a toilet better be close by. This is probably why so many detectives suffer with intestinal issues.

Violating the second most important rule: ***don't take your work home with you*** has been the cause of many a divorce among detectives. Our job forces us to become immersed in the vilest actions one human can perpetrate on another. A detective's first few cases might involve *clean kills*, leaving him feeling empowered and exhilarated. After all, this sense of winning was why you joined the force, so you talk non-stop about every little detail, and your patient wife is a good sounding board. But then you get your first "Vicks" code, and as a pup, you don't know where to file this experience. You have never had to compartmentalize something this huge, and you NEED to talk it out. As a pup, you think you know your wife better than the old stiffs at the office, so you ignore Rule #2.

Just like it felt good to throw up that nuclear waste, spewing all the goriest details also gives you a little relief—until you see that look of absolute horror on your wife's face and know you put it there out of pure selfishness. You now know you have just contaminated your safe haven.

I quickly learned there are good reasons for rules, and unless I wanted to sit behind a desk for the rest of my career, I knew I needed to find a healthy way to compartmentalize my feelings. I needed a soft place to land that was untainted by my work, and my wife Tilly provided just such a place. Tilly gently softened my cold, hard edges. I tended to feel comfortable living in my black-and-white world, but she knew my world was not healthy for me. Tilly was constantly reminding me that not everything is as easy as black and white and that motive and intent were also important—especially when it came to our two sons.

Day in and day out I was forced to work with the consequences of people's bad behavior; therefore, I had a difficult time separating what I had seen from the foolish exploits of my young sons. I felt my job was to warn them of the consequences of such foolishness, and honestly, the more gruesome the case I was currently tackling, the harsher my reaction became to my boys' unwise behavior. I could not see this harshness in myself at the time, but my Tilly understood and tried to soften my approach. But more often than not, she simply had to go behind me and clean up the emotional chaos my words had inflicted upon my sons. My poor boys paid dearly for the sins of others. So, I guess I was not as good at compartmentalizing details as I had once thought I was.

Thankfully, Tilly did get through to me before it was too late. Thanks to her, I did learn how to communicate honestly with my boys. Doing so went against everything I had ever been taught, and I'll be honest, I was a little scared, but I learned that talking about how our feelings do affect every aspect of our lives does not make us a sissy or a "girly girl"—my father's words, not mine. My dad had already died before I became enlightened, but I wish I could have had just one evening with him to talk honestly and openly about what he saw and did during his war, and sharing what I have carried with me since Vietnam. I cannot imagine how much that discussion would have brought us closer together. I imagine most men who grew up in the 1950s have profoundly similar feelings.

Because of my Tilly, I have been able to enjoy a good relationship with my boys, but only because of what happened on a hot summer day in 1980. I had caught a case late the day before and had worked it all night long, chasing leads while they were still warm. As I drove down Waterfront Avenue, heading home for a few hours of shuteye, I reflected on the difference between my life and my father's—a comparison I frequently made on my drive home. I loved my job; he hated his. Even when exhausted from the long hours, I felt elated; he felt trapped. When I closed a case, I felt satisfied, complete, and vindicated; he always felt used, unappreciated, and unfulfilled. Although frequently pre-occupied and distant from my family, I prided myself on not being the violent and sullen child-beater my dad had been. Waiting for the light to change, it dawned on me that my criteria for being a good parent had an extremely low threshold, but as long as I was better than my old man, I was pretty good.

Before really taking a measurement of how very low my threshold was, I said to myself, "At least my boys do not fear me walking in the front door." In fact, I repeated it twice as I stared off into the bright blue sky. I adjusted my rearview mirror and studied my face—the face my eight- and ten-year-old boys saw coming in the front door…but before I could draw any conclusions, horns started blazing, and I realized the light had changed. Two blocks later I turned the corner and parked my car in the usual space, but I did not get out of my car right away.

Being ten in the morning on a hot Miami summer day, I hit the universal down button on my door panel to lower all four windows and rested my head against the headrest. "So," I said to myself, "you are better than your old man? Big deal! Hardly something worth bragging about." I studied my reflection in the mirror for a moment and asked myself a much harder question, "In what ways are you still like him?" Now that was a much more difficult question to answer. Neither of us talk about our feelings. Neither of us know how to give praise without constructive criticism. Dad was a glass half-empty kind of guy… Now that I think about it, he was the glass is always-empty kind of guy; whereas I am a glass-half-empty guy. I always blame this attitude on the job of seeing the worst of humanity every day, but I realize this is what my boys see walking in their front door every day.

My mother had spent her whole life playing interference for her boys, and now my Tilly was doing the same; so, if I didn't want to have my boys look at me the way I looked at my dad, things had to change. *I have to change, but how?*

That's where my Tilly and her faith came in. You notice I didn't say her religion. I wasn't interested in religion; that much my dad and I agreed upon. But Tilly had faith—not religion. She talked with her God, not at Him. She asked Him questions, fully expecting Him to show her the answers. My Tilly was never afraid of her God, and that relationship always puzzled me…and intrigued me.

I finally stepped out of my car and headed to my front door, resolved to make a change in my life, but I quickly found old habits are hard to break. I inserted my key in the door lock, determined to start a conversation with my boys; however, as soon as I walked through that door, my routine kicked in. I walked straight over to my wall safe, removed my gun from my holster, pulled my badge out of my inside coat pocket, put them in their usual place, closed and spun the cylinder. Just that fast I was back into my routine. I shouted an empty hello at my boys, who were deep into some summer cartoons, so I let them be. *After all,* I thought, *they are not interested in anything I might have to say.*

I headed to the kitchen, knowing Tilly was busy fixing me a good breakfast that would not sit too heavy on my stomach while I caught a few hours of sleep. No heavy conversations after an all-nighter, just a peck on the cheek, a quick bite, then off with the sweat-soaked suit, and off to dreamland—if I was lucky.

A few hours later I awakened reenergized. Freshly showered, I joined my family in the living room, having forgotten all about my resolve to make a change. I looked at my two boys and realized I knew so little about them. Oh, I knew their ages, their grades in school, and the fact that they both learned how to swim last year, but only because I had paid for the lessons. I also knew they were planning to go to church summer camp in a few weeks because, again, I had written the check.

I stepped out onto our deck and sat in the shade, wearing my favorite salmon-colored OP shorts, a tank top, and flip-flops—the casual Florida attire I could muster when off duty. Hearing my boys giggling over dumb Bullwinkle J. Moose cartoons began to drive me crazy. First, the cartoons are stupid, and secondly, they have seen them dozens of times. Just as I am about ready to go inside and shut off the TV, my mind flashes back to the time I was watching *Spin and Marty*. I clearly remember how my dad stalked into the room, shut it off, and angrily ordered me out of the house.

Instead, I sat back in my seat and listened to my boys giggling and smiled, as I chided myself for my attitude. *Mike, it doesn't matter that your boys are laughing at a silly cartoon. Your boys are happy, and you should go in there and watch it with them—laugh with them. But you already know the minute you walk in there, they will stop laughing. Your boys don't laugh around you.*

I turn my head away from the patio door and stare out over the water, thinking, *I'm too late!* I wanted to know my boys, and I wanted my boys to know me, but how you do it when you've mishandled them for ten years? *I have no clue...*

Tilly came outside to join me. She brought two tall frosted glasses of sweet tea. She knew better than to ask about the current case, we had both learned that lesson. Instead, she stared off into the wild blue yonder, probably praying for me and my soul as she usually did. I did appreciate her prayers, but I wasn't that far gone. Out of nowhere she reflectively began, "Mike, Joseph wanted me to ask if you would be willing to come to church this coming Sunday? He is getting baptized, and more than anything, he would like you to be there—if you could clear your schedule."

"Why didn't he ask me himself, Tilly?" I asked even though I already knew exactly why. My son knew that I would use my current workload as my excuse, but we all knew my real reason was I didn't like church.

Tilly smiled at me. "Your being there would mean the world to him, Mike."

I started to make my usual excuses when a thought hit me. "Tilly, why is being baptized so important to him and that I be there? He is only ten years old. Is Joseph really old enough to understand the significance of baptism?"

Tilly gave me such a strange look—not hostile or cynical, but rather pleading. Then she inquired, "Do you, Michael?"

Tilly smiled, and I thought, *someday I will put that on her headstone: "Tilly Smiled."* Again, that smile was not hostile nor cynical nor condemning or even judgmental—just loving.

I turned toward her and asked, "Do I *what*, Tilly? Forgive me, I'm still quite tired from my all-nighter."

"Michael, do *you* understand the significance of Joseph's decision to get baptized? Do you know what it means to him or what he believes it means? Rather than me telling you, why don't you ask him and hear it directly from him?"

Suddenly I had this vision of going to bed every night of my last summer with my brother Charlie and never asking him how he felt about anything important. I thought about how little I knew about what made my father into the raging bully he became because none of us talked. And suddenly, I realized how little my boys knew about me and how little I knew about them, and I desperately wanted this vicious cycle to stop. Not being willing or able to talk about important matters was what had most damaged us.

Tilly, bless her heart, saw me struggling with emotion and said, "You don't know how, do you, Mike? If you can't interrogate and take notes, you don't know how to simply ask questions, not even of your boys." I remained silent. Tilly had pinpointed my pain, my family curse, my biggest shortcoming, and I had no answer for her. Suddenly, my beautiful Tilly asked, "Michael, why don't you ask for a do-over?"

I had not heard that term used in years. "A do-over? Do you mean with my boys?"

"Sure, Mike, why not? Calling a do-over simply means you recognize that you didn't do the best you could have, and you want a second chance to do it better, right? Every boy understands what calling a do-over means. Michael, what would it have meant to you if your father had been humble enough to ask for a do-over?"

I stood up, leaned over to kiss the smartest woman in the world, and went to talk to my boys before I had time to argue myself out of it. That day I asked my two boys for a do-over—the most important do-over of my life. I told them both about my dad and my brother Charlie and how no one in my family ever talked, not really talked, and how I wanted to learn how to talk with them. I told them I wanted to get to know them, and I wanted to learn how to share anything and everything with them.

Eight-year-old Benjamin was the first to respond. He flew into my arms and kissed me on the cheek, and as I looked over at ten-year-old Joseph's looking at me with his mother's smile, I knew we were going to be all right. I had not waited too long. I had grown up in a house devoid of do-overs, but thanks to my Tilly, that day I humbled myself and I gave my boys a home that would now be built on the principle of do-overs—for all of us.

One big do-over, for me anyway, was attending church with my family. With Tilly's help, I learned not to blame God for all the evils of this world, and over the years, her faith became my faith. I would never have done so simply to please her, but when you see true and honest faith lived in front of you, it is hard to deny it's reality.

3

Another Big Do-Over

IF YOU think my story is full of romance, let me set you straight. One year before starting my latest do-over in Terrebonne Parish, I buried my beloved wife, Tilly. That year was terrible. I had never felt so lost and alone in all of my life, and I have missed her every day since. We enjoyed thirty-seven wonderful years together, and I am not interested in settling for second best at this stage of the game. Tilly was an amazing woman who understood my work as a homicide detective was also my passion, and she never minded. Most, if not all, of my colleagues over those thirty-plus years either divorced or simply dreaded going home. Our work was a hard taskmaster that demanded our full attention—both on and off the job. My Tilly got it when many a detective's wife did not.

I was eighteen months away from mandatory retirement in Miami, dreading the thought of it when Tilly began having seizures. After a battery of tests, we were told she had a fast-growing inoperable brain tumor that was causing the seizures, and best-case scenario, she would succumb to it within a year. I remember sitting across the desk from that doctor as that word *succumb* came across his lips. In my mind I screamed, *"Do you really think using that word succumb makes your declaration any easier to hear?"* Instead, I squeezed Tilly's hand even harder than I had been during the last three weeks of tests. That very afternoon I turned in my papers for early retirement. Without a flicker of guilt, I handed over all of my notes on the earth-shattering case I had been working on for almost a month. While sitting in that doctor's office, my priorities had shifted. My *important* job now was to take care of my Tilly. We were given two days shy of eleven months. It is amazing how every day becomes magnified when you know they are numbered!

Tilly and I said everything we needed to say to each other during those precious months. She wanted to make sure I would be okay after she was gone, but that was impossible. Thanks to some of my do-overs, I not only understood Tilly's faith, I had embraced it as my own, so we both knew this was not goodbye forever. I knew where she was going. Although I ached beyond understanding, I was thankful and not without hope.

After she was gone, I kept myself busy making sure our sons received the keepsakes Tilly had assigned to them. I spent some time with the grandkids, but they all had their own busy lives, and I think my presence simply continued to remind my sons that their mother was gone. I knew my boys loved me, but I realized that my sons needed to deal with their loss differently than I did. They had lost their mother, but I had lost my whole world, and they could not be expected to fill it for me.

Knowing what I did, I headed back to Miami and tried to learn how to live with this gaping hole in my life. I hated the normal pastimes most men enjoyed—like fishing and golf. I hated getting up every morning with nothing to do but watch the clock tick off the long, lonely hours of same old, same old. You spend your youth preparing for your life's work. Then you spend your adult life honing your skills, garnering praise and prestige for being on top of your game. Your work becomes who you are; and one day it is all over, and you don't know what to do with yourself.

Once my Tilly was gone, many a day I asked God, "Why Tilly and not me? Why was I the one left behind? Tilly would have handled this loneliness so much better than me." I wasted the next seven months asking God why before I realized I had better start making something positive of this new normal I had. Tilly would not have wasted so much time feeling sorry for herself.

Dutifully and simply because I knew Tilly would want me to, I turned on my computer and began drafting my resume. Only then did I realize that my eighteen months before my forced retirement had come and gone, and I hadn't even noticed. Once upon a time, that date had been so important to me, but that night it was just another date. I was tempted to shut down my computer and forget about applying for another job. I would be expected to enumerate all of my wonderful accomplishments, brag about awards, continued education, etc., etc. The truth was, all of those accomplishments pale in comparison to the eleven months I had spent caring for my Tilly. Those months represented the most selfless time of my life, and I never wanted to go back to being that other person.

I took a break, grabbed a cup of coffee, and sat on my deck, pondering my situation. Tilly had always said, "Mike, it's not the number of cases you solve; it's the number of lives you touch that matters." To my shame, I never really understood what she meant. I had always answered her with "Every case I solve changes lives. The perpetrator goes to jail; the victim's family gets closure." Even though my answer was true, I leaned back in my Adirondack chair and asked God a second question: "God, if You understand what Tilly was talking about, could You show me what it means?"

That question barely crossed my lips before my mind switched to another topic. At my age, even with my stellar background, no big-city agencies would give me the time of day. But somewhere there had to be a struggling department in need of my skills. I was financially solvent and didn't need a big-city income; I just needed to work. Then another thought crossed my mind: "Maybe someone out there needs me to be his or her mentor, but how do I find that person?"

Sitting there watching the birds flying around, I remembered something else Tilly used to say: "If you ask God for guidance, don't be surprised when He opens a door." I wasn't sure about what was going on, but all of a sudden, I felt excited to head back to my computer.

I sent out a total of one hundred and two applications, without receiving a single response. Now that kind of rejection is hard on the ego! Then one day a letter came, offering me a position of investigator for a new assistant district attorney in Terrebonne Parish, Louisiana. I had to look up the place on Google maps.

Terrebonne Parish was bayou country—poor country, limited-budget country, fairly low crime-rate country, fishing country—did I say I *hate* fishing? Everything told me this offer was not what I was seeking. A man could rust in place in an environment like that! If I wanted to rust, I could stay where I was. *Just how backward is this place, offering me a position without even demanding an interview?* Disgusted with my choices, I got up from my computer desk, headed back to my deckchair, closed my eyes, and tried to imagine my Tilly sitting beside me. At moments like these, I actually ached with the sense of my loss. But then I remembered Tilly's saying, "Don't be surprised when God opens a door." *Tilly, what do you do when you hate the door He opens?*

I imagined Tilly's sitting across from me smiling back at me and saying, "Michael, you walk through it anyway! Trust God's plan for you. What do you have to lose?"

But I was a trained homicide detective, and I live in facts—provable cold, hard facts. Something told me to take the job; after all, nothing else was being offered to me. So, I signed the contract, put it in the mail and shot off a quick email notifying the Parish council I had done so. I began to pack my belongings.

If I had known what was waiting for me in Louisiana, I would have left everything behind and caught the first flight out of Miami heading to Terrebonne Parish. Instead, I calmly emailed my acceptance response to the Parish council and took my time packing up my world into my new GMC Yukon. Thus began another chance at living a worthwhile life—my next do-over.

The night before I was scheduled to leave for Louisiana, an email arrived from Terrebonne Parish, advising me that I would be expected by week's end. I clicked on the attachment, assuming my personnel documents to be filled out and turned in as soon as I arrived would be attached. I was wrong. Instead I opened a letter of introduction from my new boss, Charlemagne Smalls, informing me I had been assigned to be her personal investigator. We would work as a team—doing what, I had no clue. *Maybe they have lots of shrimp boat robberies down there or maybe the anti-oil drilling protestors are still active?* They were big-time news during the 1980s, but they had been quite successful at shutting down most of the Gulf shore drilling back in the day and had moved on to other environmental causes.

As I read the letter, a sense of dread overcame me. First of all, who names their baby girl *Charlemagne?* But once saddled with that name, what girl goes all the way through law school without legally changing her name? Then I noticed how she signed her name—*Char*, and I thought, *Better.*

I noticed a second attachment, clicked on it, and again found not what I had expected. Someone had scanned the local newspaper article announcing Ms. Smalls' hiring. As I read it, I realized I was now the investigator for the youngest assistant district attorney ever hired by Terrebonne Parish. She had graduated third in her class and had passed the Louisiana Bar on her first attempt. Charlemagne Smalls had been one of the youngest to graduate from her law school, but the article included no prior work experience for this young woman. *What's up with that?* I noted the date she had been hired and realized my offer of employment had been sent the very next day.

I realized I had been hired to babysit this wet-behind-the-ears child, and suddenly I began to regret my haste in accepting this position. Come what may, accept it I had. I unplugged my computer and loaded it the backseat of my Yukon, draped an old towel over it to protect it from prying eyes, locked up my house of more than thirty years, and left Miami behind me as I drove toward the Gulf side of Florida, heading toward Louisiana…and who knows what.

Halfway through my first full day of driving, my cell phone started ringing. I let it go to voice mail. I had investigated too many traffic accidents to be one of those who feels compelled to answer my cell phone while driving sixty-plus miles per hour down an interstate. Pleased with my progress, I pulled off the interstate just south of Tampa and checked my voice mail. I did not recognize the phone number but clicked voice mail and heard her voice for the first time. She introduced herself as Char and wanted to set up a breakfast meeting before meeting officially at the office. She didn't ramble around, giving me unnecessary data that I would be forced to swim through. She had already determined a good breakfast café in Houma, the county seat of Terrebonne Parish, my new home. She included concise directions and suggested a meeting time. All I had to do was text back, "Okay." *I'm beginning to like this young woman.*

Sixteen hours later, and after a good night of sleep in my new studio apartment, I made my way to the café Char had suggested, Ms. Clara's Café at the corner of Grand Caillou Road and Cousie Street. Luckily, our meeting place was right around the corner from my new apartment, and as I entered, I realized I had arrived first for our introductory meeting. I took a seat facing the door and waited for Charlemagne Smalls to arrive. You tend to form an image of someone you have never met through the information provided to you. Her name and her age suggested a flamboyant type—probably a silly little thing more interested in what she was going to wear that day than what she was going to accomplish. But then, her standing in law school belied both her name and age. Graduating third in your class is quite impressive, and even more impressive as a girl. Obviously, the flamboyant silly little girl image was definitely out. Maybe a stern and masculine type with her hair slicked back in order to convey a sense of control over everyone. *With a moniker like Charlemagne, I can't imagine what her life's been like; she's probably had to fight for everything. Most likely, she has a thin skin and will be ready to fight any implied or perceived slight. This will be interesting.*

"You want coffee?" The impatient sound of the waitress's voice jolted me out of my thoughts. I looked up and saw a rather robust woman in her fifties, giving me a very impatient look. She appeared clean, but disheveled and unkept. I surmised she had been standing over a boiling pot of something because her hair, although pulled back away from her face with large brown plastic hairclips, looked moist and uncomfortable as it broke free of the clips and clung to her plump cheeks. "My waitress called in sick again today, so I am doing double duty. I have three pots in the kitchen that need my attention, so, coffee or not?" Again, no smile was served up with this question.

"Please," I replied, "and might you be Clara?"

"Yes, I am," came her sharp retort as she poured my coffee. "Everything I serve is delicious so you can't go wrong. The menu is right there behind the salt and pepper shakers." Ms. Clara raised her right eyebrow in a high arch to emphasize just how seriously I should take her next warning. "However, anyone who uses those shakers on anything other than their eggs in my establishment, will never be served a second meal here because they obviously do not appreciate perfectly seasoned food."

I simply nodded my acknowledgment of her warning and made a mental note, *hands off the shakers,* as I opened the menu and began studying Ms. Clara's specialties.

Finally, a glimmer of a smile showed on her face as Ms. Clara added, "My food comes out of the kitchen ready to eat. You know what they say, 'Never trust a skinny cook.' If the cooks don't like what they make, neither will you."

I smiled back and tried pouring on the charm. "There will be two of us dining with you this morning. I don't know if the young lady is a coffee drinker, but I am." Again nothing, not even a slight smile, so I tried again, and therein made my second mistake. "Have you lived in Houma long?" I had pronounced the town's name phonetically *(Whoo-ma).*

"Let me guess, you are a NON-LA, right?"

I smiled and said, "Well, since I don't know what that means, I guess not."

Clara put her hands on her hips and said, "You are not from around here! A NON-LA means you weren't even born in Louisiana—let alone Terrebonne Parish, which would make you a LAT. Then, if you were entitlement born, around here anyway, you would be called a LAW; meaning you were born in Louisiana, and you were born to a Wilcomb." This was not a question, but rather it was a declaration. She might as well have painted a big red line on the floor between us and stood behind it. "It's pronounced, *'Home-A'!*"

I had just been schooled by a hot and sweaty ice queen, so I decided to sit quietly and sip my coffee as Ms. Clara headed back into her kitchen to attend to her pots. A fella can't put his foot in his mouth with fresh hot coffee in it. I studied the breakfast menu while I waited for my new boss to arrive.

That last item was something I would have to try—just not this morning. Clara returned to fill my now empty mug, and I gave her a thankful nod of the head and tried yet again. "Have you lived here long?"

"Just all my life," she said with a sense of pride. "I'm what the locals call a 'LAT.'" In the space of two minutes she had used two terms the locals use, and I dared not ask this testy woman to explain what those terms mean…again. I made a mental note to ask Clara once I had won her over—if that was at all possible. She was obviously not interested in chatting with a Non-LA, but I was determined to break down this woman's wall of resistance. This woman had lots of stories to tell, and I wanted to hear them.

Looking down at the menu, I knew I had lots of grits and dishes laden with heavy cream sauces in my future before I would be able to thaw out this woman. I had visions of becoming as large as Clara herself before the thaw was accomplished, but I knew she would be a gold mine of local information. Besides, her café was right around the corner from my new apartment, and I had to eat somewhere.

I made some mental notes so I would not forget to ask Clara later about the terms "NON-LA" and "LAT." I made another note that (according to Clara) locals have a term for the entitlement born—"LAW." I noted to myself, "LA" for "Louisiana-born," and "W" for being a member of the "Wilcomb" family. *Exactly what does "LAW" mean? Do they also make the law around here?*

I put away my notepad and focused on Clara's menu. In my twenties and thirties, I could eat anything and not gain weight, but then I hit my forties and all the rules changed. I began the arduous task of dieting—something I detested, but I detested clothes shopping more, so what is a man supposed to do? Tilly was really good at making me healthy dinners, but lunch was always a struggle. Detectives grab and go all the time, and my last twenty years of service to the Miami squad put more than thirty pounds on me—regardless of how careful I was.

Detectives have a uniform, which happens to be a suit, and in Louisiana, as in Miami, detectives go through suits like twelve-year-old boys go through shoes. The weather wreaks havoc on suits, and I usually got one wear before they needed to be cleaned. Like most of my squad members, I had about twelve suits I would rotate through, so gaining weight was a costly slipup. Since Tilly's passing, I had lost those thirty pounds because I hated eating alone, and I hated my own cooking. But sitting in Ms. Clara's Café, I suspected those lost pounds were going to be found real soon. And reviewing the menu, I suspected they would be bringing along a few new "friends."

Just as Clara refilled my coffee cup, an attractive young woman entered the café. I noticed she was wearing a light-gray business suit with a cream-colored blouse, accessorized with attractive gray and white pumps and a matching purse. Her hair and makeup were applied to perfection, but you would never call this woman standing in front of me silly or vain. She reeked of professionalism, with a slight shyness that made her sophistication endearing instead of standoffish. I stood up and introduced myself, "Hello, Char. I am Michael Majors, your new investigator."

"Good morning, Michael. Do you prefer to be called Michael?"

I smiled back, glad to see she had not assumed the right to give me a nickname. "I usually go by Mike, but I'm not fussy. I'm just happy to be here."

"As am I, Mike. I am glad you are not from these parts. You and I will be starting out equally unencumbered by family connections. I suspect that lack of encumbrance will be our greatest asset. I've done my homework, and I don't believe you can toss a brick in any direction in Terrebonne Parish without hitting a member of the Wilcomb family—either by birth, by marriage, or by partnership. You, me, and Dr. Harvey, the Parish medical examiner, are the only ones not yet entangled with that family. I intend to keep it that way."

I studied this young woman's face. She was not a hysterical female; rather, she was forthright, getting down to business, and I had better keep up with her. "Since I have never even heard of the Wilcomb family, I believe you can trust me, Char. I am a loyal employee. I work hard, have no outside distractions, and will give you 110 percent—as long as I feel I can trust you also. Are you okay with that?"

Char smiled. "I am okay with that. Now we both need to do some deep digging. If you were not born in this town, you are an outsider and not to be trusted. Gathering information is going to be a tedious job, and I have a strong suspicion Terrebonne Parish has lots of secrets that no one wants us to know." Leaning forward and lowering her voice, Charlemagne looked me straight in the eye and added, "I know there is no way on God's green earth that I should have been offered this position. Granted, Terrebonne Parish is not the center of the universe, but with only my grades and the fact that I passed the Louisiana

Bar on my first attempt to recommend me, I should never have been hired here. I believe someone wanted a novice ADA and a worn-out investigator on this case."

Char realized that perhaps she had just insulted me and started to backpedal when I stopped her. "Char, not to worry. I was suspecting the very same thing. Let's prove them all wrong, shall we?"

Char smiled and nodded in agreement. Then I asked, "What case are you talking about, Char? No one has told me anything yet."

Char waited until the waitress returned to her counter before answering. "Mike, thirteen months ago a young woman's body was found in the swampy north shore of Lake Boudreaux about 17.6 miles south of here. She was about twenty-six, had no visible signs of trauma, and no drugs or alcohol in her system. She was not from the immediate vicinity and had no apparent connection to anyone around here. She was fully clothed, had no evidence of assault, and was dumped premortem because the ME found lake water in her lungs. Because of the topography, she did not walk into the lake on the north shore. She had to have been dumped or jumped from a watercraft. Since no abandoned vessels were on the lake, someone threw her overboard.

"But for months, DA Calvin Wilcomb has been calling her death an accidental drowning. Dr. Harvey refused to go along with this ruling and finally wrote a letter to the state capital, demanding an outside investigation. Calvin is the son of Max Wilcomb and the grandson of the great and powerful 'Oz,' Milton Wilcomb—the man whose family has controlled this Parish for almost seventy years. I'm sure you can imagine exactly how that outside investigation went.

"Everyone clammed up tighter than anything that ever came out of these bayous. No one goes against anything one of the Wilcombs has affirmed. Most believed Calvin was simply inexperienced, but he had already spent five years as the ADA before being elected as the

DA. The only reason he got the job was the fact that he was heir to all things Wilcomb. From what I have read, the outside investigator corrected Calvin's findings and called the death 'suspicious.' The young woman was never identified, and the case was closed and classified 'cold'; that is, until a second body was discovered. Same circumstances, same location, but this time her body was identified because Calvin had dated her in high school. Therefore, Calvin was forced to recuse himself from the case because of his former relationship with the deceased. Hence, I was hired.

"Now I am not intimating anything against our boss, Calvin Wilcomb. Dating one of the victims in high school does not automatically make a person a suspect. I think his grandfather simply wants to create some distance between his soon-to-go-into-politics grandson and anything sordid. Calvin has only been the DA for three years and has yet to take anyone to trial. By the way, as an aside, Calvin was made ADA at the age of twenty-six-years, five months. He was only five months older than I am, and he did not graduate anywhere near the top of his class. He has miraculously had one after another eleventh-hour plea deals, saving Terrebonne Parish costly trials, quick closures, and as far as some would say, rather light sentences—unless you are one of the Acadians."

Seeing the puzzled look on my face, Char filled me in on some local history. "The Acadians are French colonists who settled here in the bayou in the 1760s after being expelled from Nova Scotia by the British in 1755 during their Seven Years' War. They chose this area because of its isolated geographic location, a minimum of government control, fertile land, and an abundance of fish and wildlife. These Acadian people lived in relative cultural seclusion for generations and became known as *Cajuns*, a corruption of the word *Acadians*. Rich in their family traditions of living off the land and isolationism, the Cajuns have become an easy target to blame for anything that happens in the Parish. According to records, about half the populations of Acadian men between the ages of twenty and forty have been hauled in for questioning. Someone is determined to pin these two deaths on some poor Cajun who cannot come up with a good alibi. This, my new friend, is what we have been handed."

I raised my bushy eyebrow as if to say, "Wow! Now this is some case," but I did not say a word. I studied this sharp young woman sitting across from me and reflected on how she had succinctly covered so much data without any unnecessary diatribes. My last boss was so in love with his own voice, he had us drowning in extraneous nonsense before we even saw the body.

I realized Char was staring at me, and I realized I needed to say something. "I hate chasing rabbit trails. My last boss was forever sending us on unnecessary rabbit trials because he could not tell the difference between a solid lead and someone's desire for fifteen minutes of fame. But, Char, I will follow a rabbit trail to hell and back if that's what it takes to solve a case. I am not afraid of hard work. Truthfully, I am quite hungry for some hard work. Nothing you have said scares me. I am beholden to no one, except to my deceased wife, Tilly. I promised her I would make my last years count, and I intend to do exactly that. So, when do we get started?"

"Well, Mike, I believe we already have. You and I will make a solid team. But if there is one lesson I have learned in my obviously limited experience; it is to never telegraph your strengths. Most people are so hungry for praise and adulation, they feel compelled to show off everything in their arsenal, assuming no one will notice without being told. My best law professor taught me that underplaying your hand can be the best defense against an aggressive offense. Let them get comfortable with their perceived weak impression of you and use it to your advantage. Do your work behind the scenes—not on the stage of public opinion. You do not want to make them fear your strengths; you want them to assume you are not a threat to them, so they will relax. A relaxed opponent is an ill-prepared opponent. Michael Majors, you and I will always be prepared, understated, and misunderstood; our intent will be to become the most successful team this Parish has ever seen."

I smiled as I gladly picked up the check. "I knew I was going to like this young woman." I was dying to ask her about her name, but not during our first meeting. That breakfast meeting was all business. The time would come soon enough to discover the backstory of Charlemagne Smalls.

I walked over to the register, and Ms. Clara met me there. "Ms. Clara, I suspect you will be seeing a lot of me. I can't wait to try your 'alligator and grits' dish…maybe even tomorrow."

Finally, a warm smile spread across Ms. Clara's face. "I promise you will love it. See you tomorrow."

4

The Ambush

A S AGREED, we arrived at our offices separately. No need to give off the appearance of solidarity just yet. I walked up to the receptionist desk, noting the woman who appeared to be well into her sixties, maybe older. I intuitively knew I needed to make this woman my friend. Since she was obviously not a new hire, she would prove to be a treasure trove of information. I knew better than to make a direct assault. Southern women do not respond well to rude and aggressive outsiders, so I smiled politely, commented on her lovely dress, and asked for help in finding the human resources office.

Gertrude Sanders, or so said the nameplate sitting front and center on her desk, smiled up at me as she noted, "You must be the new investigator. Too bad Calvin was never given one. The Parish council thought hiring one would be a waste of money, and now he is being blamed for not doing a good job. I don't think that reasoning is fair at all. I've known Calvin since he came into this world, and you will never find a better man. I'm sure you will find this out for yourself since he is the employer of your new boss." Standing up and extending her hand,

Gertrude added, "Welcome to Terrebonne Parish, Michael." She gestured toward a hallway. "Head right down that hallway, and HR is the second door on the left."

As I headed toward HR, I made a mental note: *Never question any of Calvin Wilcomb's decisions in front of Gertrude Sanders.*

I wasted the next three hours signing documents, including privacy laws, medical forms, the employee handbook, and so on. I finally reached the point where I stopped reading and simply signed what was put in front of me so I could get out of there before my next retirement party. As I left HR, I was instructed to head up to the third floor for a meet-and-greet with District Attorney Calvin Wilcomb. I quickly did the math. Hired as an ADA at the age of twenty-six years, five months, he had practiced law in that capacity for five years, qualifying him to run for DA. He had only served as the DA for three years, so that makes Calvin a little more than thirty-four. Since nepotism seems to be the reason why he was hired, I intended to give Calvin a little leeway until I had time to observe him for myself. *Wonder if this "Papa" Wilcomb runs the family the way he seems to run the parish. Maybe Papa pushed his grandson through law school and into this job in order to set him up for political office. It's happened before. Papa's plans are not to be questioned. If this is the case, Calvin is to be pitied. On the other hand, if Calvin is one of those "birthright babies," heaven help us.* I grinned wryly at the thought. As I opened the door to his office, I thought, *either way, I suspect I will know which one it is by the end of this meet-and-greet.*

I walked into the DA's outer office and was immediately taken aback. *You've got to be kidding!* my mind screamed as I fought to keep from smirking. *Hollywood's central casting could not have picked a more flamboyant Southern gentleman than this young man holding court in his outer office.* His flamboyance did not appear to be sexual in nature; rather, he presented a carefully studied reenactment of the beloved character, Ashley Wilkes, from Margaret Mitchell's *Gone with the Wind.* Trust me, Calvin Wilcomb could never carry off the part of Rhett Butler. He was not exactly soft, but rather too well-pampered to be believable as the rugged Rhett Butler. The suit he was wearing had to have been tailor-made. No one was selling wide-lapelled, crossover button-down Seersucker suits in 2014. He was sitting on his receptionist's desk with his legs crossed, which showed off his tan-and-suede saddle oxfords and argyle socks. *Is he kidding or is he heading down to the local playhouse after our meeting? I sure hope so.*

Calvin spotted me and jumped down from the desk and headed toward me. "You must be Mr. Majors. I'm Calvin Wilcomb at your service. You must excuse my attire. You arrived during our Spring Spectacular, and I was assigned the role of Ashley Wilkes in our edited version of *Gone with the Wind.*" He leaned in closer and whispered, "Ms. Gertrude Sanders is the director of the play, and it thrilled her heart when I came walking into work wearing this getup." He then winked and said, "You do have to keep the ladies happy."

I took a huge sigh of relief. I seldom concern myself with other men's attire—unless they are intentionally conveying a message that I need to heed. Quickly gathering my thoughts, I asked, "When is the performance, Mr. Wilcomb, and are there still tickets available?"

"Oh, we don't sell tickets to this annual affair, Mr. Majors, but we do give away tickets in order to make sure we will have sufficient seating. Gertrude always holds back three or four tickets just in case I need them. You tell her I said you are to be my guest this evening, and she will make sure you have a good seat. Tell her to give you two seats. I'm sure your new boss, Ms. Smalls, will want to attend as well."

"Thank you, Mr. Wilcomb. I shall look forward to it."

"Not a problem, Mike. Oh, and by the way, I don't actually talk like this. I need to stay in character for this evening's performance." Then slapping me on the shoulder, he ended our conversation with "In any other social situation, I would ask you to call me Calvin. But you understand that I need to maintain a professional distance—being the DA."

With this final word of explanation, I had been expeditiously excused; Calvin moved on to more important people. This young man knew how to work a room. Honey dripped from his tongue as he complimented women thirty years his senior. He had *politician* written all over him; still, I kind of liked him—at least for now.

Right then I caught a glimpse of Charlemagne standing in the far corner, flanked by two very chatty women. Not wanting to give Char the impression that I thought she needed rescuing, I strolled over as casually as I could. *She's a big girl and can handle any awkward situation without my help.* I didn't need to get very close to get the gist that these two women appeared to be the self-appointed henchmen for all things Calvin Wilcomb. Charlemagne was an interloper and an unnecessary burden to the parish coffers. According to these two, Calvin had been an exemplary district attorney and would soon be an even more accomplished state senator. Theirs was a not-so-veiled threat not to embarrass Calvin's record by being an eager beaver. At this comment, Char shot me a quick glance, as if to say, "See, I told you someone is behind all this pretense."

I stepped closer and introduced myself, trying to pour on as much Southern charm as I could muster. "Excuse me, ladies, I would love to stand here and chat with you both; however, I need to deliver a message to Ms. Smalls about District Attorney Wilcomb inviting us to the Spring Spectacular this evening. He suggested we find a Ms. Gertrude Sanders to tell her that he has requested both of us to be his guests of honor this evening. We are to get our tickets to the event from her."

Even though I was fully aware of where to find Gertrude Sanders, appearing helpless so elderly women can come to the rescue shows wisdom. "You lovely ladies wouldn't happen to know where we can find this Gertrude Sanders, would you?"

Those two women stumbled all over each other trying to be the one coming to my aid. I was certain my charm had not dazzled them; rather, I had invoked the magic name of *Wilcomb*. Southern charm fairly dripped from their lips at my referring to Calvin, and Char and I were quickly directed to Gertrude's desk. As we quickly left what could only be termed "a den of vipers," we were keenly aware of those staunchly encamped around their golden boy. If we were going to be successful, we needed to step carefully and watch our backs.

As we descended the staircase, Char whispered, "Mike, we have two separate cases on our hands: one is finding out who the killer is, and the other is finding out who is pulling all the strings around here. We must assume nothing, suspect everyone, hold our cards close to the chest, and reassess and scrutinize every piece of evidence that has been collected over the past eighteen months. These people dislike us immensely simply because we are not one of 'them.' Most of what we will be fighting will have nothing to do with the murders but fight we must. We need to keep our threat level to a minimum, cultivate a few good leads, and run them into the ground. Trust no one, and make sure I always know where you are at all times. In today's digital world, people do not die without leaving a single clue about who they are and to whom they are connected. That, in itself, is a huge red flag that smacks of a huge cover-up. Mike, I cannot afford to lose you, my only friend in this parish. Tomorrow morning, we will lock ourselves in my office and start digging; but tonight, we will go to this Spring Spectacular and begin meeting our cast of suspects."

As much as I wanted to start digging into the evidence boxes now, the gathering that night proved to be serendipitous. Char and I needed to get to know all the heavy hitters in the Parish as soon as possible, and the Spring Spectacular was the perfect cover. I picked up Char at her new apartment, grabbed a light bite of dinner, and headed over to the Houma Playhouse. As soon as we arrived, we split up to work the room separately.

Before the play, the ladies of the auxiliary hosted a social with finger foods and lemonade, where they worked the room, selling raffle tickets as part of their ongoing fundraiser. Winning any one of several prizes would prove beneficial. The top prize was an invitation to tour the home of Max and Charisse Wilcomb. As a crime-scene investigator, I would not be welcomed at that front door; but as a prize winner, the Wilcombs would have to be gracious and accommodating. At five dollars a ticket, my first response was to pass, but I needed to ingratiate myself with this well-connected woman standing in front of me. I smiled and announced, "I will take twenty tickets." I gulped as I pulled my last $100 bill out of my wallet, but I smiled at the excited auxiliary member who was carefully counting out the 20 tickets. "I'm happy to oblige you, Mr. Majors, and just remember, this is for charity. The drawing will be held right after the last curtain call tonight."

I tucked my tickets into my inside coat pocket and continued to work the crowd. I kept note of those with whom Char spent any amount of time and avoided duplicating our efforts. I strolled over to the two ladies I had briefly met at the meet-and-greet earlier that day. "Ladies, so nice to see you again. Your directions to Mrs. Sanders' desk were perfect. I didn't know she was also the play's director. I am looking forward to seeing my new boss, Mr. Wilcomb, play the part of Ashley Wilkes. Might I ask, who will be playing the part of Scarlett O'Hara this evening?"

Mrs. Treadway beamed with pride as she announced, "That would be my daughter Samantha. She majored in theater at LSU. She was really good and could have made a name for herself, but she married Stephen Sinclair, Papa Wilcomb's attorney, so these local plays are all she has time for these days."

I made another mental note: *Mrs. Treadway is the mother-in-law of Papa Wilcomb's attorney.* Just as I stepped away from the ladies, I walked right into Mr. Sinclair—hardly an accident, I believe. As much as I was working the room, I was well aware of those in the room working me. All of them knew where I was and to whom I was talking. I felt like a fish in a fishbowl, with twenty-some hooks, baited and ready to snag me. Mr. Sinclair was not a young man. I surmised that Mrs. Treadway was a well-preserved woman in her early sixties. Therefore, her daughter could not be more than forty. Mr. Sinclair had to be well into his late sixties, if not older, and I noted quietly, *Is Ms. Samantha a trophy wife?*

Sinclair wasted no time getting to the point. "Mr. Majors, the Wilcomb family has done immeasurable good for this parish. For three generations they have worked to build this community by bringing good-paying jobs to the people of the parish. We are all looking forward to having Calvin represent our state as its newest senator next year. Calvin has been a hardworking DA, and before that, he served as an exemplary ADA for Terrebonne Parish. A simple difference of opinion between the DA and the ME is why you and Ms. Smalls were hired. We all expect you to do a thorough job in discovering who killed those two poor ladies, but please tread carefully when analyzing the way these cases were handled. Calvin is going places, and we do not want a stain on his record. A careless comment offered to the wrong person could undermine years of preparation. This parish needs a senator who will look out for our interests." Sinclair ended by giving me a very condescending smile, slapping me on the shoulder, but before leaving me, he added one very veiled threat. "This parish knows who to thank for their thriving economy. If you want to get along here, you need to remember that."

I turned and watched Mr. Sinclair walk over to his mother-in-law and knew I had just been handled—or so he thought. I turned around and started toward my next target when a gentleman dressed in a full tux walked through the room, holding a handheld xylophone close to his chest in one hand and a felt-tipped baton in his other hand. He kept taping five keys as he announced, "Ladies and gentlemen, please begin making your way to your seats. Our play will begin shortly."

Since Char and I were to be seated together, I walked over to her, and we proceeded into the open vestibule together. I could see the excitement in Char's eyes and knew she felt she had just had a successful foray into the well-connected people of Terrebonne Parish—until we reached the vestibule. At first, mumbled snickers drew our attention, followed by sounds that instantly put a look of dread on Char's face. It seemed as if the entire crowd had been instructed to part the waters, so to speak, and Char came face to face with her worst nightmare.

Little did I know that the three women who stood in front of us were related to Charlemagne Smalls. The elder of the group was loud, brash, and flamboyant in every possible way she could muster. Her attire screamed, "Look at me!" Her hair was teased so high and had so much hairspray she could have used that pompadour to hide a weapon. Her garish makeup was obviously not a new style for this woman. I suspected she had never taken a backseat to anyone in her whole life. Her voice was shrill and three decibels above what was necessary at a sporting event, let alone at this type of function.

"Charlemagne, my dear girl, aren't we just the sweetest surprise for you? That precious boss of yours called me and offered to send a limo for us all the way over from New Orleans. He knew I was upset that I wasn't able to attend your swearing in, so he invited all three of us to this event to celebrate with you and all your new friends."

As I watched Char's face, the excitement drained from her eyes, and in its place, I witnessed a shy, apologetic countenance take over. Char had entered the vestibule standing tall and dignified. Although she only stood five feet, five inches tall, she carried herself well. Her shoulders had been pulled back and her head was held high, but without coming across as proud or snobbish. That refined-appearing woman was now gone. In her place stood a stooped-shouldered, evasive woman who dared not look around. I suddenly had my answer to what kind of woman names her baby girl, Charlemagne—*this type!*

This beautiful and smart young woman I had already come to admire suddenly vanished, and in her place stood a woman who wanted to melt into the woodwork. I intuitively knew this confrontation had been a well-executed setup. Calvin Wilcomb may not be a good DA, but he sure was a sharp politician. In one fell swoop, he had disarmed his potential rival in front of anyone and everyone of importance in the parish. Charlemagne Smalls was no longer the smart young ADA. She was simply the embarrassed little offspring of this dreadful, uncouth, crude, loud, and obnoxiously ill-bred woman. I thought, *Well played, Calvin. Well played.*

I was at a loss for words. I studied Char's reaction and did not notice any hatred for this unpleasant mother. Char had obviously learned to tolerate her, but what I did see was an expression revealing pain when one of these so-called, well-bred Southern ladies laughed a little too loudly at something this woman was saying. I wanted to take a mirror and walk up to one of them and shove it in her face. I wanted to scream at all of them, "Talk about bad breeding! How dare you take pleasure in the agony of another. You are as uncouth as she is, you miserably ill-trained women, who gloat in tormenting others." Instead, I just stood helplessly and watched.

Mr. Sinclair could barely contain his triumph as he walked up and offered, "Ladies, might I escort you to your seats?"

I knew I had to let the evening play itself out. I could do absolutely nothing to protect Char from this evening of embarrassments. Her mother was only slightly more obnoxious than her older sister, Jasmine, who was almost a carbon copy of their mother. The two talked incessantly throughout the play, laughing at the most inappropriate moments. I do not believe either of them knew what shame was. If they did, I feel sure they would have simply written it off and plunged even further into their tasteless behavior.

How in the world did this polished young woman grow up with these two? I wondered.

During the intermission, Char asked, "Mother, how long will you be staying?"

"Oh, we will be driven back home to New Orleans right after the evening is over. Wasn't it nice of your boss to do this for us?"

Char smiled and shot me a quick look of relief. She knew exactly what had transpired this evening. Calvin Wilcomb had struck the first blow, but she was not going down without a fight; I would have her back. After the last curtain call when Char walked her family out to the waiting limo, I did not follow. Everything inside of me wanted to protect my boss, but I was not her father; I am her employee. I could not stop the embarrassment of that evening, but I could give her privacy to handle the matter in her own way.

Instead, I joined those who were in the gathering room and attempted to keep the conversation off of Charlemagne Smalls. I could not possibly believe the whole parish could be this vindictive. *Had Char and I been dragged into something truly evil or were most of these* _people simply duped into following along with whoever was behind this evening's charade?_

I walked around the room, appearing to be invisible to everyone. I did meet Sheriff McClure who was accompanied by his wife, so neither of us felt discussing the cases would have been appropriate. I kept my conversations casual and impersonal. In the far corner of the gathering room, I noticed three men standing huddled together in deep conversation. I meandered over, making sure to change directions occasionally in order not to appear interested in their conversation. I was fully aware that my presence in that room was probably the only real topic of conversation there that night. I could barely maneuver my way around that place without everyone's knowing exactly where I was and what I was overhearing. I finally gave up, turned in my raffle tickets, and headed out to my car. The day had been long, and I was done.

I noticed that Char had not returned to the gathering and who could blame her. As I started the engine, my first thought was, _I don't have a dog in this fight. I should just grab my things and head back home._ But I no longer had a home to go back to. I had rented it out for one full year; besides, I like Char, and I never turn my back on friends. I promised her I would have her back and have her back was exactly what I intended to do.

5

Our War Room

CHAR MUST have spent the night in her office. I doubt she would have gotten much sleep after the previous night's ambush. She had already gone through all seven boxes of evidence and had them separated by case. "Mike, even though we have been told we are dealing with one killer, I want us to do our own investigation. Until we have proven to ourselves that we are looking for one killer, I want to handle these as two separate crimes."

I wanted to say something about the previous night's complications, but Char was already down to business. I suspected that was always how she must have handled her family—bury herself in schoolwork, law school, and now these cases. I decided to follow her lead. "I agree, Char. The less we listen to others, the quicker we will be able to trust the evidence. Where do we start?"

"First of all, as I went through the evidence log, I realized that two reports are missing. At first, I thought they might have just been boxed up incorrectly, but I've been through all seven boxes, and they are not here. I know I did not misplace them, and you have not been in this room until this morning. We need to find them. One is a witness state-ment taken eighteen months ago when the first body was discovered. According to the log, one guy, who was living on a boat down in Dulac, witnessed something. I will ask DA Wilcomb to check his office. I do not believe he removed those two reports as he was the one who listed them in his evidence log. Obviously, he knew they were listed there. For whatever reason, if Wilcomb was trying to hide these reports, he would have deleted them from the evidence log. He might be inept, but he is not stupid. He would have deleted all traces of those reports if he were hiding something.

"We need to find that witness statement. Mike, you could go down to Dulac and find the guy. It is only about seventeen miles south of here, and we just need to hope he has a good memory. We both know the statement taken immediately after the murder is the most reliable. Besides, the officer who wrote up that report still has his notes. The fact that it's missing doesn't make sense.

"Apart from that witness, all we have on the first case with the nameless victim is the autopsy report—not much for an eighteen-month-old case. The autopsy reported no drugs or alcohol in her sys-tem and no apparent trauma to the body. Lake water in her lungs, fully clothed when she entered the water. No fingerprint history, so she was never arrested nor in the military. She was never pregnant, no signs of prior surgeries, no dental work—so no leads there. No one has filed a missing person's report that fits the victim's description. Something smells really fishy here. In today's digital world, who can go into the great beyond and leave behind no paper trail?"

"Char, I find DA Wilcomb's calling that an accidental drowning quite unbelievable. Jane Doe's death may not be murder, but at the very least, she drowned under highly suspicious circumstances. Someone knew she was in the water and left her there to die."

Char smiled and headed to the whiteboard. Under the heading of Case #1, Char wrote, *Reaction to the findings highly suspicious!*

As soon as I read it, I suggested, "Char, until we have a secure lock on the door, I'd suggest you not put anything on that board that smacks of impugning the integrity of the golden boy."

Without saying a word, Char wiped the board clean and moved on. "The other missing report concerns the second case. The second victim was identified right away. Fingerprints proved she had been a local girl from some years earlier. Her car was found outside the marina in Dulac. Her purse was on the seat, and her car keys were found on the ground right beside her car. The ground was muddy from recent rains, and the authorities could see tire impressions that had driven over the keys, partially burying them in the muddy soil. Impressions made of those tire tracks are also missing."

I grimaced and offered, "Two reports missing is too many, Char. We need to lock down everything pertaining to these two cases. I suggest you put in a request to have the locks changed on this office. You and I should be the only ones in here from now on. No cleaning service—nothing—just you and me from now on."

"I'm way ahead of you, Mike. I already filed a request with Mrs. Sanders. The locks will be changed by the end of the day. I agree, but whoever took these reports doesn't know much about chain of evidence. The original plaster cast must be in Dr. Harvey's lab, and if not the original, then an exact copy had to have been made before releasing the original. If that copy is also missing, we need to question Dr. Harvey also. And unless that fisherman in Dulac and the officer who wrote up the interview have both met with untimely deaths, that report can be recreated as well. I don't understand why these two reports went missing."

"Do you want me to locate the officer who took that report?"

"No, at least not until I have asked DA Wilcomb to check his office. If he cannot find it, then we will call in the officer for a talk. But I would like you to head to the ME's office and check on that plaster cast. Once we have that here in my office, you and I will go through everything in these boxes, create our own evidence log, make copies of it, and take copies to our homes as backup files. This will be a late night. Plan on eating dinner here, and if the locks have not been changed by the time we are ready to leave, I intend to spend the night here. I don't want any more reports 'to grow feet' and walk away."

Two hours later I returned with the third copy of the tire impression. "Char, Dr. Harvey said something odd when I was at his office. He mentioned his habit is to keep all of his originals locked in a cupboard in his body cooler. Per procedure, he poured a duplicate copy and sent it to the DA. Because several people would be looking at this evidence, he decided to make a third copy and returned the original to his cold storage. About the time he was told the cases were being turned over to an outside investigator, that third mold was found shattered on his office floor. He was quite irritated that someone had been in his lab without permission; however, he knew the original was safe, so he dismissed the break-in. Upon hearing today that the mold he had sent to the DA had gone missing, he became as uncomfortable about the situation as we are. He decided to pour two more sets of copies. He gave me one, wrapped up the other one and decided to take it home with him. He stated definitively, and I concur, 'Michael, evidence that goes missing is *important* evidence.'"

I unwrapped the tire mold and studied the imprint. I immediately noticed four of what are called *accidental markings*—after-market cuts, gouges, or foreign bodies wedged into the tire tread. "Char, this tire tread is a gold mine. If we can find the car that has this tire, we can prove it was at the scene when the second victim left her car. The keys were on the ground before the car drove over them. No footprints showed the victim walked away from her car. The problem is we don't have any viable suspects, and three months have passed since her body was found. If the person is aware of this evidence, he or she has had plenty of time to change out the tires and destroy the evidence."

I had just placed the plaster mold in the center of our conference table when Gertrude Sanders walked uninvited into our war room. "I just wanted to let you know that I got in touch with the locksmith. He will be here within the hour." Gertrude smiled proudly as she added, "He's my eldest son Henry, and he's doing this work quickly as a favor to me."

Char smiled and thanked Gertrude—though irritated at her for barging in without knocking. Gertrude had worked in the building for more than thirty years, and obviously, she was used to going anywhere she wished. She was as much a fixture of this place as the statue of Our Lady of the Sacred Heart sitting in the courtyard…and equally revered. Char swallowed hard, smiled again and asked, "Mrs. Sanders, may I possibly requisition a coffeepot for my office? Mike and I will be putting in some long nights, and coffee would be so very much appreciated."

"Not a problem, and please call me *Gertrude*. I believe I have an extra coffeepot in the staff kitchen cupboard. And don't you worry about coffee cups. I have dozens of them at home, so I will bring in four or five tomorrow morning and have them sitting on your conference table when you arrive."

Again, Char smiled. "That would be lovely, Gertrude, but I will stop by your desk when I come in tomorrow and pick them up. Once your son changes the locks, only Michael Majors and I will have keys to this office. You are so sweet to offer your coffee cups, and one day really soon I will invite you into my office for a cup of coffee and a good old chat. But today is not a good day for me. I have so much to do before I feel I have things under control. You do understand, don't you, Gertrude?"

"Oh, certainly, Ms. Smalls. I never want to get in the way of justice. I will buzz you when my son arrives." Gertrude excused herself with just a hint of having been put in her place.

"Wowzah," I said as I closed the door behind Gertrude. "There is a woman you do not want to offend. She is the go-to person around here, Char. I think that little tea party you mentioned better happen sooner rather than later. We need her on our side."

"I know; I just need to have control of the things I am responsible for. I will make a conscious effort to smooth things over with her as soon as possible. Now let's get to work. I will tag each piece of evidence, and you record it and assign it a new tag number—one that is unique to our office.

"In the last column, we will record the original code number used by DA Wilcomb as a cross-reference. If we stick with it, we should be done with this part of the task by about 7:00 p.m. That will be a good time to take a dinner break before we actually start reading all of these reports."

In three of the four corners of our conference room, Char set up three whiteboards with a different heading on each one—"Case #1," "Case #2," and "Parish Connections." She began going through each box, identifying the item, waiting for me to issue a code number, tagging it, and then placing it under one of the appropriate whiteboards.

We had gone through three of the seven boxes when Gertrude buzzed. Char picked up the phone, listened and said, "Thank you, Gertrude. I really appreciate you getting Henry here so quickly. I look forward to meeting your son. Please send him back."

Henry knocked on our door and waited to be invited in. He got straight to work changing out the key lock. As he tested the keys, Char asked, "Henry, how hard would it be to add a deadbolt to that door?"

"Not hard at all, but I will have to drill two holes in the door. I have a drill and deadbolt in my truck. But I will need an adjusted purchase order before I dare drill into the door."

"Do you happen to know who issues the purchase orders around here?"

Henry smiled, "Not to worry, my mother does. I will stop by her desk and get that issued and be back here in no time flat."

Thirty minutes later, he was handing Char two sets of keys. "I keyed both the doorknob and deadbolt with the same calendar so one key operates both."

As Henry packed up his gear, Char casually commented, "Now these are the only copies of keys for this door, right?"

Henry paused before answering. "Well, I am required to turn over a worker's copy to the building manager. It's a safety issue."

"I understand, Henry. However, since I am new here and will be working late into the night several times a week, I would feel safer knowing there is not another key out there floating around. Let's make a deal. You give me that extra set of keys, and when I get settled and am no longer playing catch up, I will find the building manager and give him that key. Are you okay with that?"

"Sounds good to me. After all, you are the new ADA. All I need now is your signature on this invoice, and I'll be out of your way."

Char signed the invoice and locked the door behind Henry as he exited. "Now we can get down to the known facts and list our first priorities of confirmation. Let's start with the first case."

1) Confirm fingerprints, run through CODIS again.
2) Re-interview witness.

3) Review autopsy with Dr. Harvey.

4) Re-interview hotel clerk.

Char hesitated at this point and turned toward me, "I am not suggesting that the DA had anything to do with this murder, Mike; however, my law professor hammered into us that you never assume anything! You never give a pass because of power, prestige, or friendship."

"Well," I replied, "I don't believe after last night that either of us would consider Calvin Wilcomb a friend!"

"That's exactly my point, Mike. Everyone of importance in this parish witnessed my humiliation last evening. If I look into Calvin Wilcomb's motives in any way, shape or form regarding his handling of this case…Mike, it will appear vindictive on my part."

"Yes, it will, Char," I agreed without any hesitation in my voice. "Without a doubt, it will. But we do it anyway, right? Last night was an ambush designed to humiliate you and render your status in this parish to laughingstock status. That unmerciful attack was programmed to perfection by people who do not tolerate being questioned." I continued to see a look of hesitation on her face and decided to go for it and clear the air.

"Charlemagne Smalls, that your family is an embarrassment to you was obvious to everyone last night. I am sorry to speak to you so bluntly, but if we do not clear the air between us, this incident will fester and poison our working relationship. Char, everyone has family members who are awkward to have around. Some have a crazy uncle, a drug-addicted brother, a father who served time in prison, or a mother who obviously does not know her place in this world, but YOU are your own person! YOU are you! You have worked hard to get where you are. You have proven yourself to be extremely capable, especially with graduating near the top of your class. Don't let the Wilcomb tribe get away with undermining you like they did. YOU hold your head up high and do your job. Don't be unnecessarily intrusive toward the family but do your job and follow the evidence—wherever it leads."

Char finally smiled at me. "That is the second time I have been given that speech, Mike. That law professor I mentioned earlier said those exact words to me in my first year of law school. You would not have recognized me back then. Everything about me screamed, 'Don't look at me! Don't pay any attention to me! I do not deserve to be here!' Professor Armstrong and his lovely wife Elizabeth took me on…as a project of sorts. I was as plain as my mother was flamboyant. I never wore makeup or stylish clothes. Elizabeth worked with me for months, helping me become skilled at applying the proper makeup and wearing comfortably fashionable clothing. I felt clownish and overdone, but I finally began to see the value of dressing in a professional manner. I realized that no one would take me seriously if I did not change."

I did not know how to respond to this confession of sorts. Char was sharing some deep wounds, and I needed to hear her. I could not help her unless I understood what made her tick. I guess my silence was as uncomfortable for her as it was for me because I heard her clear her throat and looked up right as she said, "My mother is not a bad person, Mike. Yes, she is flamboyant and outrageous, but I have never questioned the fact that she loves all three of us girls. Being the youngest of the three, I have no memory of our father. He died when I was two, leaving my mother to raise us on her own in New Orleans. I don't even want to imagine what she had to do to keep a roof over our heads. She never finished high school, so she did what she had to do. In that town, garish and outlandish is not only acceptable, it is expected. We went without many things, but we stayed together. My oldest sister Jasmine is the most like our mother. She too is outlandish and loud. The only time she is at all quiet is when she is with my mother. As you witnessed last night, no one takes the spotlight away from Mother.

"My middle sister Camilla is a lost soul. She too grew up in the shadow of two strong and demanding women, but she was never the student I was. She never found a place of her own to shine. I tried getting her into school, but honestly, she just does not have a mind to study.

"By the time I got into middle school, I think my mother knew her days of working the streets were numbered. She found a job tending bar on Bourbon Street, and her cartoonish demeanor actually became her signature and served her well in that make-believe world of overstated indulgence. She fits right in."

Char walked over and took the seat right across from me. "I still love my family, Mike. I never want to live in the same town as them, but I hate feeling ashamed of them. Feeling that shame is the most difficult part of last night. I was ashamed of them." She buried her face in her hands.

"Char, you were set up last night, and shame was exactly what they wanted you to feel. They did not want a confident new ADA at that gathering last night. I am not the only one who would have been dazzled by your professionalism. I want to see the woman who walked into that café yesterday. Work this case. You hold your head high, do the task set before you, and prove to the world that Professor and Mrs. Armstrong were right about you."

Char lifted her face to mine with a smile that would bedazzle a blind man. "Now that is the smart young woman I met yesterday," I replied with a huge smile on my face.

"Thanks for being so honest and straightforward with me, Mike. I stumbled last evening and this morning. I was so taken by surprise, I just reacted instead of staying on the offense." Char picked up the marker and wrote:

5) Question DA Wilcomb's reason for opposing ME Harvey's findings.

6

Backtracking

I WAS up early the next morning. Char and I had worked until almost 3:00 a.m. the night before, but I could not sleep, so I headed back to Clara's for a quick breakfast. We had agreed that I would drive to Dulac, find that witness and conduct my own interview. I have always been leery of witness statements taken long after an event. Rumors start flying around, and they begin to filter into the witness's memory. Soon you cannot separate what they actually saw from what they have either read or heard, but I had no choice but to head to Dulac to find this person.

I could have contacted the officer who took the original witness statement, but since we didn't know who to trust, I decided to *go native.* At least that's what my former boss used to call "cold calling." You have no hard evidence to confirm, no time frame to prove, no cooperative witnesses to compare to. *Going native* means "it's all about your gut instincts." *Is this person a reliable source?*

Because the original report was missing, all I had was a name—Buddy Benoit. I knew he was a fisherman, so I stopped by the bait shop at the marina and asked.

"Oh sure, I know Buddy, but he isn't here this time of year. He only comes around during peak crabbing season. You see, Louisiana State Fisheries Commission forbids crabbing in state waters from February 1 to March 31. So, on April 1, it's all hands on deck. Buddy is a true Cajun boy. When he's not here, you can always find him up north in Bienville Parish. His family has roots there forever. I believe he lives right outside of Arcadia. You might ask Ben Feign. He's the one who always hires Buddy during crabbing season—even lets Buddy sleep on his boat, *The Merry Widow*, whenever he's working down here."

I smiled politely and asked, "You wouldn't happen to know what slip is assigned to *The Merry Widow*, would you?"

"Oh, sure, #77. Ben has had that slip since he was eighteen years old. Fishermen are a superstitious lot. That first season in 1971, Ben beat out every other fishing boat and made a huge haul. That was how he was able to buy The Merry Widow; well, at least put 50 percent down on her. He wouldn't dock that boat in any other slip—even if it was free."

I walked out of that shop with a treasure trove of information. I now knew who the witness was and how to find him. I knew the name of the boat he was sleeping on and where it was docked. And none of this information came from the witness. Before heading up to Bienville Parish, I took a stroll over to slip #77. No one was onboard, so I climbed aboard and stood on the deck. I decided to write down all the names of boats around *The Merry Widow*. If Buddy were a witness, maybe one of these boats had something to do with what he witnessed. I would research each of these owners and see if any suspicious names popped.

Before heading to Bienville Parish, I texted Char my intentions. We agreed to keep each other posted, and I didn't want to be so far away without knowing she was fine with my plans. Almost immediately I got back a short text: *Run with it.*

According to Google Maps, Bienville Parish was 5 hours, 21 minutes away. *This is going to be a long day.* I did not want to forewarn Buddy of my coming because I wanted his memory unpracticed. I just hoped I would find him home. I knew I would have to find a motel there. By the time I drove up there, found him, and interviewed him, I would not be able to drive back to Houma tonight. I texted this back to Char so she would not worry and then headed to LA-57 North.

It was well after four when I pulled into Arcadia. I had Googled Buddy Benoit but found nothing. I was surprised to find phone booths with phone books still in place at the corner convenience store. In Miami, phone booths had pretty much disappeared since the launching of cell phones; even the poorest of the poor in Miami had a cell phone. But I suspect that here in Bienville Parish, the poorest parish in all of Louisiana, cell phones still remained a luxury item, hence the phone booth. As I pulled up to take a closer look, I was surprised to see a phone book still hanging from the cable. In Miami, it would have been gone within twenty minutes of being installed. I turned to the "Bs" and found a page and a half of Benoits. *Must be a lot of Buddy's relatives around here.*

I started to use my cell phone but stopped as I thought, *if they have caller I.D., they won't answer an unknown number.* I went inside the store to get change for the phone. I suspected I would be making quite a few calls before someone would give me a good lead, but again, I was working with my Miami mindset. The young man behind the counter started counting out five dollars worth of quarters when he suddenly asked, "Who are you calling with all these quarters, mister?"

I took a chance. "I'm looking for Buddy Benoit."

The young man smiled and said, "Oh, Buddy just lives three blocks back. Buddy and his wife Ava just had their third baby, and half the Benoits in town are planning to stop by for our traditional Arcadian blessing. We are big on our traditions around here, mister. Buddy will surely be home today."

This was good news, but then I wondered, *how good?* I did not dare wait until morning to interview Buddy. This boy will tip him off for sure. *Is there time before this big family gathering?* I headed toward the door as if I were not in any hurry, but as I opened the door, I turned and asked, "So what time does this celebration start?"

Without hesitating, the young man offered, "Seven o'clock! They always start at seven o'clock."

"You wouldn't have Buddy's address, would you? I would love to stop by and congratulate the new father. By the way, is there something more traditional to bring as a blessing—other than flowers?"

"Money, mister. We all bring money to put in the baby's jar. Doesn't have to be much. Most of us don't have a lot of spare money, but it's the thought that counts. That five dollars in quarters would work just fine. But mister, before your quarters can become a blessing, you need to stop by Our Lady of the Sacrament and light a candle for the baby. The Benoit family has been doing this ever since our first ancestors left France over two hundred years ago."

"But I'm not Catholic," I confessed. "Will it still count as a blessing to the family?"

"Sure will! The baby is Catholic. I'm almost nineteen, and my mother still remembers every person who lit a candle of blessing for me. Every year on my birthday my mother lights one single candle of blessing and prays for every name in my blessing book. It's that important to us Acadians—especially those of us in the Benoit clan. We never spend that blessing money. We only spend some of it when one of the blessing people is also in trouble. The parents will take some money out of the blessing jar to buy prayer candles for that person. It's how we all stay connected."

I thanked him and headed to Our Lady of the Sacrament. I compared this young man with so many of the people in Miami. Getting information from people had become nearly impossible. They distrust the police even if they are not involved or have anything to hide themselves; they resist helping them at almost every opportunity. The fact that this young man didn't even ask me why I was looking for Buddy tells me that he does not believe Buddy could have done anything illegal. He did not automatically erect a protective wall of defense. To an investigator, that behavior speaks volumes. Before heading to Buddy's home, I went into the church and lit a candle.

I knew I would be early, but I did not want to speak with him in front of other guests. I pulled up to a small, slab-built house with a swamp cooler on the roof that looked like it had seen better days. A coon dog was tied up in the carport that made no attempt to warn his owner of my presence. I walked up to the screen door and knocked. I could barely see inside. Not one single light was on inside that house. I was beginning to think I had the wrong address. *No one in this house is expecting guests any time soon...* All of a sudden, the back door opened, flooding the house with light from out back. A little guy no more than four came to the door and asked, "Are you the ice man? My momma needs you to bring the ice around back. That's where the party is going to be."

I smiled and said, "No, I'm not the ice man. Is your daddy home?"

"Sure, but he's busy stringing up lights out back. You can go round back if you want."

I walked past the sleeping coon dog, and as I turned the corner, someone flipped on the lights. It was almost like daylight in the backyard. Obviously, this was where the party was going to be held. I introduced myself to Buddy and his friend who was helping him get ready for the party. "Buddy, I know this is not a good time, but I have a few questions regarding a case I am working in Dulac."

Buddy instantly knew what I was talking about. He climbed down the ladder, handed his friend the remaining string of lights yet to be strung, and said, "Gill, I'll be right back." Turning to me he suggested, "Let's take this in the house. I don't know much, but what I do know, I don't want my boy to hear."

I followed Buddy inside and took a seat in his darkened living room. "I already told that other officer everything I saw that night."

"I'm sure you did, Buddy, but just to make sure we did not overlook something you saw, I'd appreciate it if you could go over that night with me. Exactly what night was it?"

"Oh, I remember that date because it was the night before crabbing was to start. I had taken the bus from here all the way to Dulac the day before. I do that every year, so my wife has the car while I am gone. Crabbing starts every year at 4:00 a.m. on the first day of April. I had worked hard all that day getting the traps ready, checking the lines, filling the bait boxes, and cleaning up the cabin kitchen so we could eat there. The crew was going to start showing up around 3:00 a.m., and we would cast off around 3:45 so we would be ready to start dropping traps right at 4:00 a.m.

"Knowing I had to be up and ready to go by 3:00 a.m., I knew I needed to turn in early. It was right about 8:00 p.m. when I fell into bed exhausted. I turned off all the lights and was just falling asleep when I heard the sound of a boat motor slipping into gear off in the distance. I had heard that same motor start up about thirty minutes earlier, but I couldn't tell which boat was testing its engine. Lots of us do that. None of us want to be left at the pier on opening day because our engine will not turn over. Starting a boat wasn't unusual, but to put the boat in gear and head out way before the mandatory curfew is lifted…well, that could get your boat scuttled, if you get what I mean. Fishermen take first day bragging rights very seriously in Louisiana.

"So I got out of bed and went up top to see who the jerk was who was not playing by the rules. That's when I saw a 30-foot cabin cruiser, black bottom, white deck, and only one man onboard. I knew he wasn't a crabber, but I couldn't get a close view of him because he was wearing a yellow slicker and rain hat. That getup was kinda funny; after all, it hadn't rained in several days. To be honest, once I saw that it was not a crabbing rig, I didn't pay much more attention.

"I do remember seeing the word *Swamp* in the name, but that is just about every boat in Louisiana, so that was no help. I headed back down below and tried to get some sleep, but about an hour later, I heard that same engine cruising back into port. Its movements made no sense to me. Who takes their cruiser out for only one hour? I can't tell you where it docked, although I didn't see it anywhere near slip #77.

"When I was questioned by the other officer, he felt my testimony locked down the time period when the body was dumped into the lake. That's because the Intra-costal Waterway Canal that we all use to get from the marina out into the Gulf is always patrolled by the Coast Guard. Knowing crabbing season was upon us, they were out in force looking for drunks. No one was recorded coming in or leaving the canal from 7:00 to midnight that night. So, the engine I heard was moored in this marina and returned to this marina. It is a 30-foot cruiser, not a crabber or a flat-bottomed swamper or an airboat. The word *Swamp* is in its name, and oh, I forgot something else I just remembered. The stern seating area was black with white polka-dots or something like that. I forgot all about that. I also think the open-pit seating forward of the bridge was also upholstered in the same material. Does that help you?"

"It sure does. You are quite sure of what you saw and when you saw it?

"I sure am. Now I cannot say anything about a woman. I did not see one on that boat, but I know that boat was the only one to have gone out on the lake that night."

Having overheard our conversation, Buddy's wife Ava came into the room and corrected her husband, "Buddy, you didn't just remember the cushions on that boat. I remember you did tell that first policeman about them."

Embarrassed at being corrected, Buddy smiled back at me and corrected himself, "I misspoke, Mr. Majors. I meant to say that while talking to you just now, I realized I had forgotten to tell you about the cushions—not that I had always forgotten. Ava is right; I did tell the other policeman about 'em."

I corrected my notes to indicate the police knew the description of the boat cushions from the very beginning. Now I was ready to interview that officer, and we needed to see his missing report. I closed up my notepad, slipped it into my coat pocket and said, "I really appreciate your time, Buddy. You have made my job much easier. I doubt I will have much trouble finding that boat. What I would suggest though is that you keep all of this to yourself. Someone dumped that body in the lake that night, and you don't want to become a danger to someone like that. Let my boss and me investigate and find this person. You keep your family safe; and speaking of your family, your cousin Tray told me all about the blessing ceremony being held tonight, so I stopped by Our Lady of the Sacrament and lit a candle for your new little girl. Would you allow me to be the first to place money in her blessing jar?" Buddy's wife Ava beamed with pride as she left the room to get the blessing jar and brought back a beautifully painted half-gallon jar and allowed me to drop my twenty quarters into it. She then handed me the guestbook and asked me to sign my name.

As I signed the guest book, Ava asked, "Mr. Majors, do you know the whole story behind our tradition of the blessing jar?"

I confessed that I did not, so she graciously informed me. "We Cajuns have a word, *lagniappe,* which means "a little something extra to sweeten the pot." Your English word for it is a "baker's dozen." We have a lagniappe for our blessing jars that goes back a long time. When I was a little girl, my me-mere told me that her me-mere told her that many, many years ago, a young Cajun mother who was still living in Canada or even all the way back in France, or so the legend goes, added a lagniappe to our tradition. One night she was terrified that her baby boy would not live through the night. She took the baby's blessing jar and spilled the coins all around the floor and placed his bed right in the middle of the room. As she did this, she reminded God about all of the blessing prayer candles that had been lit for her baby boy and asked Him to look down on all these coins to remember all those prayers said for her baby and to honor those prayers that night. It is said that the next morning the fever was gone, and the baby was smiling. From then on and for over 200 years now, all the women started spreading the coins out of their blessing jars when they desperately needed God to protect their child. We don't think the coins are magical or have healing power on their own. The spreading of the coins is our way of reminding God about those prayers. Then when that momma dies, each of her children are given their blessing jar to keep with them for the rest of their life. The blessing jar is buried with each owner, so they are never alone and remain covered with their lifelong blessing prayers."

As I headed back to Houma the next morning, my mind kept reviewing the story of the blessing jar, and I thought about my boys. Tilly and I didn't know about this sweet tradition, so our boys never had a blessing jar, but as I drove on, the thought occurred to me that it wasn't too late. I could decorate a special jar for each of my boys and fill them with coins that represented all the beautiful prayers their beloved mother had prayed for their safety and direction. I could write out this tradition story and remind my boys that their mother believed that a prayer offered to God on their behalf was never forgotten by God and that my boys are still covered by their mother's loving prayers. I knew this would mean a lot to both of my boys. I also knew that, from that day forward, once a year, Ava would say a blessing over me, and that thought also made me feel blessed.

7

Another Body Found

RRIVING BACK at Houma right at 10:00 a.m., I intended to head straight to the war room. I had written up my witness report from the night before and planned to hand it to Char before heading back to Dulac where I was certain I could identify the boat in question. Just as I parked in my assigned space, my phone started buzzing, indicating I had an urgent text. I had set up my phone to buzz me an urgent notice whenever Char, Dr. Harvey or Sheriff McClure texted me. The buzzing did not mean there really was an emergency, only that I needed to respond ASAP.

I pulled my phone out of my pocket and saw that the sheriff had texted all three of us—Char, Dr. Harvey, and myself. I quickly entered my passcode and clicked on the text to see, "Third body found," followed by an address. I decided to run upstairs to see if Char wanted to go there together. Dr. Harvey would have immediately gathered up his gear and headed out, but I found it rather strange that I had made it all the way back to the war room without a text from Char about this new find.

Using my passkey, I was surprised to find Char still at her desk.

Before I could say anything about the text, she queried, "Mike, did you move my notebook last night?"

"No, I just returned from Arcadia. I was going to go directly to Dulac, but it's a good thing I stopped by here first. Didn't you read the text from Sheriff McClure? Another body has been found."

Angry at herself for slipping up, Char grabbed her phone and turned it back on. "Sorry, I was in a meeting with DA Wilcomb and the parish council. I forgot to turn it back on when I came back here and found that someone has been in here."

"You're kidding! You're sure of that?" As soon as the words came out of my mouth, I regretted saying them. "Of course, you are sure. We need to look into this, but right now we have a dead body, and we need to get there before half the town shows up and contaminates the area."

"All I have to do is change my shoes. High heels don't go to crime scenes. Char opened her bottom drawer and pulled out a sturdy pair of flats, and we were on our way. Right before I closed the war-room door, I grabbed my camera, locked the door behind me, and caught up with Char at the elevator. "Not sure why I bothered locking that door if someone got in there last night."

Char studied the text, "Third body found." Then she copied the address into Google Search, and thoughtfully asked, "Why is Sheriff McClure calling this the *third* body? This is nowhere close to Dulac; it's right here in Houma. This isn't even the same location, and with so little evidence on either of the other bodies, why in the world would he link this body to the others?"

I would have caught this also if I hadn't been in such a hurry to get to the war room. I marveled yet again at Char's quick attention to details. *She looks at things with a trained eye.* I cleared my mind of the interview from the day before and of any possible intrusion. I needed to arrive at this crime scene unencumbered and focused.

By the time we arrived, Dr. Harvey had already cordoned off the area. He had also placed large orange cones around the body, and as he was examining the young woman's body, his lab assistant was busy pouring plaster molds of tire impressions. "Char, walk around the back and come here for a moment." I turned on my camera as Char and I joined the ME by the body. He barely whispered, "Same tire impressions as those found near the second victim."

Dr. Harvey then whispered, "I doubt that Sheriff McClure noticed those tire impressions, so that was not what caused him to link this case with the others. He walked all over about three feet of tire marks before noticing them. I have poured so many copies of these treads, I'd know them anywhere. But Char, something about this murder is just not right. Someone knew enough to try to get rid of the molds. Why would the person not have chosen a drop off that would not leave tire tracks? Also, if the person is aware, why have the tires not been changed by now? And if the person removing evidence and the person who is driving this car are not one and the same, what motive would he have?"

"This victim had not been dumped in Lake Boudreaux. She has been shot, but not here. She was dumped postmortem from the same car used in the kidnapping of the second victim in Dulac. No car, no keys, no purse, no phone, but we have fingerprints, dental work, and tattoos. We will know who this one is in a few hours. Liver temp tells me she died somewhere between midnight and 3:00 a.m. this morning. Char, we have an unsub around here going after young, blonde, white women. Nothing about the attacks seem to be sexually motivated, which in itself is strange, given the victims' ages. Once I confirm what I already know about the tire impressions, I will be ready to call this our third body—but not until."

I decided to delay my trip to Dulac and focus on any fresh evidence we could gather on this body. Two hours later, we had confirmation of identification. Fingerprints led us to a Cynthia Young, age twenty-three, no prior history of arrest, married with two children, living in Chauvin with her mother and children while her husband was in his third month of duty on board a Navy ship, currently ported at Norfolk, Virginia.

M.E. Harvey stood in our war room and said, "That is what we know. Now this is what I suspect. This body was dressed after being shot. The clothes are not new, and all of the labels have been cut out of them. Whoever committed this murder took some serious chances. Every time someone handles a body, he takes the chance of leaving behind evidence. This person was very careful with his first two victims, but he took huge chances with this one. Why?"

Ruling out the victim's husband, Char and I drove to Chauvin to interview her mother. The duty of informing this mother of her daughter's death was going to fall on our shoulders. The Navy would handle notifying her husband. Char had never done this before, so I took the lead. "Mrs. Holder, my name is Detective Majors, and this is ADA Char Smalls. We are from Houma, and we are so sorry to inform you that your daughter Cynthia was found in Houma this morning, dead from a gunshot wound." I gave the brief report quickly and straightforward. I have learned that there is no easy or polite way of telling someone that a loved one has been murdered. We waited for the shock to somewhat subside before asking any questions.

Char began, "Mrs. Holder, is there any reason your daughter was in Houma last evening?"

"No, none whatsoever. She didn't have gas in her car, and she didn't have money to put gas in her car. We used up the last of the milk at dinnertime, so she took $3 from my purse and drove to the Stop-N-Go about 9:30 last night to get milk so the girls would have some for breakfast. I went on to bed because I had been fighting a bad head-ache all evening. I wasn't even aware that she hadn't returned until this morning. Maggie woke me up this morning begging for breakfast—something Cynthia always handled. When I got up, I saw that her car was not in the driveway. I didn't know what to do. Cynthia is as solid as a rock. She is always where she is supposed to be."

"Mrs. Holder, did you call the police?"

"No. I made the girls toast and called Cynthia's two best friends. I thought if she had had car trouble that she wouldn't call me. I had the girls, and I have no money nor do I even begin to know how to change a tire, let alone fix anything. Both of her friends have husbands, so I called them. But neither of them had heard from Cynthia. I guess I should have called the police, but I just couldn't let my mind go there. It didn't occur to me that the police could drive around and maybe find her stranded in her car somewhere. I just sat here and waited, hop-ing she would come walking in the door any time. Instead, you came knocking on my door."

Char asked, "Is there anyone who might have had a grudge against your daughter, Mrs. Holder? An old boyfriend? Someone your son-in-law owes money to? Maybe an old girlfriend of your son-in-law?"

"No! Absolutely not!" came her forceful reply. "Doug and Cindy started dating in tenth grade and married right out of high school. Nei-ther ever dated anyone else, and as far as Doug owing someone money, he wouldn't borrow money, and no one around here would loan him any. That is why he joined the Navy right out of high school. He wanted to provide for his family, and joining the military was the only way he knew how." After pondering other possibilities, she offered, "Cynthia had just signed up to sell Mary Kay cosmetics to make some extra mon-ey. She and I thought she could do that, but she hadn't actually started yet. She didn't even have the money to buy her starter kit."

Char leaned in closer to ask, "Mrs. Holder, why did Cynthia need to make extra money?"

"I know what your question is implying, young lady. My Cynthia wanted the girls to have birthday parties and presents next summer. So little is left after buying food and paying utilities each month. But last month because both of the girls had ear infections, Cynthia was in the hole. Between the $25 deductible for each girl and the meds, Cynthia was wiped out of all her extra money. It was a toss-up whether to spend the money on gas to drive all the way to New Orleans to see a Navy doctor, praying that the car would even make it that far or pay the out-of-network deductible and stay close to home. So, Cynthia chose that option."

Before heading back to Houma, we stopped at the Stop-N-Go and asked to see their surveillance tapes. We quickly cued it to 9:00 p.m. the night before and slowly watched the tape. At 9:37, we saw Cynthia walk into the convenience store wearing loose-fitting pink and yellow bottoms and a Navy sweatshirt. She had not been wearing these when her body was discovered this morning. No one seemed to be following her around the store as she purchased a half-gallon of milk and left the store. For the next twenty minutes of watching the tape, Cynthia's car never moved from the parking spot in front of the store. The car was still there when we arrived that afternoon. We needed this tape. Hopefully, with the lab's help, we could see another car parked somewhere in that dark parking lot. *Cynthia must have gotten into another car... but why?*

Before leaving the Stop-N-Go, I picked up some milk, eggs, bread, soup, coffee, and other assorted items this brokenhearted mother would need right away. We knew it was too little and a little too late, but it was something. We returned to the house and knocked on the door. A very broken woman answered the door and let us back in. The girls were sitting on the sofa, watching cartoons, oblivious to how much their lives had just changed. I set the groceries on the kitchen table, then pulled my wallet out of my inside coat pocket and took out a well-folded one-hundred-dollar bill. Tilly and I had started this habit many years ago, always wanting to be ready to help out anyone in need; and as I handed it to this woman I said, "This is from my Tilly."

As we drove back to Houma, Char and I brainstormed about all the inconsistencies. "Nothing makes sense, Mike. Cynthia had no apparent link to Houma. The first victim has no identity so far. The second was only in Houma to see an old friend but never even made it to her house. Other than that, the only outrageously vague fact we have is that long ago, she used to date Calvin in high school. She had not been back to Houma in over fifteen years, and all phone records seem to confirm his statement that he had not called her nor she him in all that time.

"Mike, I think we need to address the fact that she is a Navy spouse. I will contact NCIS in New Orleans. They have a top-notch lab, and if anyone can see more than our eyes can see, their experts can. We need to enlist all the help we can to break open this case."

"But unless you suspect the Navy husband, I doubt their lab will accept it."

Char smiled, "Remember, I grew up in New Orleans. I just happen to know one of their top lab techs. It's time for me to call in a few favors. I tutored him all the way through college English. Funny thing was, I used to tease him by saying, 'If I were to put this English assignment on a glass slab and make you study it through one of your beloved microscopes, you would ace this class.' "

Char took out her notebook, "Now set aside the video for a moment. Let's go over every anomaly in these three cases. My professor said that it is better to focus on the anomalies rather than the similarities. Similarities link cases together, but when an unsub deviates from his routine, he makes mistakes.

1] Victims 2 and 3 have been identified; victim 1 remains unknown.

2] Victims 1 and 2 have never been pregnant; victim 3 was a mother.

3] Victims 1 and 2 were found in the lake at Dulac; victim 3 was dumped in Houma.

4] Victims 1 and 2 appeared to be wearing their own clothes; victim 3 was redressed.

5] Victims 1 and 2 were drowned; victim 3 was shot.

6] Victims 1 and 2 were attractive; victim 3 was obviously unattractive.

7] Victims 2 and 3 have no history of prostitution; victim 1 is unknown.

"Mike, I have been over and over these anomalies; I see no pattern here. We know they are somehow connected. There must be a link that has not yet been found—or has been hidden from us. The question is why and who is doing the hiding?"

"Char, we are only on day four of our investigation. We control the third victim's evidence. We have not yet confirmed what is actually known about the first two victims. Do you feel comfortable with the chain of evidence, the timeline of who actually conducted the first investigations, and how they are connected in this parish?

"Mike, while you were interviewing Buddy Benoit, I asked Dr. Harvey to tell me everything he knew about the first two cases, as well as everything he suspected but could not prove. He gave me very clinical answers, and I had the distinct feeling he was hiding something. I have no idea what that could be, but you and I need to call him into the war room and get to the bottom of it. I feel hamstrung here. You and I cannot get to the truth when people hold back on us. I am going to text Dr. Harvey and ask him to meet us in my office at four o'clock today."

As I drove toward Houma, Char became quiet, finishing her notes and closing her notebook. Once or twice, I had the distinct feeling she was about to speak but changed her mind. I just kept driving. Finally, she quietly spoke. "What you did for Cynthia's mother was sweet, Mike. You told her the gift of money was from Tilly. If I'm not mistaken, that was your wife's name, right?"

I winced a little, not yet being comfortable hearing anything about her said in the past tense. "Yes, Char, Tilly was my wife, and although I lost her thirteen months ago, she is never far from my thoughts. She was my anchor, my rock, my conscience, my lover, and my best friend. When I am quiet, I can still hear her voice nudging me to do the right thing, the compassionate thing, the uncomfortable things that I would usually avoid. That woman made me a better person. I was a very blessed man, Char."

Char smiled at me but said nothing more, and I appreciated that and noted to myself, *This young woman has class. She is not afraid to ask hard questions, but she knows when to step back and let a fellow breath.*

8

Our First Confession

C HAR MADE a fresh pot of coffee while we waited for Dr. Harvey
to arrive. I took this opportunity to fill in Char on what I had
learned from Buddy Benoit. "Char, I intended to drive back to Dulac
this morning and find that boat, but then we were waylaid by a third
body. Buddy provided sufficient details to have found that boat owner
within a day or two, yet we have no report of anyone having interviewed that boat owner—or even who he is."

"Stay on it, Mike. That is the only lead we have for our first case.
The fact that we have no evidence of anyone tracking down that lead
worries me."

"Worries me too, Char. I am not a big believer in conspiracy theo-
ries. They require too many people knowing your business. No one is
so powerful that he can control an entire parish. Maybe he can control
one or two, but unless the killer has access inside these walls, how is he
manipulating every scrap of evidence?"

Char started to answer when Dr. Harvey knocked on our war-room
door, and Char asked me to let him in. Dr. Harvey was noticeably

uncomfortable as he entered and took a seat at the conference table. Char placed a fresh cup of coffee in front of him and took a seat. "Dr. Harvey, I will come right to the point. Michael Majors and I have been hired to solve the murders of the first two victims, and now we have a third victim who is loosely connected to the first two. I do not have time to play games with you. Women are being killed, and I suspect we will have more bodies to autopsy if you continue to hold back on us."

Dr. Harvey kept his head lowered, studying the cup in front of him. Char and I could both tell he was struggling within. I knew he wanted to come clean; he just needed a little persuading. Char stood, pushed her chair around next to Dr. Harvey's chair, and as she sat down, she took hold of the arm of his chair and spun him around so they were sitting knee to knee. Char flashed him one of her brilliant smiles that contain no animus as she leaned forward and asked, "Dr. Harvey, you do have something to tell us, don't you?"

Char and I remained quiet as we watched a man struggle with a weighty decision. I assumed this was not the first time he had pondered his options. Finally, Dr. Harvey lifted his head and looked Char right in the eyes, "Okay, I'll tell you what I know and what I suspect. But first, I need to tell you how and why I became vulnerable. I do not speak of my vulnerability as an excuse. I simply tell you because I need to clear my conscience."

Again, Char flashed him a smile and said, "Take your time, Dr. Harvey."

"I have never been one who strived for fame or fortune. During medical school I realized I was not cut out for looking across my desk and telling a patient he or she was going to die. My professors said, 'You will grow a thick professional skin, and after the first few times, it will stop hurting.' I hated that thought. I never wanted to become so 'professionally disconnected,' that I didn't feel the pain of others.

———

"I wanted to be of value, but I had no interest in becoming a great surgeon. My heart was always drawn to finding answers as to why someone had died and to be able to provide the families with answers. That was when I knew my destiny was to become a medical examiner. I did not mind living my life practically alone with the dead. I was able to help people; after all, the great medical staff had failed to keep their loved one alive. At least I could give them some answers that would help heal some of the loss, and I have done that for thirty years.

"One year before the first body was discovered, my wife of thirty-five years died of colon cancer. My life was in turmoil as I watched her fade away, but I kept my professional demeanor intact while she and I faced the fact that she had no hope of a cure. I had buried my wife a mere six months before that first victim was placed on my slab. After my wife died, I had started drinking a little too much and a little too often. I was numb, and I was lost. Three weeks before that first body arrived, I met my lawyer to sign a bunch of documents, removing Clare from my will and putting our three daughters in her place. That was a difficult lunch meeting, and I drank a little too much that day. I should have called in sick and gone home to sleep it off but heading home that day was the last thing I wanted to do.

"Foolishly, I returned to my office. I never would have touched a body that afternoon. I was not too far gone to know that. I would have ordered the body be transported to another ME. After all, we don't get suspicious deaths around here every day. Medically supervised deaths can always wait a day, so I felt safe returning to my office. How wrong I was!"

Char leaned in again and asked, "What happened that day, Dr. Harvey?"

"Nothing! Absolutely nothing went wrong." Dr. Harvey's eyes filled with tears as he continued. "I did not perform any medical procedures or write any medical reports that day. But I found out that simply being in my office while intoxicated was a breach of conduct, and that is how I was snared. I should have reported myself and taken whatever the reprimand would have been. But at the time, I could not imagine my life without my job to distract me from my pain."

I sat watching Dr. Harvey talking about going through exactly what I had experienced after losing my Tilly. I understood his pain, and I wanted to tell him about my Tilly, but now was not the time or the place. I made a mental note to invite Dr. Harvey to have dinner with me when things settle down. The two of us have a lot in common.

Trying to give Dr. Harvey some room to breathe, Char leaned back in her chair and asked, "Dr. Harvey, tell us about this snare and who orchestrated it."

"Char, what I am going to tell you now is both fact and supposition, but I do not believe in coincidence. The day after that young woman was pulled from the lake, Mr. Sinclair and DA Wilcomb came into my autopsy room—something DA Wilcomb tended to avoid like the plague. They had both just returned from a business trip to Houston, Texas, and heard that we had an unidentified body with suspicious circumstances. Both men wanted to see the body. I had taken photos, but they wanted to see her. Calvin also wanted to see my preliminary autopsy report and looked rather relieved at what he read—until he came to my cause of death, which I had recorded as *drowning by suspicious means*.

He showed the report to Sinclair, who immediately asked, "Why are you calling it suspicious? Maybe she jumped and committed suicide. Couldn't that be a viable conclusion? You state in your report that there were no bruises on the body, so she wasn't held under, right?"

At this point I didn't wait for Char to respond. "Dr. Harvey, why was Sinclair in autopsy?"

"That's exactly what I asked." Dr. Harvey turned to Char and said, "Would you, as an ADA, feel you needed to bring along your personal attorney?"

"Wait a minute," Char responded, "So Sinclair is not only Max Wilcomb's attorney, but now you are telling me that he is also Calvin's attorney?"

"He is more than just Calvin's attorney, Ms. Smalls; he is Calvin's campaign manager. Three years ago, Papa Wilcomb hired Mr. Sinclair to set up and manage a campaign to ensure Calvin's bid for the Senate seat coming open next year. Max Wilcomb has been funding it, and everything Calvin has done for the past three years has been carefully orchestrated with that election in mind. Calvin could not afford to lose a case, so every case was settled out of court.

"Even the trip to Houston had been a bid for position. Sinclair and Wilcomb were organizing a world-class fishing competition. Their idea was to make Terrebonne Parish well-known by having the parish host most of the competition. Lots of press, lots of tourists, lots of local economy, and therefore, attention, attention, attention for Calvin Wilcomb. Those two do nothing without that objective in mind."

Char looked puzzled. "But how does any of this ensnare you, Dr. Harvey?"

"Because when I refused to change my findings, they got ugly. Sinclair did not want a murder case in the parish at this point in the campaign. They had spent an abundance of money setting up the world-class fishing competition, and they could not afford to have DA Wilcomb distracted and unavailable for all of the photo ops and publicity gatherings. They also could not afford a possible unsolved murder case on his record so close to the main campaign. He argued that because this young woman was not from around here and as yet unidentified, I should simply classify it as a suicide and put it to bed.

"When I still refused to go along with him, Sinclair played his trump card. He pulled out the original bar bill from three weeks earlier." Seeing Char's look of shock, Dr. Harvey confessed, "Yes, I know how foolish I was to hire Sinclair as my lawyer, but it was just a codicil to my will. Sinclair reminded me that even crossing the threshold of my office made me guilty of gross negligence. He cited that pilots do not have to actually fly the plane to be charged with gross negligence. All they have to do is board the plane while intoxicated to be found guilty. He said, 'The same goes for doctors.' A doctor who enters the hospital facility while intoxicated would be found guilty. They do not have to wait until that doctor actually treats a patient. Entering my autopsy lab that day was all I had to do to lose my job and my license to practice my profession."

I was puzzled and asked, "Wasn't Sinclair your attorney, Dr. Harvey? Isn't he bound by attorney-client privilege?"

Char answered my question. "Mike, Sinclair's privilege only pertained to the will he was drafting for Dr. Harvey."

Dr. Harvey confessed, "I wish I had called his bluff that day and turned myself in and let the chips fall where they may. But I couldn't imagine how I could go on without Clare and my job, so I offered to water down my findings. I agreed to rewrite my report and simply state, *Drowned.*" Dr. Harvey then looked directly at Char and confessed, "I knew I had been handled and that I had given in. I was quite certain neither of these two men were involved in the murder; they were eight hours away in Houston for four days prior to her entering the water. They wanted this whole thing to go away quietly, and I let them—for a whole year."

"What changed your mind, Doctor?"

"Because, Char, I do have a conscience. Wilcomb took over all of the evidence. He and his best friend, Officer Tate, did all of the interviews and found no evidence to warrant further action. I knew that was wrong, so after I came to terms with what I had to face regarding my own involvement, I wrote to the state's attorney general.

"I asked the attorney general to review District Attorney Wilcomb's ruling on this open case. Under the Louisiana Constitution of 1921, the attorney general is an officer of the judicial branch of government. He is vested with statewide criminal jurisdiction to initiate original criminal prosecutions or to intervene in existing ones. Implicit in this power is the independent prosecutorial discretion as to when and how to exercise it. To date in Louisiana, this jurisdiction has only been exercised twice, so before stepping in and exercising his power, the state's attorney general ordered an independent investigation. We have been told that he found no chargeable action against DA Wilcomb; however, he strongly recommended the hiring of outside investigators. Hence, you two were hired."

Char leaned forward again. "Dr. Harvey, you said that DA Wilcomb took over all the evidence. Might you have made backup copies as you did with the tire impressions?"

"Yes, I always do, and I did not tell the DA that I had. Granted, there is limited evidence, but I suspect Wilcomb didn't care to look too hard. He just wanted it to go away."

Turning to me, Char ordered, "Mike, I want you to get Dr. Harvey's fingerprints of the first victim and take them to Baton Rouge. Since we do not know who we can trust, I don't want them in our computer system just yet. I don't want anyone to know we are looking at them. I want you to stay there while the prints are run through CODIS. Someone must be looking for this woman. We also need to verify that Wilcomb and Sinclair were in Houston that entire time. We cannot afford to assume anything. We need to return to Dulac and find that boat owner. Unless he was just a passerby, someone will remember that boat.

"As for you, Dr. Harvey, I need to talk with my law professor before I make any promises or decisions regarding your situation. My heart wants to keep you on these cases, but I am not really clear as to the repercussions to my office if I were to do so. I am concerned for you, and I am concerned for the ongoing protection of these cases. If you are suspended, pending a hearing, I do not trust who will be put in your place. So, until I know what I can legally do, everything that has been said in this room stays in this room."

Since Baton Rouge was only two hours away traveling via US 61 North, I decided to follow Dr. Harvey to his lab and collect the fingerprints. I wanted to be on the road by 7:00 a.m. the next morning. I spent that evening writing out all of my notes, keeping some things coded in case my notepad mysteriously went missing. Feeling a little overly cautious, I moved all of my work papers into my bedroom so I could get a good night of sleep and was on the road earlier than planned.

I was about thirty minutes out when I realized that Char and I had not returned to her original question of the day before. I turned off my car radio and said, "Siri, text Char for me."

"What do you want to say?"

"Concerning war-room privacy: suggest we sweep for bugs. Should have done so before yesterday's meeting. Protect your notes. Warn Dr. Harvey. See you around 3:00."

Almost immediately came an answering text: "Agree to all. Watch your back."

I had to wait two hours for my turn on CODIS. I suspected this was a little territorial war wrangling, seeing as how Houma is generally treated like the orphaned child while Baton Rouge is the privileged state capital. I had to enter my badge number, our case number, and electronically sign into their log before the officer could enter our fingerprints.

I commented to the officer, "We never had to do this in Miami. What's with all the security?"

I was told that four years earlier, a rogue cop had used the system to stalk women, and after multiple complaints by women, this system had been instituted.

It only took thirty minutes for a match to pop up on the screen:

IDENTIFICATION INFORMATION

Name	**Gender**
Sandra Green	Female
Date of Birth	**Race**
May 5, 1986	Caucasian
Current Age	**SSN**
31	099-09-9990

NO OUTSTANDING WARRANTS

ARREST RECORD

Arrested 2003, age 17, charged with prostitution in Cincinnati, Ohio; suspended.

Arrested 2008, age 22, Charged with embezzlement in Toledo, Ohio; suspended.

Arrested 2011, age 25, Charged with identity theft, probation and time served.

| THUMB | INDEX | MIDDLE | RING | LITTLE |

LAST RUN: 3/14/07 by Calvin Wilcomb

As the officer clicked the print button, I sat puzzled as I read the screen and wondered why this woman had gone unidentified for eighteen months. As the printer spit out the findings, the officer asked, "Do you want the CODIS report of activity as well?"

"Yeah, sure." Then suspecting it might be a long report, I asked, "Is that a nationwide report or just your system?"

"It is only our system, sorry." I was relieved at his answer…until I saw what came up on the screen. Only one name was listed, and Char and I were now in for a major battle. Calvin Wilcomb's name was the only name on that report.

9

Dirty Hands

DECIDED not to call Char with my findings. I was only two hours away from home, and I wanted to be there when she learned this interesting bit of information. Not having had time to check for bugs, I texted, "Char, meet me at our first meeting place at two o'clock."

Two minutes later came, "Understood!"

Char was already at Clara's Café when I arrived. She was sitting in the last booth, facing the front door—exactly where I would have chosen to sit. The booth in front of her had a "reserved" sign sitting in the center of the table; I assumed Char had made this handwritten sign and had brought it with her. Once again, my admiration for this young woman deepened. I said nothing. I simply took a seat across from her, handed her the two reports, and waited. Char read the reports several times before placing them on the table. "Wow! Where do we go from here, Mike?"

"We tread very lightly, Char. Being an investigator, I am careful not to assume facts not in evidence." Keeping my voice down, I suggested, "Char, since I have had two hours longer than you to absorb this new information, why don't I share what has been running through my head for the past two hours?"

Flipping her notebook open to a clean new page, Char readied her pen and said, "Run with it, Mike."

Facts

▶ Wilcomb knew who the first victim was two days after she arrived on Dr. Harvey's slab.

▶ Wilcomb knew she had a history of criminal activity since she was seventeen years old.

▶ Her involvement in identity theft means we do not know what name she was using in Dulac.

▶ We have proof that Wilcomb received this report and hid this report. Why?

Suppositions

▶ Possibly bad timing, distracting Wilcomb from his big publicity events?

▶ Possibly Sinclair does not trust Wilcomb's ability to actually walk a murder trial into court?

▶ Possibly simple prejudice: once a prostitute, always one, and good riddance to bad rubbish?

Improbabilities

▶ Wilcomb was somehow involved in the murder? Confirm his alibi!

▶ Sinclair is somehow the puppet master, using Wilcomb to hide his involvement? Confirm his alibi!

▶ Unlikely that Dr. Harvey lied about being blackmailed; confirm before charging them.

▶ One of them could be protecting the killer?

Conundrums

▶ Two additional bodies. Would they protect a serial killer?

▶ If Sinclair is protecting Wilcomb, we need independent witnesses to confirm both alibis.

▶ Figure out how to confirm the blackmail—a possible wiretap?

▶ How and when do we confront Wilcomb with this evidence...or go straight to the attorney general?"

Char put down her pen and grimaced painfully. "Mike, sometimes, as you know, sweet news can often come with a bitter pill chaser."

"Well, Char, I have always found it best to swallow a bitter pill quickly."

"Mike, it's about the blackmail. While you were up in Baton Rouge getting this evidence, I was on the phone with my mentor. Because of the potential serious nature of having Dr. Harvey's confession, I requested our conversation be off the record. After I laid out the entire timeline, he said Dr. Harvey is safe; the problem is, so is Sinclair."

Frustrated by this explanation, I blurted out, "Even if we get him on tape admitting to it?"

"I asked the same question, Mike. The issues are that everything was verbal: the blackmail held for one full year, and seven additional months have passed since Dr. Harvey finally called Sinclair's bluff by refusing to continue cooperating and wrote the attorney general. By his doing that, the blackmail became moot in both parties. The sweet part is Dr. Harvey is safe; the bitter part is that Sinclair is also. Let me explain point by point:

1] Sinclair cannot produce this evidence now without explaining why he held onto it for over a year. His action would substantiate Harvey's allegation of blackmail.

2] The length of time from Harvey's alleged violation to when Sinclair could have turned him in is long past. My mentor does not believe a medical review board would consider acting after such a lengthy time period, especially with no evidence he touched a body or wrote a medical report during that time frame.

3] Allegedly, Sinclair blackmailed Dr. Harvey because two years of preparation for the 2016 Bayou Bass-Fishing Classics was just about to start filming, and they were promoting Terrebonne Parish as a safe and pristine place to come. Dr. Harvey's one year of silence allowed their plan to go off without a hitch.

4] Once Dr. Harvey wrote that letter and called Sinclair's bluff, my mentor believes that once someone like Sinclair lost control, he could never be baited into talking about the blackmail.

5] Three weeks after losing that control, the second body dropped. If Sinclair was simply maneuvering for political benefit, he got what he wanted and will remain silent—especially with bodies piling up. If either Sinclair himself, or his golden boy Calvin are involved in the murders, we will have to go after them another way."

I interrupted Char's train of thought. "Char, to think these two could be involved in these three murders is a big stretch." But as this statement came out of my mouth, I remembered a case from Miami and suggested, "Well, on second thought, I worked a case back in the late '70s where several bodies showed up over the course of about six weeks. Like these, we had a hard time linking them together because they had just enough similarities to tell us we were looking for the same man, but they were not similar enough to make sense of all the evidence."

"So how did you solve it, Mike?"

"Once we realized we were being played by someone who understood evidence, we stopped paying attention to the anomalies because they were not errors; rather, they were intentional rabbit trails. Only one of the bodies was actually linked to the killer; the others were smoke and mirrors."

"So, Mike, we study each body as an independent case until we can link one of them to someone. At least now we know who all three victims are; at least that is a starting point."

"But, Char, Clara's Café cannot become our war room. What are you going to do about Wilcomb and Sinclair?"

"Mike, I am not paranoid; however, I am rather obsessively compulsive. I always have a place for everything, and I never deviate once something has been given a place. I started this habit when I was young. I think that habit was my way of controlling an uncontrollable world. I lived with three people who never did a deliberate action in their lives. Because of their indolence, they never paid any attention as to where an item was placed because the thought would never occur to them. I could always tell when one of them had been snooping in my room.

"This became a habit for me. I like the feeling of being in control of my little space in this world. The other day while we were setting up the war room, I set up my desk. In doing so, I determined "where" everything would go. Once I have decided, that is exactly where items will always be placed."

"Okay, Char, I get it. I'm not like that, but I get it."

"Well, like I told you, my notebook had been moved. Not a lot—but enough that I knew someone had been snooping in our war room. So now we know that you and I are not the only ones with a key. How is this possible?"

"You are absolutely sure about this, Char?" Even as these words left my mouth, I regretted saying them. "I know you are sure, Char. I think I need to go have a talk with our local locksmith."

"Mike, trust me, I'm not being paranoid. I don't think we should confront the locksmith. We have no idea how he is connected to Wilcomb. Maybe his mother just demanded a set of keys because she runs that building, and no one tells her how to run her building. Maybe her snooping is simply her way of proving to herself that she is still in control. Do you know how to change a deadbolt lock?"

"I can figure it out! When I leave here, I'll go to the hardware store and buy a whole new mechanism and have it installed within an hour. Are we going to waste time trying to solve the case of an illegal entry or are we going to secure our world and move on?"

"I suspect Wilcomb is nervous about what we might know. We have him on withholding evidence in a murder case. Right now, we can only prove that he withheld the fingerprint identification; we cannot prove he destroyed the tire impressions. But the fact that two additional bodies have been added to the count could sit directly on his shoulders. If he had aggressively pursued the first case, they might have connected the killer to the first victim and stopped the killing."

"That is assuming that all Wilcomb is guilty of is tampering and not murder."

"True, but Char, either way, once the Wilcomb family realizes we are looking at their golden boy, a reign of terror is sure to come down on us. The longer we can protect our sources and our plans, the easier and safer we will be. Just changing the lock is going to send a huge message to SOMEONE. But that cannot be helped, we need our privacy."

"Mike, do you know how to sweep a room for bugs?"

"Again, Char, I've never done it, but I will find a way to either hire an outsider or learn how to do it myself. I wish I had thought of that while I was still up in Baton Rouge. Maybe it's worth another four-hour round-trip drive to make sure our buying these items does not get reported to Wilcomb and Sinclair. I'll get started right away so I can be back here by 8:00 tonight and get us buttoned down. But Char, I need to go back to Dulac tomorrow and find that boat owner."

"Okay, Mike. I've already warned Dr. Harvey about the break-in and that someone now knows about the extra set of tire impressions and the fingerprints. I shipped the video directly to my friend in New Orleans early this morning. Now I'm starting to second-guess my every move. Maybe I should have sent the video with you to Baton Rouge and had you mail it from there."

"Char, conspiracies can only go so deep and so far. Yes, this is a "well-connected" town, but not everyone can be involved. Having said that, I think I will simply drive back to Chauvin. It's only a thirty-minute drive, and it will just look like I am working the third case. We need to protect our cases, but we don't need to get paranoid."

10

Resistance

BY ELEVEN o'clock that night our war room had been re-keyed and had been swept for listening devices. We agreed that no important information was ever to be passed between us via the city hall telephone system; we were to communicate via our cellphones only. As much as possible we would contact each other by text. We also decided that any time we had a suspect or a lead in the war room, I would sweep for bugs before we let anyone into the room. I wished we had taken these precautions before meeting with Dr. Harvey, but who would have guessed we would need these to implement these safety measures. Finally, we felt a little more secure. I did not find a bug, so Char and I felt Dr. Harvey was still safe. I left for Dulac the next morning, fully expecting to find the boat and the owner in very short order.

Not wanting to draw attention to myself, I didn't want to ask questions just yet. I started at one end of the marina and walked up and down every dock, looking for any 25- to 30-foot cabin cruiser, black hull, white deck with an open front lounge, with dark-blue or black polka-dot upholstery, and the word *Swamp* in its name.

After almost two hours in the Louisiana sun, I headed back to the bait shop. I felt cartoonish as I walked in the door. I could not have done any more to scream, *I am not a fisherman*, then to have walked the docks for two hours in my street clothes; I just hoped it worked. My sport coat was drenched in perspiration. I was tempted to take it off, but my wet shirt was clinging to my body.

The old man remembered me from my last visit and smiled, "Did you find Buddy?"

I smiled in return, thankful this old man was still being gracious. "Sure did, thanks. He's a good boy, and he has a nice family."

The old man kept filling the shelf behind the counter with snack food as he changed the subject. "You know, back in the day, I sold mostly fishing gear—hooks, grappling gear, knives, rope. Nowadays, even the old-timers buy their gear online. I can't beat their prices, so now I stock my store with snack food. Those boys climb off those boats starving to death and will about clean me out. Such is life these days. But bait is one thing they can't buy online; that has to be fresh, so I'm still doing okay."

I purchased a cold soda and two bags of chips. While the old man counted change, I casually commented, "You must know every boat owner on these waters, don't you?"

"I know most every *fisherman* around here, but all those fancy-pants boaters think they are too good to come into my bait shop—even for snacks and cold drinks. Most of them bring their fancy food and imported drinks and make absolute pests of themselves out on the water with real fishermen."

I smiled after downing the cold soda in about three gulps, "I guess I'm looking for one of those fancy-pants boaters. If I described his boat, do you think you might know him?"

"You should go ask at the marina office, mister. They know every boat in this marina. But as for me, if they don't have a crane, winch, and at least 50 crab traps on their boat, I'm not interested. Wish I could help you."

I thanked him for the cold drink and headed to the marina office. Char and I had discussed the problems I would encounter if I had to interview the marina staff. We knew that Sinclair and Wilcomb had pulled off a huge fishing event the year before, and most of the professional fishermen felt extremely beholden to them both. After seeing the films on the TV Sporting Channel, not only did the fishing revenues skyrocket, most of the commercial rigs were now hosting wannabe fishermen, willing to spend top dollar for few days of hard work and adventure. Anything, or anyone, that threatened this new burst of economy would be dealt with in the harshest of ways. One misdirected question and I would be driven off the dock and into the water before I could finish my question.

Char and I were very much aware of how totally immersed Calvin Wilcomb's name had been interwoven into these films. As soon as any scandal leaked out regarding Calvin, the Sports Channel reruns would be dropped, and we would undoubtedly be blamed. If we were going to move forward, we had to make sure we found sufficient evidence to make this fallout worthwhile.

Opening the office door, I quickly noticed three individuals. I immediately knew the man in his late fifties sitting behind a desk by the back window was in charge. His face screwed up into a snarl as soon as he laid eyes on me. I had made it obvious that I was not a fisherman, so he dropped his gaze and continued reading the newspaper in front of him. The second man, who was several years his junior, walked up to the counter and asked, "What can I do for you?" His question sounded more like a statement rather than a question that I was expected to answer.

I instantly wished I had taken the time to review all of the fishing films before coming there. I might have been able to play off a pretense of having watched them and was here just checking out the area. Even as this thought crossed my mind, the man at the counter said, "You're that new investigator, aren't you?!"

That question closed another avenue of conversation. "Yes, I am. My name is Mike Majors. I've been sent down here to follow up on a witness statement that was taken eighteen months ago…"

Cutting in before I had finished introducing myself, the older man put down his newspaper as he bellowed, "Yeah, we know. Buddy Benoit was the witness—sort of. You are aware that Cajun fishermen drink a lot, aren't you? More than one of them falls overboard every single year 'cuz he can't handle his liquor. On top of that, by his own admission he was roused from a sound sleep. Can't rightly believe you boys would put much stock in Buddy's tall tale."

"Nonetheless," I plowed on, trying to sound as disinterested as the old man was, "I am required to follow up on this *tall tale*. It should be easy enough. Either the boat exists or it doesn't. If it doesn't, Benoit will be considered a fame chaser, and we drop him." Sounding as disgusted as I could, I added, "I already walked the whole marina and couldn't see a boat that looked anything like Benoit described. You might just have something there about him drinking."

A snicker escaped the guy at the counter while the older one responded, "Yeah, we watched you walking up and down the docks dressed in that sport coat, no less."

I thought to myself, *I knew you would be watching me. At least that was not a waste of my time.*

The old man continued, "Why didn't you just come here and ask? I'd a told you we only have seven cruisers docked here. Only two of them have an open hull lounge up front. One of them has been docked for four years with a blown engine that old Charlie can't afford to fix. The other one is an aqua-blue hull with a white top named *Betsie's Bum*, and she belongs to me. I bought her the month my divorce was final in the fall of 1983, and I named her that 'cuz I was proud to be Betsie's ex-bum. Those aqua-colored pads have always been on her since she was new in '71."

I knew this guy was offering too much information. He was giving me extra details, and he had a reason for doing so.

"Besides all that..." he continued, and I thought to myself, *So here comes the real reason he is being so unusually chatty with me.*

"I loaned my boat to my boy that month, so my boat wasn't even in Louisiana waters. My boy took her down to Tampa, Florida, 'cuz he started a new job and needed a cheap place to live until he got settled down there. He lived on my boat from March 10 until he returned her to me the following winter. You can check out my story if you want. I'm only telling you 'cuz I don't want you to go think'n my boy could have done that murder."

As the old man gloated, thinking he had both debunked Buddy's story and had protected his own boy from becoming a suspect, I let him get comfortable because that's when they let down their guard. I let my shoulders roll ever so slightly forward, making sure I didn't overact. "Benoit has cost me almost three hours in this Louisiana heat."

The old guy chuckled, and I believe he almost felt sorry for me, but I didn't want his pity; I wanted him to get cocky and forget to watch his step. I dared not look over at him because he would take that look as a challenge, and that would be that. I had been in the office for thirteen minutes and had yet to catch the eye of the third man. I had learned to quickly size up the pecking order among co-workers. The old man was definitely the alpha dog, and this guy was absolutely the omega dog—the grunt, the disrespected putz—just the guy I wanted to befriend. *He views me as an equal—a fellow putz.* If I had come in here flashing my badge, over-talking his alpha dog, he would have turned stone cold toward me. All I have to do now is get him alone, and he will spill his guts.

As I left the office, I noted that the old man did not say there had never been any other cruisers docked in his marina—only that right now there were only seven. An investigator has to pay close attention to words. People who are lying to you tend to use too many words as a way of covering up what they do not want to tell you. Men tend to talk very little, and they usually get right to the point. This guy had been prepared to give me the full accounting of every cruiser currently in the marina. *Why?* I wondered. I would have understood if he had told me about his boat. *He wants to make sure his boy was in the clear.* That made sense, but why the others…and so quickly, without any probing from me? Being so helpful was where the old man had made his mistake. *He knows about the boat I am looking for, and he is protecting someone.*

I sat in my car for another hour before my "omega dog" came walking to his car. He was at least six-feet-seven inches and thin as a rail. I let him get into his car and leave the marina parking lot before I followed him. He made two quick stops before parking in front of a house that was little more than a shack. I stayed put and let him get into his house and settle in for a few minutes. As I waited, I noticed a café right down the street that specialized in shrimp and grits and ice-cold chocolate shakes. I got out of my car and walked up to the door he had entered a few minutes earlier and knocked.

Fear was his first response when he came to the door and saw me. I suspected that was always this man's first and only response. He reminded me of a dog I once owned that had been a rescue project of Tilly's. The pound was about to put him down, so Tilly brought him home. He had obviously been beaten and starved for a long time. I had to learn to move slowly and deliberately around that dog because quick moves sent him into a shaking fit. I suspected this guy would act much the same way. Whenever I had accidently moved too fast and sent Duke into a panic attack, words would never get through to him. I started keeping a box of doggie treats next to my recliner because usually during a football game I would forget the dog lying at my feet, and I would jump up, screaming at some call made by a blind and stupid ref that would send that dog into a painful panic. Once I realized what I had done, I would sit back down and offer Duke a treat. I did not try to talk to him, and I had learned the hard way not to try to pet him during a panic attack. That poor dog could not tell the difference between good touching and bad touching—but he sure understood treats. I was going to use that same technique on this guy. I could tell he didn't know what to do. He just stood at the door staring at me.

I smiled, making sure not to make any sudden moves. "Remember me, Sid? I was thinking I'd get a bite to eat before heading back to Houma. I was driving by here looking for a good place when I saw you pull in here and recognized you. I hate to eat alone, so how about you join me for some shrimp and grits down the street—my treat. I noticed they even serve chocolate shakes. Care to join me?"

Sid stood there for about a minute, trying to decide what to do. *I suspect Sid never makes quick, concise decisions.* "Uh…I just took out a TV dinner."

"That's okay, Sid. Just toss it back in the freezer for another night. I don't know about you, but the idea of a frosty-cold chocolate shake sounds pretty good to me. How about you? It's just about four doors down, so we could walk. Remember, it's my treat."

"I don't know about that place; I've never eaten there."

"Then pick someplace else; I don't care where you choose. As long as the food is hot, the shakes are cold, and they have good grits, I'll be a happy camper."

"Well, I guess that place is as good as any. The guy next door eats there all the time, so it must be okay." With that last statement, Sid pulled his front door closed behind him, and we started walking toward the café. Neither of us said a word until we were seated and checking out the menu. I smiled and suggested, "How about the all-you-can-eat shrimp and grits dinner special?"

Sid's eyes lit up as he nodded his head in agreement. The waitress came over and took our order. When I told the waitress we both wanted a double-thick chocolate shake with whipped cream, Sid actually smiled. I sat back and looked out the window. When you are working a wounded creature, man or animal, you must give them breathing room. Pushing too hard could spook him. I wanted to continue playing the part of an omega dog; they know their place in this world, and they never take control of any situation…sadly, not even in their own home. But here in the café, Sid and I were equals. I just had to fill up Sid's empty stomach and get him to relax.

After Sid's third bowl of shrimp and grits, he began to unwind. "Don't you just hate Old Man Barry?" Sid asked. "He really is a bum. His wife was right. All he ever does is shout orders."

I stayed quiet. I just gave Sid a knowing smile.

"Barry thinks he knows so much. You should have seen how he kept trying to get himself interviewed by all those film crews. He actually did get into one of the films when they filmed the marina." Then giving me a knowing look as he polished off his second shake, he suggested, "You might want to go look through those films, Mike. I think if you study them real hard, being careful to pay attention to all of the boats in the background, you might find one or two answers for yourself."

Signaling the waitress for yet another bowl of shrimp and grits, Sid smiled, "Remember, I didn't tell you anything. It's not my fault if you suddenly get interested in fishing competition films and especially the ones that film the different boats in our marina."

I have what I'm looking for, I thought triumphantly. After Sid polished off that last bowl of shrimp and grits, I paid the bill. The two of us walked back together. Full and satisfied, Sid waved as he entered his shabby little place.

I too was satisfied. I had a really strong lead, and I smiled as I headed back to Houma, determined to watch all of those films very carefully. I could have taken a heavy-handed approach by threatening to bring a subpoena and force Barry to open his records, but Char and I knew she would have to run a request for a subpoena by her boss. We had decided to go in a different direction in order to keep our investigation private for now. *We shall see if our plan worked.*

That evening I joined Netflix because Sid had hinted that I might like to stroll through their documentaries and sporting films. Being an old-school kind of guy, it took me a while to figure out how to navigate their website. I miss the old days of looking through the *TV Guide* and just turning to channel 7. Who needs 250 channels of the same stuff? But once I found what I was looking for, I adjusted my opinion. In the old days, if you missed a program on the television, you simply missed it. Nowadays, everything is on reruns, on demand, and available on Netflix for months on end. *Maybe not everything new is bad.*

I made myself a cup of tea and hunkered down on my sofa, ready to watch hours of fishing commentaries. I was fairly sure Sid's hint specified "watch for Old Man Barry's famous minute of fame," but I just didn't know where in all of these films that one minute would be. I started speeding past films that were taken out at sea among the crabbing rigs, and endless interviews of fishermen talking about current, reading the water, baiting, etc. I have told you that I hate fishing! Have I also told you just how much I hate listening to fishermen telling their fishing whoppers? Well, I do, but I endured them that night.

About midnight I clicked on yet another film and there he was—Old Man Barry in all of his glory. He looked like he thought of himself as Hemingway's *The Old Man and the Sea*. He was standing on the deck outside his office, talking to the cameraman about how many commercial rigs his marina could host. I sat up straight and studied every boat in the background, but none of them were cruisers docked behind him. All were commercial vessels. I was beginning to think Sid had pulled a fast one on me when all of a sudden way off in the background, I spotted a 30-foot cruiser with a black hull, white top, open front deck with a lounge, moving slowly under the bridge that links the marina to the Houma Navigational Canal that links the marina to the Gulf. I watched that boat turn left and head south toward the Gulf before the camera moved and I lost sight of it. The cruiser was too far away to make out who was piloting that boat, but if I could get my hands on the original film, the crime lab could perform certain enhancements to the film and maybe, just maybe, we could see *who* was at the wheel.

"But again," I argued with myself, "the owners will not release their film without a subpoena, and we do not dare tip our hand."

I couldn't wait to show Char what I had found. I clicked "Start from the beginning" and used my iPad's camera to capture the segment of film Char would be interested in viewing. I knew it wouldn't be a great copy, but it would show her we had enough to warrant a subpoena. I also filmed all of the credits so, if we could obtain a subpoena, it would be for this one film alone. I knew the hour was late, but Char needed to know this was coming.

"CHAR, DO NOT GO INTO THE WAR ROOM TOMORROW MORNING. MEET ME IN THE PARKING LOT AT 7 A.M. SHARP. WE HAVE A LEAD!"

Immediately came a response: "MAKE THAT 6 A.M. OR DO IT NOW. THANKS, NOW I WILL GET NO SLEEP AT ALL TONIGHT."

11

Wowzah!

As soon as I showed my find to Char, we both started plotting how we might obtain the original without involving Calvin. We batted around several ideas before Char stopped and asked, "How much time did the state's attorney general give that original investigator, Dwight Lennord, to investigate these crimes? I'm wondering if the time he was authorized to investigate has expired. If so, did it expire when I was hired? If not, maybe we should drive to Baton Rouge and talk with Investigator Lennord. We should tell him what we know, what we know but cannot prove, and what you have found. Maybe he can obtain a subpoena for those films without anyone down here knowing about it. He could use the labs there to enhance the film and help us get an answer."

"Char, I'm glad I filmed the whole episode, including the film credits. That should make it easier to get a subpoena since we are not asking for a blanket subpoena to go on our own 'fishing expedition.' Judges hate them and seldom sign off on them."

"Mike, our first order of business is to convince Dwight Lennord to put his oar back in the water. If we can convince him we are simply following legitimate leads, I think he would want to help us. We need to make sure we do not come across as 'going after Wilcomb.' We can show him we have sufficient evidence to prove our distrust of our boss; hence, we are coming to him. We need to make it absolutely clear that we are not suggesting that Wilcomb is or is not our unsub, rather that he has gone to great lengths to hinder this investigation for his own purposes. Politically connected people rarely care to step on powerful feet. We do not know what Lennord learned during his investigation to conclude that DA Wilcomb was not chargeable."

"Char, he might bite back just because he did not discover any of this, and he might resent the fact that we have gotten this far."

"Either way, Mike, we have no choice but to approach him. We need that film, and we cannot get it without Dwight Lennord, so let's get going and let the chips fall where they may."

We agreed not to call ahead, deciding it was worth a wasted trip rather than give anyone advanced notice. We were sitting outside Investigator Dwight Lennord's office at 9:30 that same morning. Neither of us felt comfortable with our options. While driving to Baton Rouge, we discussed how the poison of suspicion can paralyze a person into a prison of indecision. Conspiracy theorists count on the fear of "Big Brother" being too big to stand up to. Very few are truly that powerful, but most use this fear to their own advantage. If people are afraid of what you might do to them, you seldom have to do anything. The fear alone is enough to get them to do what is best for you.

I think using fear to their advantage is exactly what the Wilcomb family had been doing for years. Everyone feared the retribution of saying anything against a Wilcomb that could be construed as criticism or disloyalty. Who knows what will come of it—maybe your job would disappear. I doubt that the family had ever exercised anything close to the reprisals the people of the parish had imagined; hence, bullying works. Fear makes the bully become bigger than he actually is, and people who already live at the bottom of the societal ladder fear the bully the most because they have no means of recovery.

I had just thought, *I wonder where on the societal ladder Mr. Lennord stands?* when his door opened, and he invited us to come in.

I was so proud of Char. She wasted no time getting to the purpose of our meeting. She laid out our case succinctly, avoiding any unnecessary character assignations. She presented our evidence in the order in which we had discovered it. She made it clear why we were asking for his help, and she laid out exactly what it was we wanted from him.

I studied this twenty-three-year-old woman who had grown up at the very bottom of the societal ladder, had worked hard to overcome her limited opportunities by educating herself, and had refused to back down to those who would view her as being inferior. Although strikingly beautiful, Char did not use her beauty to her advantage; rather, she downplayed her looks to her detriment. She was not militant and aggressive. She was also never petulant, expecting the world to clear a path for her because of her unfair start in life. Charlemagne Smalls did her homework and knew her stuff. All she expected from others was a fair hearing, and she received exactly that from Investigator Lennord.

Lennord leaned back in his desk chair and smiled. "You two are doing a great job. I knew there was more to everyone's story than I had time to uncover. I was sent down there to determine what course of action the State's Attorney General should take regarding Dr. Harvey's petition. My recommendation was to hire an outside ADA to take over the case, and then I suggested the attorney general persuade the Terrebonne Parish Council to hire you, Mr. Majors."

Startled by his statement of confidence, I looked at him puzzled and then corrected him. "You mean you persuaded them to hire an investigator who turned out to be me, right?"

"No, that is *not* correct, Mr. Majors. You do not remember me, do you?"

I shook my head and confessed, "No, should I?"

"Well, it was a long time ago. Do you remember attending a conference on investigative techniques at Quantico, Virginia, in 1977? We were both in our early thirties. I was your roommate during that conference. I was so impressed with how you looked at cases, how you conducted the mock interviews, and how you seemed to catch clues that none of the rest of us saw."

Embarrassed, I said, "I am sorry, but I still cannot place you. I remember attending that conference, but I don't recognize you."

Dwight smiled and slid open his credenza door and pulled out a photo album. Maybe this will help jog your memory, Mike. As you can see, I was two hundred pounds heavier back then. I've lost the pounds and I've lost my hair, so it is no wonder you don't remember me; but I never forgot you, and when your resume came across my desk, I held onto it. We didn't have an opening right then, but I held onto it and when Terrebonne Parish needed a smart investigator who would not be intimidated, I used every bit of influence I could muster to make sure you were hired. I am glad to see how right I was about you."

I thanked Dwight for the kind words, making sure he knew that Char was every bit as instrumental in getting to this point as I was. But inside, I knew that something much bigger than just being remembered all these years later had brought this about. I am memorable, but not that memorable.

As Char skillfully presents the rest of our evidence, our suspicions, and our concerns, my mind cannot help but stitch together this new information that I had just learned from Dwight, and I smile because this is what my Tilly used to call, "a godly intervention." During our early years of marriage, these remarks drove me crazy, and I would painstakingly explain to her how God had nothing to do with it.

Tilly would simply smile and reply, "Mike, as a trained detective, I know you do not believe in coincidences. You study the facts and follow them to other facts, which eventually leads you to more hard evidence, right? Why don't you do the same with faith, Mike? When God puts things in front of you—you write them off as coincidences because you disregard it as being faith talk. Why don't you use the same principles with matters of faith? I challenge you to study the facts and stitch together each of these clues until an irrefutable truth emerges. If nothing comes of it—so be it, but do not simply disregard it as coincidence and ignore it."

I look over at Lennord, deep in thought as Char presents our case so far, and I remember what I was like back in the days when Lennord met me back in 1977 at that Quantico training camp. I was thirty years old and arrogant beyond words. That young thirty-something that Lennord remembers was so full of self-confidence and pride, I doubted a case could ever come which I could not solve. Was I that good? On my good days, yes. Was I better than most? Yes, I was, but was I as good as I believed I was? Certainly not—hubris blinds you to your shortcomings. Back then I thought I did not need God, did not believe He existed, and did not understand why my beautifully intelligent Tilly felt the need to lean on someone imaginary. Broken people need God, and I was not broken—hubris! As a young boy I was kind to everyone. As I became a young man, I intentionally patterned my behavior completely opposite to that of my father; I prided myself on being everything my father was not, and I was good at it. *How could that be called broken?*

At thirty, no one felt more complete, in and of themselves, than I did. At the age of thirty-five, my Tilly challenged me to stop ignoring God, but rather to put God to the test, to determine for myself, if there was sufficient evidence to support my belief or lack of it in God, but then Tilly hit me with an even greater challenge. "Mike, this time use a different measuring tool. Instead of using your father as the measure, I challenge you to look at God as your measure."

That conversation was in 1982, and my Tilly knew I needed "rock-solid evidence," a phrase I loved to use, often with such a smugness that to this day, I blush at my audacity. Tilly loved me, so she endured my insults for which I am forever grateful. That summer Tilly gave me a book to read. The title alone—*Evidence That Demands a Verdict*—grabbed my attention. Written in 1972 by Josh McDowell, the author set out to disprove the value of faith, of Jesus, and of all things related to Christianity. For months, as a fellow agnostic who simply disregarded everything faith-based, I devoured and argued against every one of his points, but in the end, I found too much irrefutable proof, and the evidence convicted me of my hubris and convinced me that, by my life-changing experience, I too could say that the evidence did demand a verdict. I surrendered my life to Jesus at the age of thirty-five.

Did my work suffer? No, actually I became much more focused and clear-minded—once my ego stopped getting in the way. Self-sufficiency and an over-inflated sense of superiority is blinding. I finally realized that my lifelong striving for perfection was how I compensated for feelings of inadequacy—something almost every child of an abusive parent will battle. Subconsciously, my whole life I had been trying to prove that my father was wrong—I wasn't a nothing, and that if I worked hard enough, I could prove him wrong. Constantly feeling the need to prove my worth eventually faded into a drive for perfection, and I forgot the reason behind the drive. I married, moved to Florida, and locked away my father as a bad memory—or so I thought.

As I studied, I learned that being broken before God allowed me to finally understand exactly how much worth God placed on me—allowing me into His family because He loved me. What I had strived for through my hubris to earn and had failed to achieve, God gifted to me through my surrender to His love. Some think it is pure audacity to believe that a God powerful enough to have created everything could possibly bother with loving sinful man. But now I know that walking through this broken world believing you do not need God is the highest form of vanity and arrogance.

I met Dwight Lennord in 1977 for a total of five days, yet he remembered me in 2009 when my resume came across his desk thirty-two years later. I was not *that* remarkable! But he had held onto it for almost a year and pushed the Parish council to hire me, which makes absolutely no sense—except when you add God to the equation. God wants me here, not just to help solve these murders, but to do for Charlemagne what Tilly did for me—exchange the emptiness of driven perfection for a soul at peace, knowing that God loves her without reservation. The striving to prove ourselves worthy is a bottomless pit of effort that will never be satisfied, but God's love fills those deep pits and brings healing contentment.

Solving the murders is my profession, but helping Char is my mission—the real reason I am here. She reminds me of my former self—driven to succeed, but never satisfied, relentlessly pursuing perfection but feeling perpetually unworthy. I know only God can heal this void. Our working together was not coincidence; it was ordained.

Suddenly, Char's voice drew me back into the conversation. "Mike, give Mr. Lennord your iPad."

I quickly removed my iPad from the satchel and Lennord accepted it, connected it to his computer and uploaded my copy to his computer. He quickly fast-forwarded to the credits, made a print screen and sent it to his printer. "It will only take a few hours to secure a subpoena; however, it might take several days to track down these films and present the subpoena. I will text you when we have them before I send them on to the lab for enhancement. I'd like you both to come back here when the lab has finished, so we can view the film together and then decide what to do next."

Handing me back my iPad, he speculated, "I found it odd that after one full year of silence, the killer chose to drop a second body when I started looking around. Then five days after you two arrived in town, another body was dropped. I can't help but feel like the second two were dumped to keep you from looking too closely at the first victim. I sure hope the film tells us something."

Char smiled and shook his hand. "We fully agree with you, Mr. Lennord. We simply need to work quickly and efficiently, so we can stop all these unnecessary murders. I would hate to have any more bodies show up because I didn't do my job quickly and find this killer."

Lennord continued to hold Char's hand as he said, "You will not survive this job if you do not protect yourself from self-incrimination, Char. The killer has an agenda, and we must find out what that is if we are to stop him. Just focus on that and don't worry about whatever else is coming. It is not on you."

12

Know Your Opponent

URING THE ten days it took for Dwight Lennord to track down the filmmaker and get his hands on the film, Char and I were able to confirm both Calvin's and Mr. Sinclair's alibis. We had rock-solid evidence that they were both in Houston for several days prior to the first murder. Throughout the four full days before the body was dumped, both Wilcomb and Sinclair were in meetings with the film producers, working out the filming schedules, filming promo ads, and helping write filler pieces that Wilcomb would do for the production company. The time factor would not have allowed either man to leave Houston, return to Houma, commit the murder, and return to Houston. Additionally, from the production company's schedule for post-filming rewrites, we learned that Calvin was in Memphis doing post-production color commentary pieces the weekend the second body was found. Though no mention was made of Sinclair's accompanying him, we could not imagine that he would have let Calvin go alone.

As Char and I drove to Baton Rouge, we were relieved to know for certain that Calvin Wilcomb was not our killer. Although we still could not trust him, it was not because he was a stone-cold serial killer. We were anxious and ready to see who was steering that boat. Once we had the pilot's identity, we felt sure we would have our killer.

Lennord directed us to the huge forensic lab where the three of us pulled up lab stools and watched the big projection screen as the film we had watched on my ten-inch iPad came up and started playing. I had watched this film one hundred times in the past ten days, so I knew exactly when the boat would enter at the top right corner. At this magnification we could see that the pads were no longer showing on the deck. The deck had been stripped bare, and the cabin curtains were pulled closed. As soon as the bridge of the boat came into camera view, Char gasped and said, "That's Sinclair! Don't you agree, Mike?"

"That is defiantly Stephen Sinclair, but we know he could not possibly be the killer. We have time-stamped his every move for the four days prior to the killing. Yet here he is removing the only boat in that marina that could possibly be the boat Buddy Benoit spotted on the water that night. We need to find out where he took it and why? If he and Calvin are not the killers, who are they protecting? Who holds so much power over them that they would take such a risk?"

Char finally said the name we were all thinking. "Max Wilcomb? A seventy-six-year-old man who suffers from arthritis? Do any of us believe he could have piloted that boat that night? Not to mention tossing a 126-pound woman overboard?"

Lennord affirmed, "The time has come to call in both of these men for questioning. I would suggest you start by showing them this film. You need to get them talking because they know facts that you need to know. Whatever those two are hiding, it cannot be as bad as murder, and you need to put enough pressure on them that they come clean—the sooner the better!"

Char and I were both quiet all the way back to Houma. We knew what needed to be done; we were just not sure how to go about confronting Calvin and Sinclair. We agreed that the best way to deal with this team was together, not separately without giving them any warning. Put them in a room, start the film, and hopefully Wilcomb will jump ship like the rat that he is.

In preparation for our upcoming meeting, Char wanted to know as much as possible about the Wilcomb family. She went online to Google the name. She quickly scanned the three pages of recent activity. She had already read everything pertaining to Calvin before she had accepted the job. She was looking for old history when she spotted an article published in a well-known nationwide publication in 1956 titled "The Making of a Millionaire: The Joseph Wilcomb Story," as told by his older sister Josephine.

As I ran out to grab us some dinner, Char printed the entire article and had it sitting on the conference table when I returned. Across the top, Char had written "Know Your Opponent!" I read the article while eating my shrimp and grits. The extensive, three-issue series painted an excellent picture of the Wilcomb family. Papa Max's father, Joseph, was the first-generation Wilcomb to reach true wealth and power, but according to his sister, he would never be revered by the Parish people because they had known him when he was just "one of them."

In 1886 Joseph Wilcomb was born in Terrebonne Parish to a lowly European immigrant couple looking for a safe place to rear their new family. Joe, their third child, was the first one born as a true American. His sister reminisced how their mother put so much stock in this birth privilege, Joseph's opinion of himself was grossly distorted and conflicted with everyone else's opinion. After all, Joe Wilcomb was only the son of a hardworking grocery store owner, whose family lived above the store.

According to the article, this dichotomy between Joe's sense of entitlement and how his world looked at him must have fueled his determination to prove their view of him was wrong. In 1904 when Joe was eighteen, he refused to follow his father in the grocery business because he wanted wealth and that resource would never come from following his father. Since 1901 Joseph had been reading about the new oil rigs being built in the Oklahoma territory, and in 1904, the speculators hit it big in the Muskogee Oil Fields. Joseph left for Oklahoma and stayed for ten long years. His sister was quoted as saying, "Joe never ever came home during those ten years. He slept in their free bunkhouses to save money, never drank, never gambled, or caroused. He was a man on a mission who learned how to save every penny he earned." But when he realized he could never compete with the big oil corporations, he began plotting his next move.

By 1914 Joseph had saved a healthy nest egg and wanted to start investing it; thus, the only reason he came home. His ten years of savings could go a long way—if he played it smart. In 1914 people in Louisiana were selling anything and everything they had for ten cents on the dollar. Josephine shared her thoughts about her brother's search for the right investment:

> My brother would never even think of taking our father's path. Endless hours of work for meager pay were never going to take him where he thought he deserved to go. Joe's heart wanted a big city life, but even at ten cents on the dollar, his money would not go very far in the North. Here in Terrebonne Parish, where everything was already cheap in comparison, he could make a killing.

The article reviewed how Joseph found a struggling cannery in the Louisiana bayou located on prime land that already had good, serviceable equipment. The first cannery had opened in 1904, but people were slow to cultivate a taste for canned tuna, and this owner had no head for marketing, so when Joseph showed up in 1914 with an offer of working capital for a 55-percent interest share, the owner bought into his proposal.

When World War I hit, every other American felt like his world was falling apart, but Joseph saw opportunity. Ten years of dreaming, sacrifice, and planning was finally coming to fruition. On April 6, 1917, Joseph, now the 80-percent owner of the largest fish cannery in the Gulf, took the train north to be the first one in line to negotiate a lucrative contract with the military. Canned fish is nutritious, cheap, easy to transport, and has a long shelf life. Joseph rode the train back to Terrebonne Parish a rich man—as long as the war would last. He immediately started negotiating contracts with Bayou fishermen, locking in more than 70-percent of all the commercial fishing rights before anyone else realized there was money to be made.

By the end of the war, Joseph had made his millions; by 1920 he had married a well-connected woman, and in 1926, at the age of forty-two, he had fathered his one and only son, who he laughingly named Maximillion. The Wilcomb empire was in place. Joseph bragged that his son's name sounded "like one of those European royals"—even though the royal families spelled the name with an "ian." Joseph insisted on spelling his son's name with an "ion" to represent the millions of dollars sitting in his bank account. And since money begets money, Joseph continued buying up whatever he set his mind to possess. Few could resist his persuasive methods or his money, and the Wilcomb empire continued to grow.

The closing comment in the article must have angered Joseph Wilcomb. Although not a direct quote, Josephine Wilcomb had been heard to have said, "My nephew Max was deliberately raised with this sense of entitlement. By the time Max was five, the Wilcombs were the richest people in town. Although I love that boy, Max was given whatever he wanted; after all, his father believed that was what being born of privilege meant."

I had just finished reading this article when Char handed me another one, saying, "Mike, it does not pay to speak ill of the Wilcomb men. I Googled Josephine, and sources say that after this article appeared in the magazine, she and her brother never spoke again. Handing me yet another article, Char said, "If that last comment banned his sister, I wonder what kind of hateful response this article produced?" The next article, quoting an old college mate of young Maximillion, was an eye-opener. The article stated,

"Max's views of life were rather strange," according to his dormmate. "He bragged openly about what was expected of him. He had attended the best schools, had traveled the world extensively, and had anything and anyone he wanted. But his Papa Joe drew the line when it came to marriage. Max was going to be someone, and his marriage had to connect him to another with wealth and connection. Max grew up knowing that his marriage would be comparable to a business merger and that everyone would turn a blind eye to his affairs of the heart. After all, he believed, women of privilege grow up knowing these are business deals for which they will be paid well and have a life of continued privilege—as long as they bear their husband a son. Remaining deaf, dumb, and blind means life will continue to be good."

When I finished reading, I placed the clipping on the conference table and mused, "This article was obviously from a disgruntled ex-friend. This kind of disloyalty would definitely ensure that he would never be invited back to the Wilcomb home. But if even half of it is true, the roommate's observations are very revealing as to the Wilcomb men's blatant sense of entitlement."

Before we left for the night, I used my iPad to photograph all three white boards, making sure the photos were legible before Char wiped them clean. We boxed up all of our evidence, carefully noting each piece in our evidence log. I then carried each box into Char's inner office and carefully stacked them in her closet and locked the door with yet another new locking mechanism.

Char painstakingly gathered her evidence log, both sets of films, the CODIS reports along with her notepad and placed them in her oversized purse. "Mike, I believe we are ready. Wilcomb will be expecting my weekly update on our progress with these cases. He will get a little unnerved when he enters this room tomorrow and finds it wiped clean and empty of everything. Only this projector and a blank white board will be here to greet him tomorrow morning."

I was standing at the door, sweeping the room for anything we might have missed when Char added, "I did what you suggested, Mike. When I called Wilcomb and asked that our weekly update be conducted in my conference room, he hesitated at first, but then I confessed that in order to prove that I was capable of conducting an unbiased investigation, I had had my investigator verify both his and Mr. Sinclair's alibis and found they are rock-solid. Mike, you should have heard the relief in his voice. He must have assumed that we were still in the dark as to his other involvement because he offered to invite Sinclair to come along pointing out, 'Mr. Sinclair is not accustomed to being interrogated and having his reputation questioned, Ms. Smalls. This might be an excellent opportunity to clear the air between the two of you. What do you say? Should I bring him along?'"

I smiled. "'Come into my parlor,' said the spider to the fly."

13

A House of Cards

DA Wilcomb and Stephen Sinclair walked into Char's web rather cocksure and full of themselves. Feeling vindicated as usual, Sinclair was attempting to orchestrate everything and everyone in the room. Char let this bluster go on for a few minutes. We both observed DA Wilcomb's reaction when he noticed how clean and empty the room was. With three homicides on her hands, he knew this room should be filled with evidence, potential leads, photos, etc. Staring at the projector, Wilcomb chided, "Don't tell me you are one of those techno geeks, ADA Smalls! Are you part of this new generation of people who turn everything into digital format? Weren't you warned about doing that in law school? Courts demand hard evidence; besides, digital records are easily corrupted or even fail all together."

Char simply smiled and suggested they take a seat. "Gentlemen, I asked you here out of courtesy and respect for your positions within this parish." Sinclair, not liking the sound of this introduction, immediately stood up and started to protest, but Char took two steps forward and suggested, "You might want to take your seat, Mr. Sinclair, unless you would rather I waited for you to enter your fancy office, be arrested, handcuffed, and given the perp's walk of shame in front of everyone in the parish?"

Sinclair was immediately placed at a distinct disadvantage with not knowing what we knew. He begrudgingly returned to his seat as Char took control of the room. "Gentlemen, I am very much aware that you each hold a degree in jurisprudence; however, because of the nature of this meeting, to advise you both of your rights is incumbent upon me." It was now Wilcomb's turn to protest. "That is just about enough out of you, young lady! I am your boss, and I will not have you threaten me or my attorney!"

Char did not miss a beat. "Would you rather have the state's attorney general advise you of your rights?" Calvin's face turned ashen as he lowered his gaze. Char, undeterred, repeated the Miranda Rights and demanded that both Wilcomb and Sinclair verbally assent before proceeding. "Having been advised of your rights, I must also suggest that you, Calvin Wilcomb, might not want to assume you have your attorney present with you as I am charging you both with tampering with evidence in an ongoing murder case. Be advised that I am not charging either of you with the murder, but rather with tampering and interference. Both of these charges can spell the end of your careers and any future political ambitions."

Pulling the fingerprint report out of its folder, Char explained, "Usually, I would interview each suspect separately, but after extensive investigation and observing you both, I strongly feel you two have been working in collusion for several years, so my intent is to confront you together as a team." She placed identical copies of the reports in front of each man. "I am quite certain that you both have already read this CODIS report."

Sinclair's jaw muscles were twitching, but he held his tongue. He did not return Calvin's pleading look for help. As Char slid the second report in front of each man, I observed a slight change in Sinclair's posture as he must have been racking his brain for a way out of this. He could plead attorney-client privilege. Surely, he had known about this report, but to act on this evidence, he would break his sworn oath. If what he was looking at was all we had, Sinclair could argue his way out of trouble. However, his trouble was only beginning if Papa Max thought he appeared to be abandoning Calvin. Char and I had walked through every possible reaction the two men could have, and we knew that this excuse would be Sinclair's only ace in the hole. He simply didn't yet know what we knew.

Leaving Wilcomb to postulate his own dilemma, Char stepped over to the window and closed the blinds. She wanted both men to have a clear view of what was coming next. She said nothing—simply stepped over to flip on the projector.

As I observed both men, I had the distinct impression that they had no idea of what was coming. Lennord had asked his lab to splice together the three transitions of the same film, so like the rest of us who first observed this film, Calvin and Sinclair focused on Old Man Barry and wondered why Char was showing them that film. But then the second splice zeroed in on the distant background, and both men became visibly shaken. I knew Sinclair would be, but Wilcomb seemed even more upset than Sinclair at seeing the cruiser in the enhanced background—even before the driver of that boat was yet visible.

Char walked over and sat directly across from Sinclair as the final splice began to reveal Sinclair piloting the boat out of the marina. Lennord had instructed the lab to insert the filmmaker's stamp of authenticity with the date and time of filming. As the film came to an end, Char said, "We have proof that two days after your trip to Dr. Harvey's autopsy room, Wilcomb was in Baton Rouge running this

CODIS report. One day later, we have proof that you, Mr. Sinclair, removed the very boat described in the missing witness report. Well, gentlemen, what do you have to say?"

Seldom do investigators have the privilege of enjoying the very moment when all of their hard work deflates someone as cocky and entitled as these two men. Oh sure, Char and I had not yet solved the murders, but we had solved the case of who had absconded with the evidence though we still did not know why.

Trying to salvage whatever he could of his visibly dissolving future, Wilcomb asked, "So where do we go from here?"

Char maintained her composure as she stated, "As I told you last night, Calvin, we are more than certain that neither of you could have committed the first or the second murder. I just don't understand why either of you would take such foolish chances that will cost both of you your careers? Can you explain that to me?"

Sinclair, a more seasoned attorney, set his jaw and refused to talk. He obviously needed time to come up with a plausible explanation, but Wilcomb, not having the protection of client privilege to fall back on, desperately wanted to make a deal. "Okay, what do you want to know?"

"Let's start with Sandra Green. Why did you withhold her identity?"

No longer feeling quite so entitled, Calvin turned toward Char and pleaded, "Because she was blackmailing me...but I didn't know her as Sandra Green, and I did not kill her. I knew her as Crystal Martin, and I had been having an affair with her for several months. I met her in Memphis on one of our trips to interest the film company in our project. I was unknown in Memphis, and Crystal was wild, fun, and an enjoyable distraction. We hooked up several times, but then she showed up here in Houma. I told her I could never be seen with her here and suggested she get a room in Dulac near my boat."

"Wait a minute, Calvin," Char interrupted. "you don't own a boat. We did an extensive search, going back twenty years. You have never had a boat registered to you in the last twenty years."

"No, you wouldn't have found anything because Papa Max had Sinclair create a shell corporation in the early '80s for the sole purpose of keeping our world private. The boat, which was my twenty-first birthday gift, was purchased, registered, and maintained by the corporation. Annual marina fees, repairs and fuel were all paid by my corporate credit card. The only restriction Papa put on its use was never to drink when piloting the boat. An accident involving drinking would shatter the veil of privacy and expose the Wilcomb family."

"So that is why we could not link you to that boat," Char responded before asking, "but everyone in Dulac must know who you are?"

"Yes, and that is exactly why I haven't used the boat in years. Oh, I've taken one or two causal cruises around the lake or if the weather were good, a day trip out into the Gulf with friends. But my wife hates boating—just like she hates just about everything else I like. She hasn't been on that boat in eight years, so it became a safe and private place to entertain women outside the view of prying eyes. My slip was secluded and only steps away from my private parking space. I could slip in and out without being seen; the setting was perfect because we paid the marina well to remain blind and quiet."

Char leaned in and asked, "So what went wrong, Calvin?"

"I'll tell you what went wrong," Sinclair bellowed. "Calvin has a terrible time reading women! That's what happened. After years of planning and shortly before all of our hard work was finally going to pay off, Calvin here, got involved with a professional blackmailer, and he was too stupid to protect himself."

I remained silent while Char continued the interview, but I started thinking, *Maybe they did hire a hitman. Maybe these two are still guilty.*

After all, they have a lot at stake. But if so, why is Calvin being so open about the situation now?

Char asked, "Protection from what? Having your wife find out that you cheated on her?"

Calvin stared at Char with such a look of derision that my soul was sickened. The very idea that his wife could possibly have any say in his personal dalliances was beneath his station. "No, ADA Smalls, that issue would have been handled in house. What we feared was exactly what this woman was threatening—to take all of her "proof" public and ruin my bid for the Senate seat."

"What proof? Did she show you her proof? If so, why wouldn't Maximillion Wilcomb have paid her off?"

"Exactly, ADA Smalls," Sinclair chimed in, "and paying her off is precisely what we were in the process of doing when she was found murdered. I had negotiated a healthy sum to which she had agreed. I had already transferred the sum to the shell corporation so it could not be traced back to us, and that next week we were to make the exchange. Even in making the deal, we knew we were still vulnerable. It is not like the old days when once you got your hands on the negatives, you were safe from further blackmail."

"How were you going to protect yourself? Again, what was her proof?" Char asked.

"She was good. I believe she must have made a duplicate copy of my boat keys because she had obviously been in my cabin for hours without my being onboard. She had hidden sound responsive video recording devices in several locations around the cabin in order to capture our meetings. I'll just say that nothing was left to the imagination, and the video had obviously been shot on my boat."

Sinclair, wanting to move away from this conversation, added, "Because Max has dropped millions of dollars into Calvin's future, what was a few more? But she wasn't going to get the settlement all at once. For every year she remained silent, I would transfer another $500K into her account. We knew that time and success would only give her about four years to do any real damage. Once Calvin won his seat and had made a few deals that benefited his voting public, the people would not turn on him if dirty laundry came out. So, we structured her payments to ensure our window of exposure. So, Char, what possible motive would we have for killing her?"

"But someone did, and that someone used your boat to do it," Char declared.

"Yes, and again," Calvin argued, "why would we use my boat to do that? It makes no sense. But if this Crystal, or Sandra, or whatever name she used was blackmailing someone else at the same time, and the two of them were also using my boat, maybe that person decided killing her was cheaper than paying her."

I had remained silent up to then but found myself blurting out, "That explanation would be plausible were it not for the two additional bodies. What possible motive would anyone have for those murders? They were not connected to Sandra Green, so they were not a threat to the one being blackmailed."

"We agree," Sinclair muttered. "We've been trying to figure out who could possibly have a motive for killing three young women. Is it just coincidence that the woman who was blackmailing us was one of them?"

Char declared, "I don't believe in coincidence!" Then feeling that she had come to the point of no return, Char proposed, "The two of you have rock-solid alibis. I expect that you, Mr. Sinclair, could, if pushed, produce equally solid evidence to support your claim that you were ready to pay off the blackmailer. That being the case, might I propose another possibility? Calvin, your Papa Max has spent millions to see his plan come to fruition. Is it possible, since he has no credible alibi, that upon becoming overwrought with rage at seeing his golden boy's future in jeopardy, he decided to take revenge rather than let her win?"

Everyone in the room sat quietly contemplating this possibility until Calvin protested. "Papa would certainly have thought of that reprisal. No one touches his family—no one. But there is no way Papa Max could have pulled it off. First of all, he is eighty-three years old, and he has not driven in ten years. The arthritis in both of his feet makes driving unbearable for him. Secondly, it has been years since he has done anything on his own."

Char winced in disbelief. "You expect us to believe that, Calvin? Someone as powerful as Max Wilcomb could do just about anything he cared to do, and no one would dare try to stop him."

Both Char and I could see that Calvin was obviously struggling with some undisclosed knowledge.

Char urged him on, "Calvin, if there is something you know, now is the time to tell us."

"No one knows any of this. Papa Max is a proud man, and our first order of family business has always been to keep our secrets. If he finds out that I have told you, he won't care that I am his grandson. Betraying him is an unforgiveable sin."

Char leaned back in her chair and suggested, "Would you rather I haul him in here and ask him what you are hiding?"

Chagrined at this possibility, Calvin shook his head in defeat and started talking. "About eight years ago, we started seeing signs of dementia, so in order to protect the family fortune, Mr. Sinclair convinced Papa Max that in the best interest for the family, he should be tested. Wanting to protect Papa's privacy, Sinclair arranged to have a doctor in Memphis do the testing. And since we were going, Grandma

Charisse, my mother, and I all talked Papa into taking along my father to be tested as well."

Having jumped down the proverbial rabbit hole, Calvin had obviously decided continuing to hide the family secret was useless. "You see, for nearly my entire life, I have known something was wrong with my father. No one ever spoke about the matter. Papa Max is a proud man and would never tolerate anyone suggesting that a son of his might not be altogether right in the head. Papa spent an outrageous amount of money keeping this family secret. Pride is a hard taskmaster, Ms. Smalls."

Knowing this was probably the most difficult confession of his life, Char wisely remained quiet, and Calvin continued. "We took them both to Memphis and put them both through a battery of tests. We finally learned that Papa Max was in the early stages of dementia, and that my father, who we all know was not quite right, actually suffers from high-functioning autism. Though Papa Max worked hard my whole life to keep my father's odd behavior a secret, he understood even then how vulnerable his fortune was if my father had ever inherited the estate. While still capable of doing so, Papa Max ordered Mr. Sinclair to rewrite his will, bypassing his son Mitchell and leaving everything to me. Sinclair was ordered to file both of those medical reports with the will as evidence of my father's condition as reason for simply setting aside sufficient funds to ensure my father's ongoing care for the rest of his life, but first and foremost, the intention was to protect the Wilcomb family fortune."

Char interjected, "But what about Max's wife, Charisse? Was she willing to allow her husband to set her aside as well?"

Calvin stared at Char with a look I could only describe as incredulous. "Ms. Smalls, the Wilcomb family fortune will never be turned over to outsiders. Charisse is Papa Max's second wife, and both of his wives, my mother, and my wife were forced to sign ironclad prenuptial agreements. They will be quite comfortable, but they will never control the Wilcomb fortune. It has always been so, and it will always be so."

Then with a look of pride that made me feel disgusted, Calvin added, "Even with early onset dementia, my Papa Max knew how to protect what was his. His name was removed from all of the accounts, and we changed them all to require three signatures to move any money from one account to another. The three signatures were mine, Sinclair's, and my mother Catherine's; however, my mother's privileges do not extend beyond being a third signature. Papa Max would never give a non-blood relative any power over his estate. Once Papa is gone, I will inherit everything, and the other two signatures will no longer be required. Papa demanded that during his remaining lifetime, in order for anyone to pay out any amount in excess of $5,000, all three of us needed to agree. So, you see, Papa could not physically do the killing, and he could not pay for someone to take care of the matter for him."

Knowing this information would be easy to verify, Char decided to go in a different direction. "Mr. Sinclair, where is the boat?"

"I took it out into the Gulf of Mexico and went around the bayous below New Orleans and into the harbor at Mobile. I hired a private investigator to fingerprint the entire boat, inside and out. He also took extensive photos, swabbed everywhere for DNA, and then I ordered that the boat be shrink-wrapped for preservation. The boat has been lifted out of the water and placed in dry dock, secured under lock and key ever since. I can return it in a few days. I know you cannot use any of this evidence in a court of law because you cannot swear to the chain of custody, but you can use it to eliminate some and maybe figure out who to go after. Everything collected from the boat is locked in my office."

Char stood up as she ordered, "I want all of that evidence within one hour, Mr. Sinclair. I also want the name and address of the dry dock, and a notarized letter giving Mike permission to remove it from storage. I could get a subpoena, but we still have a serial killer loose, and keeping our actions quiet for as long as possible would be best."

Char collected the copies sitting in front these two men and added, "You both will be formally charged and prosecuted for these crimes; however, I have spoken to the state's attorney general about the sensitive nature of this case, and he agreed to hold off charging you until we have determined who is killing these women. We do not need every newspaper in the country muddying the water down here. Someone close to you, Calvin, took advantage of your private little world. He might be trying to set you up, so I would suggest you watch your back. But I still do not understand why you destroyed the tire impressions. I understand the fingerprints and the witness statement, but why did you destroy the tire impressions?"

Calvin face turned ashen. "I didn't, Ms. Smalls. I received my copy of the impressions from Dr. Harvey, and they sat in my office for three months. I recorded them in my evidence log and turned everything over to you—except, as you know, the fingerprint report and the witness statement. The second killing had nothing to do with Crystal, so why would I even think to tamper with evidence from that case?"

Char looked Calvin right in the eyes as she asked, "Calvin, have you been in my office?"

"You mean since this became your office? No, I swear I have not!"

Char studied Calvin's face for several minutes. "Those tire impressions link cases 2 and 3. Sinclair, you swear that the boat has been locked up in dry-dock since April 12, 2008, yet the second body was dumped in the same area of the lake almost a year later. Why? Who is behind all of this?"

Sinclair looked like someone had pulled his plug and let all the air out of him. As he stood up, he appeared to have aged ten years in the space of two hours. "I will bring that letter and all of the evidence within the hour. We were only trying to protect Calvin's reputation and his political future aspirations, but we are not killers. We are willing to do whatever it takes to stop these killings."

Char headed to the door, but before opening it, she warned, "My office has been violated twice so far. Someone who has access to this building is snooping and removing evidence. I would advise you both to keep all of this to yourselves. Do not talk in public. Do not use any building computer system, fax or otherwise. We are not in a secured system. The less the killer knows, the safer we all will be. And Calvin, do not go anywhere alone. I am not convinced that this has not been a personal attack against you."

The two men who walked out of that office were not the same two who had entered. They no longer felt entitled and privileged. They know their Judgment Day was coming, but even having just presented all of their corruption, I seriously doubt that either one of these men feel they deserved what is coming.

Char closed the door behind them and asked, "Mike, assuming we get that notarized letter this afternoon, would you be willing to make the trip to Mobile, hire a boat transporter, supervise it being loaded on the transport and follow it back here? I know caring for this task is a lot to ask of you, but I don't trust anyone else."

"I'd be happy to do it, but Char, we cannot trust anyone in this town to touch that boat. I suggest we deliver it to Dwight Lennord in Baton Rouge," I advised as I pulled two evidence bags out of my jacket pocket and carefully dumped the remaining coffee out of both Calvin's and Sinclair's cups, carefully marking the bags and sealing them. I then dropped both into my briefcase. "I'll drop these off at the New Orleans forensic lab on my way to Mobile. We already have Sandra Green's

DNA; now we need to figure out a way of obtaining the rest of the Wilcomb family's DNA."

Char joked, "I wish DNA results were as quick as they are on television. On *CSI* or in Abby Sciuto's lab on *NCIS*; they have their results in minutes! Here in real-life situations, the analyzing will take several weeks. So, the sooner we get the other samples, the better."

"Char, I am going to go to my office, research a boat transporter, and grab some lunch. You want me to bring something back for you?"

"I'm okay, Mike. I packed my lunch today. Once you have the transporter scheduled and have had your lunch, come back and we can start planning our next strategy. I will call Lennord and ask him if you can take the boat to Baton Rouge. I would feel much more confident if he were supervising that part of this investigation for us."

14

The Spider's Web

I was in my office researching boat transports in Mobile when my iPhone buzzed, and I read a text from Char: "ASAP," and I took the stairs two at a time back up to Char's office. As I entered, I saw Stephen Sinclair sitting in the same seat he had occupied earlier. "What's up? Do we have the letter?"

"It's right here, Mike, but Mr. Sinclair has something he wants to tell us before he turns over the evidence he has collected. Apparently, he did not want to speak in front of Calvin, but I am sure he will tell us why that is in short order. I told him he had two choices, either I recorded our meeting, or he would agree to have you sit in as a witness. He preferred you."

I took the same seat I had occupied and let Char direct the conversation.

"Okay, Mr. Sinclair, what exactly do you want us to know?"

Sinclair stammered around a little before pleading, "If I tell you something that has no direct correlation to the case and I can prove what I am about to say beyond a shadow of a doubt, would you be willing to consider keeping it quiet?

"You know I cannot make any promises without knowing exactly what it is you want kept quiet. What I can promise you, Mr. Sinclair, is that I take no pleasure in destroying people for no reason. If whatever you feel the need to reveal is of no use to the case, and if I feel I have been given sufficient evidence to that effect, and if withholding it will not jeopardize the case's standing in court and under appeals, I will do my best to protect an innocent party."

Sinclair studied Char for a moment before saying, "I never said the person was an innocent party, Ms. Smalls. I said her situation has absolutely no bearing on this case. I know I broke the law hiding that boat. I knew Calvin had not killed that woman, and for certain that I had not killed her, but sometimes a spider creates a web, and others accidentally get caught in the labyrinth created. As much as I hate the idea of the public humiliation, the loss of my career, and most likely probation and legal fees, all of which I deserve, I need to disclose some facts.

"Maximillion Wilcomb took a liking to me and made me his counsel of record. He was the most powerful man I had ever met. The heady intoxication of power and privilege began to bleed over, and I began to view myself as one of the privileged ones. Max had been born to a father who knew what it felt like to be poor, and he drilled into his son the responsibility of managing that wealth. Sadly, Max did a terrible job of passing on that training. But to be fair to Max, I doubt that any training would have changed Mitchell.

"By his own admission, Max had given the boy too much freedom. Mitchell was Max's only son and was only a few years younger than me when I 'joined' the family circle. I watched as Max did all he could to light a fire under that boy to accomplish something. Truthfully, Mitchell reminded me of a boy trapped in a man's body. His whole life he had been tutored, which was actually glorified babysitting. His problem was not exactly an absence of mental acuity; rather, his absolute lack of interest in anything and his inability to focus kept him from accepting any responsibility.

"By ninth grade, no one could work with Mitchell. He refused to cooperate and began having complete meltdowns, which forced Papa Max to begin hiding his son from the public. That year Mitchell's mother was paid off and sent to Europe. She became very wealthy just to go away and never talk about her son again. I don't believe Mitchell thought about her or even missed her. I suspected he was not be wired quite right, but you must remember this was thirty-seven years ago when so little was known about high-functioning autism. Even so, in Max's world, no one dared suggest any defects.

"I was charged with the task of finding Mitchell a suitable bride and to convince Mitchell that marrying was all his idea. Mine was a formidable task that I dared not fail to achieve. Max wanted a grandson to fulfill all his dreams that Mitchell would never fill.

"Mitchell's odd behavior made it nearly impossible for him to interface and interact with others, especially women. After several complete failures with promising choices, I knew I was running out of time. In my quest to find Mitchell the perfect bride, I had not yet married, although I had enjoyed the company of a steady love interest while I established my practice.

"I decided to take Mitchell to New Orleans during Mardi Gras, and Catherine accompanied us on the trip. How was I to know that Mitchell would take a shine to the light of my life? Catherine was easy to talk to, easy on the eyes, and she had a way of getting people to open up and tell her their most closely held secrets without feeling judged. Mitchell had never before experienced that type of togetherness, and he mistook this feeling of amity for love. He came home bubbling incessantly about Catherine, telling Max, "I met the girl I want to marry!"

"Max turned to me and said, 'Make that happen.'"

"Mitchell had absolutely no idea that Catherine was my girl, and Max would not have cared. Power and privilege get what they want. I knew I had better produce a wife for Mitchell or I would be gone. I knew Mitchell didn't really want a wife. He showed absolutely no inclination in that direction. All he wanted was for Catherine to make him feel wonderfully happy—like she had at Mardi Gras.

"She and I talked about this dilemma for weeks. Could we actually even consider such a thing? Catherine would be financially set for life. Mitchell would seldom, if ever, request her personal attention, and I would always be right there for her.

"After several short trips together, with me along as chaperone, she and I decided we could do it, so Catherine married Mitchell while I stood as his best man. That day and their honeymoon were the most difficult days of our lives. As I suspected, Mitchell never consummated the union. He loved for Catherine to talk to him while he drifted off to sleep but wanted nothing more. Of course, Max was unaware of Catherine's secret.

"But Max began to fuss about not being a grandfather, and we began to worry. Mitchell hated the insults hurled at him by his father. Catherine would tell me that Mitchell would cry himself to sleep in her arms, and she would tell him it would all work out in time. And in time, Calvin came along, and everyone was happy. Max was elated at becoming a grandfather, Mitchell was happy that his father no longer cared what he did or did not do, and Catherine and I were thrilled that our baby boy would have all the comforts and privileges of wealth and power—as long as we kept our secret."

I studied this power-hungry ladder climber, trying to convince us that he had done all of this with absolute altruism. *Sinclair reminds me of a spider spinning his glistening web of lies,* I argued in my head, *He is wanting us to believe he was simply trying to give his boss the desire of his heart. In actuality, Maximillion Wilcomb had just been tricked into placing the Wilcomb fortune into the hands of three people who have not one drop of Wilcomb blood in them. Sinclair says that Calvin has no idea, but for this to work for Sinclair, Calvin must know.*

Sinclair sounded so sincere as he confessed, "I dread facing a judge for my crime of tampering with evidence, but that would be nothing compared to having Maximillion Wilcomb find out that I tampered with his family. Even Calvin does not know."

Char and I both had been quiet throughout this painful confession, but finally Char asked, "Stephen, why did you choose now to tell us your secret?"

"For two reasons. First, because Calvin's DNA is all over that boat."

"Which is expected," replied Char.

"Secondly, because Catherine and mine are also in that cabin. You see, for years we were careful and discreet. Being together watching our boy grow up was enough. But years of enduring Mitchell's lifestyle had begun to wear on her. She was everything he was not. She was imaginative; he was dull beyond endurance. She was well-read; he would get lost in the comics. She loved to travel; he was content to ride his four-wheeler around the family compound. She loved to have deep, theoretical conversations; Mitchell could not, or would not, express more than a five-word pronouncement.

"About the same time as we were having Max and Mitchell tested, Catherine was at her breaking point. We both had sacrificed so much—she by marrying Mitchell, enduring his endless meltdowns, Papa Max's treating her like excess luggage, and me, at age fifty-seven, planning to marry Samantha Treadway, the most boring and self-centered girl on the planet simply because people were beginning to talk. The pressure was too much. Samantha bored me to tears, but Catherine, fearing my heart might stray, began asking me to meet her on our son's boat. We knew his schedule, and we were certain he would never catch us. Our trysts made the last five years tolerable, but then we were almost caught by an unscheduled handyman. We both vowed never to meet again at the boat." Sinclair handed Char some papers. "In case you dare to think Calvin's mother had anything to do with any of this, here is a copy of her flight to Paris, and her hotel bill, all of her charges during her ten-day shopping trip. This has been Max's annual gift to Catherine for the past thirty years. You can verify it all. She was not in the country."

"Okay, you can be assured that we will confirm this trip, but again I ask, why did you feel you needed to confess all of this?"

"Because if those DNA results are ever made public, everyone will know about our affair. Calvin will know, and Max will know. Mitchell will not care, but Max will. He is now an old man who loves his grandson with all of his heart. Seeing that boy disgraced and prosecuted, and having his dream shattered will be hard enough, but if he finds out that Calvin is not his son, the knowledge will kill him."

With a look of absolute disdain, Char asked, "And you want us to believe that Max Wilcomb's feelings are your driving concern, Mr. Sinclair? As I see it, for all of Maximillion Wilcomb's wealth and power, he was used and manipulated by you—a simple hireling. You used the most personal and valuable desire of Max's heart, his desire for a grandson, to attain your lofty position in this parish. Max, a man born of privilege and entitlement, could not protect himself from the greed of equally self-entitled men."

Char stood up and walked over to the window. Sinclair remained silent as I studied this now shell of a man. Once an arrogant power broker who could suck the air right out of the room by his very presence and a master manipulator who had enjoyed the heady life as one who believed he could make or break a man simply by choice had been caught in a trap set for another, and his world was crumbling around him.

I felt zero sympathy for him. Silly women might romanticize the circumstances keeping soulmates apart, but all I saw was a greedy and power-hungry man who was willing to use the girl he loved and the son he sired to ensure his place of power among the powerful. I wondered what Char was thinking. *Will she be taken in by this eleventh-hour plea on behalf of poor old Max Wilcomb? Is she buying into Sinclair's suggestion that his reason for keeping this disgusting secret is for the sake of others—not himself? Or will Char fall into the trap that so many others have fallen prey to—the heady feeling of power and being able to destroy another simply because it is within her newly acquired power to do so? If Char chooses that path, she too will be caught in the snare of the spider.*

A British politician once said, "Power tends to corrupt, and absolute power corrupts absolutely." I agree that power does corrupt, but if Sinclair and Max are an example of anything, it is that absolute power is a myth—a snare that grabs you as you grab for it. The allurement of a spun web glistening in the moonlight looks enticing until you get too close. Though appearing delicate and harmless, easy to manage and overpower, when the sticky threads of your desire catch hold of you, you have become its powerless prey.

Thinking of how all these webs of deceit have been played out among these power-hungry people, a person could not help but feel a tinge of pleasure at their upcoming destruction. Right then my mind raced back in time as I remembered something my Tilly taught me long ago. Tilly was always patient with me, listening to every detail of the cases I was working. But when I started sounding a little too invested, desiring my own sense of retribution, Tilly would often warn me, "Mike, be proud of all your hard work. Take great pleasure in using your skills and instincts to capture a dangerous criminal. Enjoy the fact that you have made the streets safer because you were instrumental in putting someone in prison who needed to be removed from society. But, Mike, don't ever take delight in having beaten 'that person.' Always protect your soul from finding joy in destroying another person! Pity these souls who chose such a sick path. Be proud of stopping them, but never enjoy the powerful feeling of crushing them because you become like those people."

I needed many a reminder from my Tilly before I fully understood the difference between glee and self-admiration. Glee focuses on the effects of my actions on the perpetrators, where self-admiration focuses on the good I accomplished for society.

As I studied this man in front of me, I suddenly felt exceedingly rich indeed. Trust me, I have very little in this world except the knowledge that I have had the love of a good and faithful woman, untainted by this world's lust for power, position, and greed. I am one of the fortunate ones.

Char turned away from the window and drew me back into the moment, and I was anxious to learn what path she had chosen. "Mr. Sinclair, I will not agree to being part of any collusion that continues this charade against both Maximillion and his son, Mitchell, however…."

Both Stephen Sinclair and I triggered on the "however" with a sense of hope, but certainly for different reasons.

Char continued, "…however, my mandate to this parish is to find the murderer, bring him or her to justice, and to stop these killings. If, and only if, I do not need to use any of the DNA evidence to accomplish my task, I would agree not to use that evidence. Therefore, your hidden life remains private. I will not expose you simply because I can. I will not keep your secret simply because you ask. Do you understand what I am saying, Mr. Sinclair? I will not be a party to your treachery, and I will not be intentionally destructive to your future. In whatever way this case plays out, it will be the evidence that will orchestrate what happens to you—not me. I promise you nothing beyond that."

As Sinclair stood up to leave, he acknowledged, "That is fair."

"Oh, one more thing, Mr. Sinclair, since Maximillion Wilcomb is the owner of record for that shell corporation that owns that boat, I will need to interview him. I expect you to do whatever you must do to make that happen. I expect you to make sure that both Max and Mitchell will be available as well as both of their wives. I will only give you seventy-two hours to make that request happen, or I will start hauling everyone associated with that boat into this office. Make it happen, Mr. Sinclair."

Once Sinclair was gone, Char and I sat together absorbing every-thing we had learned during those two meetings that day. We wrote until our fingers could no longer hold our pens. Years of deceit and treachery had been revealed—but not the killer. We were certain that blindsiding them the way we had with our irrefutable evidence gave them no time to conjure up a story, and as wildly outrageous as their stories were, they fit seamlessly into what we did know.

Char finally put down her pen and stared at the pile of notes in front of her. I noticed circled words, arrows drawn from one comment to another, double underlines, question marks everywhere. She gath-ered up her stack of notes and shook them in the air as she announced, "Mike, have you ever heard the term *blitzkrieg?*"

I put down my pen and smiled. "Yes, but only because I am a stu-dent of German military history. It's a military technique for over-whelming a stronger opponent. If you are outnumbered and cannot win in a straight-forward assault, you rapidly come at your opponent from all sides in an unrelenting fashion. This forces them to change their strategy and split up their attention. For a short time during college, after my hitch in Vietnam, I was enthralled with military history. I know what the Germans meant by the term, but how do you interpret the word in regard to our case?"

Char smiled at me as she continued to shake her stack of notes. "I interpret that word the same way the Germans do! I believe you and I have just experienced a deliberate *blitzkrieg*." Replacing her stack of notes on the table, Char warned, "When someone does not want you to look too closely at a certain fact, they bombard you with so many facts that the one fact that can truly hurt them gets lost in the maze of facts staring back at you.

"Mike, we ambushed these two men with irrefutable evidence of the crime of tampering with evidence. Both of these men should have remained silent. Any half-decent attorney would have advised them to do so, yet they both immediately confessed. Wilcomb confessed to having had an affair with the dead woman, and Sinclair confessed to fathering Calvin Wilcomb."

I corrected Char. "Wilcomb, yes; Sinclair, no. I believe that Calvin assumed we had gotten our hands on those tapes, and he panicked. Sinclair, on the other hand, sat here during the first meeting, pushing all of the focus toward Calvin. But if Sinclair had orchestrated the killing of Sandra Green/Crystal Martin, he would have made sure he had all of those tapes, and he would not have confessed to having used that boat as a love nest with Calvin's mother. Sinclair had that boat in his possession from Dulac to Mobile. Why didn't he sterilize that boat?"

Char chimed in, "Why didn't Sinclair simply scuttle the boat at sea?"

"Exactly," I replied. "Sinclair does nothing without a plan. If he is breathing, he is plotting ten steps ahead of everyone. I'm sure he never expected us to get our hands on the video of him removing that boat, but once we had evidence, Sinclair had to come up with another plan. Maybe he kept that boat for insurance. Maybe he thought he now had a golden hold over Max and Calvin that would ensure his position for life, but he needed to have those cabin tapes in his possession for that plan to work."

"But wait a minute, Mike. Maximillion Wilcomb would never have agreed to pay out $2,000,000 over four years, without having seen the videos, so we know the videos exist. What if Sinclair did hire someone to take out Sandra and collect the videos, and now he plans to use them himself?"

"That would be plausible, Char, were it not for the other two murders, and the fact that he told us about the tapes. Those two murders would in no way help Sinclair. For him to be able to pull off a second blackmail, he needed Max to relax, thinking his money could assure their privacy. These other murders only highlighted this case. Sinclair would see no profit in ordering the other two killings. I think Sinclair is not the killer, but he was planning to use the boat as a bartering piece. He would have no other reason to have the boat sealed up and stored away."

"I agree; but if he has those tapes, why would he tell us about Catherine?" Char hesitated for a moment before adding, "He knows their DNA is all over that boat, right? He could have sterilized the whole boat, but then evidence about whomever killed that girl would also be gone. Maybe he didn't scuttle that cruiser because, deep down, Sinclair is still trying to protect his son."

"The tapes, if they have not yet been destroyed, most likely would not show us who the killer is. The victim was the one who was making those tapes—unless we find DNA of another blackmail victim turned killer. If that person got his or her hands on those tapes, they have been destroyed. But one thing we can be assured of…at one point, both Sinclair and Papa Max have seen portions of those tapes. Might they have a copy because the blackmailer, Crystal or Sandra, would not have allowed a face-to-face meeting? She must have made a copy and sent it, most likely to Sinclair.

I concluded, "And since he knows that someone else does have those tapes, he cannot protect himself from being exposed; therefore, I believe Sinclair's confession today was his attempt at plotting his way out of being exposed."

Char opened her calendar and reviewed our daily progress. "Mike, we have been on this case for four weeks, and all we have accomplished thus far is confirming in our own minds exactly who is not the killer."

"No, we have confirmed the identity of the first victim, we have rock-solid proof of Calvin's actions, we have tracked down the missing witness, we have our hands on the only film that showed Sinclair removing the boat from the marina, and we forced him to produce the boat."

"I know, Mike, but now that we know that Calvin has not been in here snooping, we still do not know who has been breaking into our war room and who destroyed the tire molds. If this intruder is the killer, we now know that he has access to this building."

"Char, we also know that Calvin's boat was not used to drop that second body in Lake Boudreaux because it had already been in dry storage for almost a year at the time of the second killing. Whoever is doing this is trying to pin it on Calvin Wilcomb. Maximillion would have no reason to do this nor would Sinclair. We need to find out who would possibly want to bring down the Wilcomb family."

Char stood and started gathering up her things. "Mike, I sent that Stop 'N' Go video to New Orleans ten days ago. While you head to Mobile to retrieve the boat, I plan to drive to New Orleans and put a fire under that lab. Besides, I haven't been home in five weeks, so I will check in with my family while I'm there. Text me when you have possession of the boat and give me your ETA for Baton Rouge. I think I want to meet you and Lennord to go over all we know and suspect before the cruiser is handed over to his lab."

15

Trouble at Home

URING OUR two separate interviews, Char's phone had buzzed no less than twelve times; none of which had she answered. After the first interruption, Char put her phone on vibrate, but that, and the fact that her phone lit up each time, continued to annoy all four of us. Twice, I was in a position to see her mother's photo on Char's iPhone, signifying the calls were coming from her. I have known Char for five weeks, and apart from the ambush of our first night on the job, Char has not been forthcoming with information about her family, that is, until her phone would not stop ringing.

Once Sinclair left the office, Char picked up her phone and pressed voice mail. For the second time in five weeks. I watched a self-assured professional transform into an apologetic little child right before my eyes. Just hearing her mother's recorded tirade seemed to emotionally throw Char into her past—a place I suspect she dreads to revisit.

I wanted to give Char privacy and started to excuse myself, but Char signaled me to stay. We still needed to confirm each other's schedule. While I drove to Mobile, Alabama, Char planned to drive to New Orleans to pick up the enhanced video from the Stop-N-Go security camera. All week her intention had been to drive there and back in one day, but after listening to the twelve voice mails, Char was struggling with a well-entrenched sense of responsibility. "Mike, I think I need to stay in New Orleans for the weekend. Neither of us feels comfortable being too far from our home base with a killer on the loose, but I need to do this."

My place was not to question Char or to put her on the spot with embarrassing questions, but obviously Char felt she needed to explain. "Mike, this is the longest I've ever gone without checking in on my family. Even as a ten-year-old, I always felt like I was the stabilizing factor for my family." With a quick look of embarrassment, Char smiled. "You saw my mother and my eldest sister. I love them both but honestly, they live for drama. If it does not come, they both go looking for it. Mike, these are the two most foolish women you will ever meet; the problem is, they love that life, and they live in a city that lends itself to their flamboyance and foolishness. They are not going to change, but my middle sister Jewel needs me. She has always needed me, and most of my choices in life have been because of and for her."

I sat quietly, realizing Char was not so much talking to me, as she was working out a difficult personal dilemma out loud. I diverted my eyes and gave her time to work it out.

"Mike, I can't bring Jewel here. She requires a lot of babysitting— time I do not have right now. She is a sweet trusting little girl in a woman's body. Her skills are limited, and her level of naïveté makes her a soft target. She is not flamboyant at all—unlike my mother and older sister, neither of whom feel any responsibility to watch out for her. But Mike, we are right in the middle of a triple murder case, and I need a quiet life in order to process everything. I am not being selfish, Mike, even though it isn't safe for her to stay in New Orleans, we still have a killer here in Terrebonne Parish. What am I supposed to do?"

Again, I remained quiet and Char continued, "School had always been my escape from the humiliation and drama that always surrounded my family. In elementary school, while Mother was still 'a working girl,' I ignored the constant insults and shunning of the other children because their parents told my classmates about my mother's business. I hated the rejection, but I could do nothing about it. I knew my mother was doing *that* to keep us fed and clothed, and I loved her for that. So, I focused on being a top-notch student, which became my only protection. That focus paid off for me. Did I tell you I was awarded a full-ride scholarship to both LSU and Tulane Law Schools? My heart wanted to go to LSU but being 80 miles away from home might as well have been on another planet for me. Attending LSU would have been my chance to move away from home and all that chaos and finally focus exclusively on my studies—something I had never been allowed to do. I just could not shake off my lifelong sense of responsibility to watch out for Jewel, so I chose Tulane. Don't get me wrong, it's a great school—but I chose it because it was right there in New Orleans, not four blocks from where I grew up so I could stay home with Jewel."

I could see that Char was struggling with the decision of whether or not to bring her sister back with her. I could not help her make this decision, nor was she asking me to. I felt honored that Char trusted me enough to share her personal pain and use me as a sounding board.

I wanted to say something, but felt I needed to be careful not to intrude or offer advice. I also wanted to know more about this amazing young woman sitting across from me, but I did not want to press too hard. "Char, you just said that you lived only a few blocks from Tulane. If I'm not mistaken, that is in downtown New Orleans, next to the French Quarter, right?"

Char smiled as she said, "And you are wondering how a "streetwalker" could afford to live in that area, right?"

I could feel the blush coming to my face as I realized my question was more than a little intrusive. "I just thought the rents down there were very pricey."

"Oh, they are, Mike. But, you see, my mother was once married to a successful businessman. The house he grew up in was three doors down from Ferret Street on Audubon. The estate had been in his family for three generations, and he inherited it when his parents both died while he was away at college. After graduation he returned home and married my mother, who was way too young and too foolish to be married to anyone—much less to a young man who had grand intentions. They quickly had two little girls, but my mother soon tired of the role of housewife, and he realized that she would never be a help to him. Actually, he knew she would always be an albatross around his neck. He suspected that Jewel was not even his child, and he wanted out of the marriage so badly that he offered to sign over the house to my mother if she would grant him a quick and quiet divorce. My mother agreed, and she was already pregnant with me even before the divorce was final.

"I've always known that he was not my father, even though I was given his name and grew up in his family home. I often wondered why my mother never sold the house during some of our times of extreme hardship. That she never did seemed so unlike her, and I didn't find out until right about the time I was a first-year law student at Tulane. My mother asked me to read her divorce agreement to see if there might be a loophole in her favor. As it turns out, Martin Smalls was a wise man who knew my mother and her careless ways. Therefore, to ensure his only daughter, Jasmine, would always have a roof over her head, he kept the deed in his name, paid the taxes and insurance, and only gave my mother permission to dwell in the house for as long as Jasmine lived at home."

I could see how painful the telling of this story was for Char. I doubt she had told very many people about her family story, and I felt honored again that she trusted me enough to share. "Char, does your sister ever see her father?"

"No, I suspect she is too much like my mother for his tastes. I've never met him myself. He was long gone before I was born." Then giving me a crooked smile, Char corrected herself. "Well, that isn't exactly true. I have met him; I just didn't know who he was at the time. You see, when Katrina hit in '05, I was in my last year at the University of New Orleans. Many insurance agents trying to settle claims were coming and going all over New Orleans. For more than a week, a man came who acted like he owned the place. All three of us girls thought he was from the insurance company, and Mother did not correct us. Much later, once he was gone for good, Mother finally told us he was Martin Smalls. I suspect he was making sure his family home would be in good condition when it was returned to him."

Char smiled. "So, you see, Mike, Jewel has no one in New Orleans watching out for her. She is a dull girl, though sweet and caring. She never finished high school, and while I was in college, I was worried that Mother might put her out to work the streets, so I found her a job in a laundry. She is a hard worker as long as the work is repetitive, and she does not have to interact with too many people. As long as she brings my mother her paycheck every week, my mother leaves her alone. But you heard the phone messages from my mother. Jewel is losing her job at the end of the month, and my mother is in a panic. Jewel is now in real danger because Mother will put her to "work" without any care of what might happen to Jewel. Mother's attitude is 'If it was good enough for me, it's good enough for her.'"

I could hold back no longer. "Char, is your place big enough for two people?"

"It would be tight," she admitted, "but Jewel and I are used to that. I cannot afford the distraction she would bring to my life right now, and I am really worried about having my sister here with a killer roaming around. She trusts everyone and would not know to be careful."

"What if I agreed to help watch out for her?" *There, I said it.* I had given my opinion about what Char should do, and I had offered to help.

"I appreciate that offer, Mike; I truly do. Jewel will need a job, but not just any job. She is very limited in what she can do, and I don't have time to do all that research right now."

I smiled a very fatherly smile and said, "I have an idea, Char. Before I leave for Mobile, I need to make a stop and check out a possibility. If I can make it happen, I'll text you. If it works out and you approve of it, you can then make whatever arrangement you feel is best for both you and your sister. I promise I will not question your decision. Is that fair for you?"

"Okay, Mike, and thank you. But remember, she cannot handle anything but repetitive work and very little interaction with people without getting overwhelmed."

I headed home to pack for my quick trip to Mobile before going to Clara's for my usual dinner special. As I walked in, I mused to myself, *this extra five pounds and my five weeks of schmoozing Miss Clara just might pay off.* During this entire five weeks, her waitress, Cindi Sue, has missed more shifts than she has worked. It has taken me two weeks to elicit any information from Clara. Being an outsider in Houma has put me at a distinct disadvantage, but my people skills have surely been sharpened.

Three weeks earlier, on an exceptionally hot evening, Miss Clara let it slip that Cindi Sue was actually her son's girlfriend, and just about the time Char and I showed up in town, Clara learned she was going to be a grandmother. I took my usual seat at the counter so Clara didn't have to walk so far to serve me. I placed my order and sat there quietly. I have learned that you do not intrude—not with Clara. I finished my dinner, paid my bill, and was about to leave when Clara said, "Mike, I'm not sure what I'm going to do. I need to hire a waitress who can show up to work every day, but I cannot fire Cindi Sue because she is family."

I counted to ten before saying, "You know, Clara, my Tilly had a really hard time with food smells at the beginning of both her pregnancies. I know it's hard on you, but I feel really sorry for Cindi Sue."

"Yeah, even when she shows up, she spends more time in the privy than on the floor. My cooking doesn't get to her so much; it's the dirty plates with half the food eaten that turns her stomach, not to mention the dirty dishwater. She cannot seem to handle any of that."

I smiled and offered, "Miss Clara, why not hire a girl to clear all the tables, do the dishes, and reset the tables for poor Cindi Sue? If she only has to greet your customers, take their orders, and collect their payments, maybe Cindi Sue could handle that."

"Hmm, not a bad idea, Mike. On the days when Cindi Sue just cannot make it in, that person could take some of the work off of me when I have to come out here and service my customers. But I couldn't pay very much, and this person would have to be dependable and not talk my head off. I simply can't abide chatterboxes. I know Cindi Sue can't help it with being is six weeks pregnant. I think she really wants to quit, but she and my son, Clifford, need her to work. This job is too hard on her, but she doesn't want to give it up."

"I'm so sorry, Clara, but you need some help around here. Doing double duty has to be so hard on you."

"It is, but I don't dare hire a new waitress. I don't want Cindi Sue to feel like I am shoving her out. The days she feels strong enough to work makes her feel like life is still possible for her. My son makes a fair living, but they do need Cindi Sue's money with the baby on the way."

"I get it." I smiled, trying to talk with a casual tone, "but what if you hired someone to help out in the kitchen as well as clear the dirty dishes for you? That person would not be a waitress, but a part of the kitchen staff. Wouldn't that help you out? You could even teach that person how to prep the food for you so your days wouldn't be so long. After doing all your prep work, that person could keep the dishes moving and even deliver the dishes to the tables for you. Wouldn't that take a big load off of you, Clara?"

Clara, exhausted from another fourteen-hour day, leaned back and pondered the idea. "That used to be Jeff's job, but when Cindi Sue started calling in sick all the time, and I had to be out front more. Jeff began taking over more and more of the cooking. It never occurred to me how much easier my life would be if I hired a second kitchen helper. I was just trying to get through the days when Cindi Sue was a no-show."

I smiled and let the idea percolate for a few minutes before asking, "Clara, do you have anyone in mind for such a position?"

"No, and I don't have time to go looking." Clara's exhaustion was at the tipping point.

Not knowing if Char would even go along with such a plan, I dared not be too specific with Clara. But I did not want her moving ahead of me and hiring someone else. "Clara, I have a young woman in mind for you."

"Now wait a minute here, Mike. I've hired help before and learned the hard way. Some just want to work here long enough to steal my recipes. It takes weeks to train a good prep cook, only to have them leave with my secrets and start their own place. Does your girl have goals of opening her own place someday?"

I smiled, being careful to stay non-specific. "Clara, this young woman is a little challenged. I doubt that she has big dreams, but I've been told she is very good at following direct orders and doing repetitive tasks. She has faithfully held down a job over in New Orleans for more than ten years. The company is closing down, and she is looking to relocate and will be looking for work. She probably would not make a good waitress, but I think having a second pair of hands in your kitchen might be just the right fit for you."

"Mike, just how challenged is she?"

I hesitated for a moment because I couldn't honestly answer this question. "Clara, how about if I bring her here for dinner one night, and you can observe her and talk to her. That way you can decide for yourself before you actually interview her. If you decide she wouldn't be a good fit for you, you simply don't bring up the job." I smiled and added, "No harm, no foul."

Clara stood and gathered my dishes, signaling we were now done. She still had another two hours of work in the kitchen before she could go home. "Mike, bring her by, and I will check her out. "How soon could you bring her, Mike?"

"Not wanting anyone in Houma to know that I was heading to Mobile, I sidestepped Clara's direct question with another question. "Do you think you should talk to Cindi Sue and your son before I bring her by? You don't want to ruffle feathers among the family."

"You're right, Mike. My son is the one who would get miffed. They need every penny Cindi Sue makes, but if I can convince him this will help Cindi Sue be able to stay working longer and make more money, he would go along with it. Mike, can you give me the weekend so I can work on Clifford? If I think it will work, on Monday I will give you the high sign to bring her by on Tuesday or Wednesday. How does that sound to you?"

"Sounds like a right good plan, Clara."

I paid my bill and left, knowing I had just stepped into it. If this goes badly, I have lost weeks of hard schmoozing, but if it works out everybody wins. I sat in my Yukon and realized that everything I had just done was based on Char's assessment of her sister. I had only met this young woman once on the night of the ambush, and all the attention had gone to her mother and older sister. I do remember thinking she was a pretty young woman, but apart from that, I knew nothing about her, except for Char's description. I reread Char's texts and realized exactly how much I have come to trust this young woman's opinions. I had spent the past five weeks trying to ingratiate myself to Clara, my best source of local gossip, and I have made some huge inroads. So, what did I do? I decided it was a good idea to sell Clara on the idea of hiring Jewel. I sighed. If this goes badly, I will have to start all over again.

I picked up my cell phone and text: "I MAY HAVE FOUND A JOB FOR YOUR SISTER."

"WHAT KIND OF JOB?" Char immediately replied.

"CLEAR TABLES, WASH DISHES, CUT VEGGIES, PREP FOOD."

"MY SISTER COULD DO ALL THAT. BY THE WAY, MIKE, MY SISTER'S LEGAL NAME IS CARMELLA JEWEL, BUT EVERYONE CALLS HER JEWEL. WHERE IS THIS PLACE?"

"MS. CLARA'S CAFÉ, BUT DON'T TELL JEWEL JUST YET."

"WHY?"

"CLARA WANTS TO MEET HER FIRST."

"I UNDERSTAND. THANK YOU, MIKE."

I put down my phone and started the engine as I looked into the Louisiana sky and said, "Tilly, it's been a long day. I butted into Char's business, and I might have ruined five weeks of hard work winning over Ms. Clara. Tomorrow I'm heading off to retrieve the boat, and it looks like Charlemagne Smalls might be on her way to rescue her sister, Jewel. I know you would have helped her, regardless of the fallout. I sure miss you, Tilly."

16

The Retrieval

THE NEXT morning, I headed to Mobile, but my mind was on what Char was going to face when she arrived in New Orleans. I took Barrow Street up to Main, hung a left and turned left again onto New Orleans Bridge for the seven-mile trek to US 90 East. Once I was on the highway, I had twenty-three miles of straight driving before I had to worry about my next transitions to merge onto Interstate 10 toward New Orleans. Once I got close, I would need to focus on my driving in order to bypass the city congestion. For the next twenty-three miles I could sit back and worry about Char, or I could use my time to better advantage and begin mulling over everything that had been said the day before. As usual, I turned on my mini tape recorder and began going back over what we knew and what we suspected.

Char had done an excellent job of presenting our evidence. I did not see a flicker of intimidation. She had played them like a pro and had maintained control of the room at all times. When confronted with irrefutable evidence, most people react one of four ways:

1] They fold and confess everything.

2] They fold but blame someone else.

3] They look you right in the eye and continue to blatantly deny it.

4] They ask for a lawyer and shut up.

Wilcomb had folded and confessed everything. What else could he do with our cold hard evidence? I'm not sure we got the whole story, but we got enough to ruin his political future—if that had been our only goal—but it wasn't.

Sinclair, on the other hand, is a real piece of work. If the man is talking, he is conniving. Sure, he gave up the boat, but what choice did he have? The look on his face when the videotape showed him behind the wheel of the boat reminded me of a rat in a maze. His mind was flying from one track to another, believing he was still smarter than we were and fast enough to outmaneuver us. But when rats reach a dead-end and knows they are finally trapped with nowhere to go, most surrender. Sinclair, on the other hand, is not the surrendering kind. Quite simply, He has worked too long and hard to surrender; that man has something up his sleeve.

On the surface, we already had enough evidence to destroy Sinclair's relationship with the Wilcomb empire, but with Max Wilcomb possibly succumbing to dementia (a fact not yet established), Sinclair might already have positioned himself in such a way that he has probably protected himself from injury.

He did not volunteer that boat out of altruism; he was maneuvering and manipulating the evidence he could no longer hide without jeopardizing himself more. Everything Sinclair does is about and for himself; after all, that man handed over the love of his life for position and power.

We are certain Sinclair is not the killer, and if he knew that Calvin could not have been the killer because they were together, why take such a big chance by moving the boat? They had not used the boat to dump the body, but in the political arena, merely having your name linked to a dead body would ring a death knell over your campaign. No doubt, sordid details will be released with the DNA evidence and then there are the blackmail tapes....

Picking up the recorder from beside me on the seat, I talked loudly into it:

1] Where are the blackmail tapes? Sinclair admitted they existed, but he did not offer them into evidence. Why else would the family agree to pay such a huge blackmail compensation?

2] Sinclair admitted that they have watched some of the tapes; no doubt the most salacious parts, but someone still has his hands on all of those tapes.

3] We need to find those tapes. If Sinclair destroyed them, he will never admit to it.

4] We need to get a search warrant for both Sinclair's office and home.

5] We need to secure search warrants for the Wilcomb compound, all their bank accounts, including their shell corporations, and Calvin's office.

6] We need to interview the guy Sinclair hired to "clean out the boat, as well as serve a search warrant for his home and office and force him to turn over all the lab results he performed under Sinclair's authority. They may not be legal in court, but they should provide some solid leads.

7] We need to secure a warrant that includes this guy's business and his personal bank accounts. We need to follow the money.

Seeing the highway sign to merge with I-10 East, I clicked off my recorder and paid attention to traffic as I merged onto I-10. Once securely in the correct lane, I allowed myself to get back to business. Char and I had only been on this case for five weeks, and we now knew a lot, and yet we still knew very little. Clicking my recorder back on, I postulated:

1] No clue who the killer is

2] No clue who has the tapes

3] No clue who keeps getting into the war room.

4] No clue who removed the tire impressions

We have wasted five weeks focused on the Wilcomb family because their behavior reeked of guilt—just the wrong guilt.

I picked up my recorder and said, "Switch gears. What else have we learned?" Then setting the recorder on seat beside me, I pondered, *Well, I've learned that it has cost me seven pounds of eating Ms. Clara's rich food in order to win her over.* Ever since arriving in Houma, I've eaten breakfast and dinner at Ms. Clara's Café, wearing down that woman. The first week or so, I was almost afraid to eat what she placed in front of me because her hostility level was so high. She had been told that we were the enemy, and she believed it. I have never had to work so hard to make a sweet old lady like me, but I kept at it.

I needed to earn her trust and loosen her lips. That woman knew things that I needed to know. The first thing I learned was that woman can cook!

I then learned that during the 1920s through the 1980s, almost everyone worked for the Wilcomb empire. Everyone knew that their livelihood depended upon the Wilcomb family doing well. During that time, her husband worked at the Wilcomb cannery, as did nearly everyone in the parish in one way or another back then. You either collected a paycheck directly from the cannery, as her husband did, or you were a fisherman who was under exclusive contract to sell your catch to the cannery. That symbiotic relationship bred a tremendous amount of blind loyalty among the old guard that seems to be still present in many.

In the 1980s, other businesses began building up in their prosperous parish, and the younger generation ceased to appreciate exactly how much they owe to the Wilcomb family. When driving through the parish, many family names other than Wilcomb can now be seen on the mailboxes. These younger families arrived long after the cannery days, so the younger ones don't hold to the same loyalty as do the older generation.

After two weeks of schmoozing this rather standoffish lady, she spoke a kind word to me. Once I had broken through her resistance, I began uncovering a gold mine of information. Just as I had suspected, this woman knew a lot. Oh, she doesn't run in the inner circles of Terrebonne Parish, but as anyone who has ever lived in a small town knows, everyone knows more than you wish they knew. Now, they don't know everything, but they know enough, and that was what I needed to know. I mentally ran through the past three weeks of gleaning:

1] Mrs. Treadway, who went to school with Clara, believes Sinclair has been cheating on her daughter.

2] Mrs. Treadway is not someone you want to have as an enemy.

3] Did Mrs. Treadway learn of her son-in-law's unfaithfulness to her beautiful daughter and how he has treated her? Could she be working a revenge angle?

4] Back in the day, Maximillion had dallied with most of the young women in the parish. He was rich, handsome, and fun, but everyone knew the casual relationship would go nowhere.

5] Back in college in the late sixties, Maximillion had even dated Gertrude Sanders.

6] Ms. Clara made it quite clear that Gertrude, although a resident of the parish since the late '60s, had not grown up here.

7] Maximillion had married his first wife Sarah from old family money in Fairhope, Alabama. Everyone knew the marriage was a business deal between Papa Joseph and her father. Once Mitchell was born and they began to see signs of trouble, Sarah spent more and more time away from home. Servants say she had no tolerance for his tantrums. Maximillion continued to have affairs, and no one in the parish blamed him.

8] Right after Papa Joseph died, Maximillion was finally free and divorced Sarah. When he married Charisse, he broke lots of wishful hearts around the parish. Charisse eventually won over the admiration of most, but Gertrude never liked her.

9] Max's son Mitchell from his first marriage continued to be odd, and everyone was shocked when his upcoming marriage was announced. When Catherine was found to be beautiful and smart, everyone knew she had been bought off—why else?

10] You could have knocked everyone over with a feather when Catherine turned up pregnant. Because Maximillion loved Mitchell's son, so did the whole parish. Calvin became everyone's golden boy.

11] No one liked the outsider Calvin married. Even using the Wilcomb family attitude as a comparison, Jacqueline Westbourough Wilcomb is the most self-entitled, obnoxious woman to ever meet. No one in the parish would fault their golden boy for fishing in another pond.

Seeing the sign for my off ramp, I reached for my recorder and right before clicking it off, I said, "Check out where Mrs. Treadway was during the murder. Sure, she is in her sixties, but mess with a Momma Bear and see what you get. Could it be that Mrs. Treadway mistook the girl as Sinclair's folly by mistake? CHECK THAT OUT! *Click.*

I exited off the highway ramp onto Front Royal in Mobile and worked my way down to 5470 Front Royal Street to Robert's Royal Yacht Storage, where everyone's boat is treated like royalty.

I parked my car, tossed my recorder in the glove box, and walked over to the waiting transporter. "Hi! I'm Mike Majors, thanks for meeting me here on such short notice."

A toothless grin greeted me. "Not a problem, Mike, but the clock starts ticking now and won't turn off until I offload the boat in Houma. And as agreed, however long it takes to drive there, I will tack on the bill to cover my return trip, right?"

"Sounds fair to me, Neil. I'll just go into the office and get them started loading the boat. Be right back."

I had instructed the storage owner not to touch the boat until I was present. Robert O'Cleary, the owner, was waiting for me, "You have the authorization letter, Mr. Majors?"

I handed him Sinclair's letter, written on his own stationery that had been notarized, a photocopy of Sinclair's driver's license, and my photo I.D. "Here you go, Mr. O'Cleary, and I want a copy of your contract with Mr. Sinclair and a copy of his payment history as well. Mr. O'Cleary, did your company do the shrink-wrapping of the boat?"

O'Cleary nodded as he pulled out the Sinclair folder. "I have the invoice right here."

Looking at the invoice, I see two signatures at the bottom and ask, "Do both of these men still work for you? If so, might I have a word with them while the boat is being loaded?"

"Sure, they still work for me, but talking to them will have to wait since they will be loading the boat for you. Those two are my best men. Moving a 30-foot cruiser around a tight storage yard is not for amateurs."

"O'Cleary, has that boat been moved or touched since your boys shrink-wrapped it?"

"Nope, it hasn't—not even last summer when I called Mr. Sinclair about removing the wrap for the summer. You know, if you don't let a boat breathe during the summer, you can cause all kinds of rot and mold, but Sinclair was insistent that the boat stay wrapped. This is Mobile; we don't wrap boats down here unless they are being transported a long distance, and we want to protect the paint job. They wrap boats up north during the winter, but even there the wrapping is removed at the first sight of spring." Slapping his finger on the invoice I was holding, O'Cleary said, "See the disclaimer I wrote and made Sinclair sign. I warned him leaving a boat wrapped during an Alabama summer would destroy a boat, but he insisted."

As I stood examining the invoice, the thought occurred to me that O'Cleary is a man who takes his work seriously, so I asked, "Were you warned ahead of time that this boat was coming?"

"Not by much," the old man groaned. "I think he called the day before to make sure I had a space and the rigging to hoist the boat out of the water. Why?"

"Mr. O'Cleary, once the boat arrived, how long was the boat left in the water before it was hoisted up and set on one of your trailers?"

"Right away, Mike, because that was what Mr. Sinclair wanted. He piloted the boat right to the hoist and wouldn't get off the boat until Jimmy was ready to swing the hoist over and drop the strappings. No one is allowed on the boat while Jimmy handles that procedure because it is too dangerous."

"Now, once you hoisted the boat out of the water, did anyone ever enter that boat again?" I knew the answer; I just wanted to see if I was dealing with a trustworthy witness.

"You mean besides my boys?"

I simply nodded, "Yes."

"As soon as the boat was securely on the trailer and the hoist strappings had been swung away and the boat was strapped down to the trailer, Sinclair had a man go into the cabin and do a lot of stuff. We were not allowed to board the boat, but I ordered Jimmy to stay there and keep watch. I was already suspicious, and I told Sinclair that before we would shrink-wrap that boat, I wanted to have a look inside. For all I knew there could be a dead body in there."

"Did you look inside the cabin?"

"I sure did, and the place was a mess as you will see when you get the boat back to Louisiana and have it unwrapped. That black fingerprint dust was everywhere. I didn't see any signs of blood anywhere, but I didn't actually go inside. They were obviously looking for something in there, and I didn't want my prints or DNA in that cabin."

"So you knew what that man was doing in there?"

"Sure, I did. I watch *CSI*. He took almost three hours in there before locking the cabin, taping it off like a crime scene, and handing

Sinclair the keys. Only then did Sinclair give us the okay to start wrapping the boat. He stayed right here until the job was completed and we moved it to where it has sat ever since."

"Mr. O'Cleary, do you remember either of those men removing anything from that boat?"

"No, sir, and we watched them like a hawk. Queer stuff. I demanded to see the other man's I.D. before he left. I took a photocopy of it. You'll find it in the file. I didn't want anyone thinking I was hiding a drug-runner's boat, although they generally don't use gutless cruisers like this one. The fact that they were being so squirrelly had my attention."

O'Cleary signaled Jimmy to bring the boat forward and position it under the hoist, where Jimmy carefully placed the hoist straps around the underbelly of the cruiser and lifted it high above the trailer of the transporter. He locked the hoist and guided the transporter bed into place and lowered the cruiser down. Jimmy started to strap it down, but Neil, my transporter, waved him off. "I'm responsible for the cruiser from here on out," he gruffly stated, "so if you don't mind, I will strap it down."

Jimmy gave Neil a knowing nod and stepped away. Thirty minutes later we were back on the road heading for Baton Rouge. As we drove west on I-10, passing north of New Orleans, I couldn't help but think about how things were going for Char. I clicked off the air conditioner so I could send a text. "Siri, text Char."

Siri, "What would you like to say?"

"CHAR, HAVE CRUISER IN TOW. HEADING TO BATON ROUGE. WILL YOU BE JOINING ME THERE?"

Almost immediately came her response: "NO, BRINGING JEWEL BACK WITH ME. SEE YOU TOMORROW."

By the time I turned over the cruiser to Investigator Lennord, signed the evidence log, and gave him copies of all the storage documents, I knew it was too late to drive back to Houma in time to get to Clara's before closing. "Hey, Dwight, how about catching a bite to eat, my treat?"

"Sure thing, Mike. There is a LuLu's right down the street."

If felt good being able to talk with Dwight about the case without having to filter every single word. I went over every single loose lead, picked his brain about how he would go after them, and although he couldn't think of a single thing we had missed, it sure gave me a good feeling that Char and I were on top of the case—as much as anyone could with the convoluted mess we were tackling.

I arrived home at almost one in the morning and dropped into bed, exhausted and more than a little frustrated, but that is always how a detective feels when there are too many clues and not enough real leads. Just as my head dropped on my pillow, I repeated that thought, "Too many clues and not enough real leads." As I turned off my side-light, I moaned, "We are being played."

As arranged, I spent Monday running DMV records on Jeeps owned in the parish since 1980. I knew this list would be long, but I was looking for any names that might be connected—how, I did not know. My first pass through this long list was focused on any corporation names. We knew about four of Wilcomb's secret corporations, but there could be more. Just in case, I intended to track down every one of them.

Throughout the day, I texted Char several times to keep her abreast of my progress...or lack thereof. I resisted asking anything personal although I was dying to know what was going on.

17

A Flawed Jewel Is Rescued

I WALKED into Ms. Clara's right at seven o'clock Monday evening and took my usual seat. As had become quite common, Clara's waitress was a no-show, and by this hour, Clara was now frazzled beyond measure. Her cook's helper was doing his best to cover everything in the kitchen while Clara called out the orders from the front window.

In the five weeks that I had been dining there, I had learned to order simple meals when Cindi Sue was missing. My fail-safe order was always shrimp and grits with a side salad and Clara's fabulous cornbread puffs. These puffs are nothing like traditional cornbread, which is dry and stiff. Somehow, Clara makes them heavenly—lighter-than-air muffins. The crown looks dry, but when you bite into them, they are airy and light and need no butter or honey. The puffs are Clara's pride and joy and have become one of my favorite items.

Clara finally noticed that I was intentionally keeping my orders simple after I had placed two or three uncomplicated meals, and though she would smile at me in appreciation, she said nothing.

Neither did I, but I could tell that I was beginning to wear her down. This woman prided herself on serving great food, and when she was forced to cover the front, she knew her customers were not getting her best. That thought bothered her greatly. Those rare smiles of gratitude from Clara were a sign that I was winning her over. Honestly, I have never worked so hard for a smile in my whole life, so hers were the smiles that I valued most.

At eight o'clock sharp Clara flipped the sign that hung on her front door. She was officially closed for the night. Four of us were still eating, so I took my time and enjoyed my last cornbread puff with a final cup of Clara's hickory-vanilla coffee. As she poured, she announced her usual, "This is the last refill of the day, Mike; enjoy it."

"You know I will, Clara," I said with a grateful smile. I wanted to be the last customer to leave so I could have a private conversation with her. Finally, the threesome paid their bill and left. As the cook's helper was busy cleaning in the back, Clara gathered up dirty dishes and carried them to the kitchen before returning to my table with one last refill. Our routine of late was Clara's taking a seat across from me and giving her feet a rest after a long day of waiting tables. "So, where were you this morning, Mike?"

"I thought I told you I wouldn't be here for breakfast this morning, Clara. I'm sure I did. Remember? I told you I had to go out of town on business." I dared not tell her what that business involved or where I had been—not just yet.

"Oh, I remember you telling me that. It's just that when Cindi Sue calls in sick, my whole world turns upside down. Speaking of that, I talked to Clifford over the weekend, and he thinks it would be a good idea for me to hire a kitchen helper. So, when can you bring her by?"

As I had not yet talked with Char about how the weekend had gone, I was feeling a little uncertain exactly how much I could promise.

"Ms. Clara, because I did not want to presume, I thought it best not to talk to my friend until after you and Clifford discussed the possibility. Now that you have, I will talk to my friend and bring her by for dinner either tomorrow evening or the next night. How does that plan sound to you?"

"You might want to bring her by tomorrow evening, Mike. I will be serving your favorite dinner, Chicken Fricassee."

"I'll be here—with or without her. Now, how about boxing up a dozen of your corn puffs so I can use them as bait for my friend?"

I climbed into my Yukon and set the box of corn muffins on the seat then texted Char: "HOW DID IT GO WITH YOUR FAMILY?"

"GIVE ME FIVE MINUTES, AND I WILL CALL YOU."

I answered my phone on the first ring, "Hi, Char."

"Good evening, Mike." I noticed immediately that she sounded exhausted. "It was not fun. My mother did not want Jewel to leave because she has always been a source of steady income for my mother. I believe my suspicions were correct about her hoping to start Jewel in the street trade. Honestly, I just don't understand how my mother thinks."

I did not comment on this admission, instead asking, "Do you think your sister would feel comfortable going to dinner with me to-morrow evening?"

Char hesitated, "She will if I come along."

"What if I came over to your place this evening, and you intro-duced me to her? I don't think it would be a good idea for you to come along to Ms. Clara's Café. Breaking down her animosity toward me has taken five weeks. You and I are still the interlopers—the enemies—and I don't want to remind Clara of that status."

Char groaned in a strange voice. I suspect this mother-hen strug-gle comes from years of Char's watching out for her sister, and if I do not tread carefully, this might become an issue between the two of us if I push too hard. I tried to back up and give Char a little space. "Char, it is not my intention to take over here. Jewel is your sister, and you know best what her capabilities are."

"No, I understand, Mike. I just have never had anyone I could trust to watch out for her before. She is sweet, innocent, and sadly, not the brightest bulb on the tree. I don't say that in a mean way, but rather to say that people tend to take advantage of her. I also think my not being there would be a good idea. If I were present for the interview, Jewel would not talk at all. She is used to me taking the lead and would not show herself well. Why don't you come over tonight so she can get to know you? But Mike, no talking business around Jewel. She has no filtering system. She cannot handle bad news, and she cannot keep things to herself. She looks quite normal, but believe me, she is far from it. Therefore, you and I need to turn off the case when she is around."

"Char, I'll be there in about ten minutes."

"That would be fine." Right before hanging up, I heard her add, "And Mike, thank you."

I pulled into a parking spot right next to the stairwell that Char had said led to her apartment. I grabbed the box of corn puffs and headed upstairs. Hearing how exhausted Char sounded on the phone, I wasn't sure of what to expect. "No shop talk," I repeated, before realizing I had sent Char twenty-plus texts throughout the day, so she already knew everything I know. I knocked on the door as opposed to ringing the doorbell, a habit many Southerners use to alert the dweller that this is a friend rather than a stranger or a salesman. Char answered the door in casual attire—bright yellow cotton pedal-pushers (at least that was what Tilly always called them), a mint green and yellow striped sleeveless cotton top, and bare feet. At first, I was taken aback, never having seen Char in anything other than professional attire.

She smiled and waved me in, calling out, "Jewel, take a break from unpacking and come meet Mr. Majors, my investigator."

Both women were glowing with perspiration, and I quickly realized that some of Char's exhaustion was pure fatigue. I quickly counted four large empty cardboard boxes by the door and three still unopened ones stacked by the hallway as Jewel came out of the bedroom to greet me. "Hi, Mr. Mike."

Char pushed the empty boxes out of the way and offered, "Would you like something cold to drink, Mike? I have Pepsi, sweet tea, and club soda."

"Sweet tea would be nice, Char." Then holding up the box of corn puffs, I said, "I brought these. Thought you two might enjoy them."

As Char opened the box, Jewel reached over and took one. Tasting the corn puff she said, "Boy, these are soft!" Then quickly taking two more, Jewel grabbed her drink and headed toward the sofa. "Mr. Mike, my sister, Charlemagne, is really, really smart. She never gets her words all tangled up or nothing."

I smiled and nodded my head in agreement. "Yes, you are so right, Jewel. Char is smart and brave."

Jewel's face brightened, "Oh, she sure is brave, Mr. Mike. You should have seen how she stood up to my momma and Jasmine the other day; I could never do that. When those two get hop'n' mad, all my words fly out the window, and I just have to leave so they won't hit my face. But my Charlemagne just stood up and argued at them both like one of those important men on TV. I don't know how many big words can live in that pretty little head, but they flew out of her mouth so fast that my momma had to sit down and let me move here with Charlemagne."

I leaned forward and spoke in as gentle a voice as I could muster, "Jewel, she must love you a lot to stand up to your momma like that."

"Oh, she does love me a whole lot, Mr. Mike. Did you know when Charlemagne was just a baby that I saved her life? I surely did, didn't I, Charlemagne?"

Char came over and plopped down next to her older sister, put her arm around her neck and gave her a hug and kiss before explaining, "She surely did, Mike. I was just barely four years old, and Jewel was almost six. Right, Jewels?"

"Yes, that's right. Momma had to go out that night and make some money for us, but my big sister, Jasmine, who was ten years old, did not want Momma to leave cuz she was hungry and wanted her dinner—but Momma went out anyway."

I leaned even closer and asked, "So what happened, Jewel?"

"Well, you know how little kids should never turn on the stove, right?"

"Yes!" I said emphatically.

"Well, Jasmine broke Momma's rule. She was mad and she was hungry, so she put a pan on the stove and turned it on. Then she got in the fridge and took out some gumbo we had the day before, but by now the pan got too hot for Jasmine, so she got Momma's blue and white dish towel and tried to wrap it around the pan handle. I warned her not to. We are never supposed to turn on Momma's stove because that belongs to her. But when Jasmine gets mad, she doesn't listen." By now Jewel's eyes were sparkling with excitement as she relived that night. "Well, Mr. Mike, Momma's dish towel caught fire, and Jasmine just tossed it from her and ran away. I didn't know what to do. Jasmine ran off, but the towel was still burning, and then the curtains started burning. I started crying but Jasmine wouldn't come back and fix it."

Getting another glimpse into Char and Jewel's childhood, I asked, "So, what did you do, Jewel?"

Char chimed in and said with a well-rehearsed voice, "My sister

Jewel got me out of the house and got the neighbor to put out the fire before we lost the whole house. Wasn't that smart of her, Mike? Not even Jasmine thought of doing that smart thing, did she, Jewel?"

"Nope, just me. I saved Charlemagne's life, didn't I, Sister?"

"You sure did, and that is why I love you sooo much, isn't it, Jewel?"

"Yes, it is, and that is why I never ever touch the stove, isn't it, Charlemagne?"

"Right, because fire is scary, and we do not want another house fire." Then, seeing the time, Char suggested, "Jewel, say good night to Mike. He has to get up early tomorrow."

"Good night, Mike, I liked your corn puffs."

"You did, Jewel? Well, how would you like me to take you to dinner tomorrow night? I could take you where they make those corn puffs. Would you like that?"

"Can Char come too?"

"Oh, Jewel, remember I told you I have a meeting tomorrow evening, but you and Mike can go together."

"Okay, Mike, I can go." With this settled, Jewel stood and shook my hand. "Good night, Mike, I'll see you tomorrow."

Char suggested, "Jewel, while I walk Mike out to his car, you jump in the shower. When I return, I will have your bed made up."

We were both quiet as we walked to my car. I didn't know quite what to say, having witnessed this much-rehearsed story of Jewel's brave moment. Char was well aware of how much her storytelling had exposed a child lacking in parental care. At the same time, the story also revealed how caring and compassionate Char has always been to her sister. So many neglected children only focus on how neglected they had been, and rightly so, but Char had chosen a different response. This story, although factually accurate, has been woven into a story that Char has used for years to remind her challenged sister of the night she was the smart one, the brave one, the one who had saved her life.

As I got into my Yukon, I rolled down the window and said, "Thank you, Char, for trusting me." I wanted to say more, but nothing else was coming to me.

Char reached into the window with huge tears in her eyes, gripped my forearm, and with a tremulous voice, said, "Mike, thank *you* for everything."

Sensing I was going to brush off her gratitude, Char gripped my forearm even harder and almost whispered, "No, Mike, I really mean thank you for nudging me to go get Jewels. I think I snatched her out of the fire just in time, and you helped me make that decision. Thank you." Then knowing we were both feeling exposed, Char turned on her professional demeanor and said, "I will see you in the morning, Mike." She quickly stepped away from my truck and waved goodbye.

18

Leads and Leaks

ERTRUDE SANDERS greeted me as I entered the building on Tuesday morning. "Good morning, Mr. Majors. Clara tells me that you two have become quite good friends."

"Good morning to you, Ms. Sanders. Ms. Clara can surely cook, and I have five extra pounds to prove it."

"Well, Mike, you hide it well. I didn't see you here yesterday. How was your trip to Mobile?"

I hesitated for barely an instant before recovering from the shock of her question and answering. *I know I did not tell anyone where I was going, so how does Gertrude know about Mobile?* "Uneventful, Ms. Sanders, how was your weekend?"

I noticed her hesitate ever so slightly, and I suspected she was sorry she had asked the question. "Boring as usual, Mike—full of laundry and cleaning, but my husband Phillip and I were able to get in some good fishing on Sunday. Do you like to fish, Mike?"

"Sadly, no, Ms. Sanders. I know living here in the heart of fishing country and not liking to fish is a shame. I guess you have to start that habit as a young boy in order to get it in your blood."

I considered asking Gertrude how she knew about my trip to Mobile but doing so would only confirm where I had been. I quickly excused myself, and as I headed toward our office, I reviewed all of my conversations since deciding to drive over to Mobile last Thursday. I was certain I had not slipped up, but maybe Char had. I made a mental note to ask Char and warn her to keep everything close to the vest. *Loose lips sink ships!*

As I unlocked the door to our war room, I was dying to ask about Jewel, but work had to come first. As I suspected, Char was already there and deep in paperwork, so I locked the door and took a seat.

Without looking up, Char greeted me with, "We have a great lead, Mike."

"From the video tape of the Stop-n-Go," I asked?"

"Yes! We now know the make and model of the car, but sadly, no matter how much they tried, the camera did not catch the driver or the license. We are looking for a rather common Jeep, between 1990 and 2005, dark blue in color, a beige rag top two-door with a winch on the front bumper. There were no telltale stickers to help us identify it, but actually my friend said the fact that it had no stickers was probably quite helpful since most Jeeps sport a ton of stickers."

Thrilled with this new lead, I added, "And we know, thanks to Dr. Harvey's tire impressions, that this Jeep has three different tire types—unless the killer has changed the tires. But with this new information, we can run a search on any blue Jeeps getting new tires in the last four months. That should narrow it down for us."

"Mike, I ordered a BOLO on all blue Jeeps with a rag top. If this vehicle is still on the road, we will find it."

"Char, can you change your BOLO? I wouldn't limit it to a rag top. Maybe the killer also has a hard top that can be interchanged. My son switches his all the time."

"I can do that," she agreed as she stood to leave. "I know putting out a BOLO is tipping our hand, but we need to find that car."

Char returned and announced, "BOLO is changed, now on to other business. How long before our techs go through the cruiser? I know we have a problem with chain of evidence, but leads are leads."

Shaking my head in agreement, I added, "It will take several days. The cruiser has been wrapped for over a year and that alone caused lots of damage. And talk about a polluted crime scene, I am not hopeful of finding anything beyond what Sinclair offered up to us."

"Well," Char groaned, "we can't use anything that Sinclair collected since he is going to be charged with tampering with evidence."

"True, Char, but at least the storage owner was quite thorough. He documented everything, and his description of the timeline matches Sinclair's."

"I'm not sure how we could get around the chain-of-evidence issue, let alone the fact that Sinclair is the source of this evidence. Talk about fruit of the poison tree. It might help us know where to start looking, but we will have to find another inevitable lead if we want to use that evidence." Then, switching back to the Jeep, Char added, "At least the Jeep is a clean lead. I want you to get right on a search of all blue Jeeps getting new tires. Run every lead to ground and get back to me ASAP."

"I'm on it," I said as I gathered up my notepad. "Oh, Char, I wanted to ask you something. Did you happen to mention to anyone that I was going to Mobile?"

Char stopped what she was doing and stared at me in bewilderment. "No, I did not. Why?"

"I didn't think so, but this morning Gertrude asked me how my trip to Mobile went. I tried not to react to her question, but she caught me off-guard, and I hesitated momentarily before answering her. I could see by her expression that she was sorry she had asked. I know I did not tell anyone. I am certain I did not tell Ms. Clara where I was going, so Gertrude could not have heard about it from Clara. I've gone over and over everything I have done since we made the decision to go retrieve that cruiser. There is no way Gertrude could have known."

Char sat back down in her seat. "And yet she does...."

I nodded, "And yet she does. We had agreed never to put any of our notes in the trash, so she could not have gone through our trash cans and found it. We swept the room for bugs. Maybe it's time we did it again." Then the image of a stack of mail sitting on Gertrude's desk that morning, ready to be delivered to the different offices, came to mind. "Char, what if Neil, the transporter, dropped off his invoice, thinking he would get paid faster? I'm going to text him and find out. I can't imagine he would drive all the way here to deliver an unsealed bill."

Char almost barked her response to this. "When people are a living hand-to-mouth existence, no telling how far they will go to get paid. Even so, Gertrude Sanders has no business opening even unsealed bills directed to this office. But before we dare confront her, we need to confirm that Neil even did this. I cannot think of any other way she would have known. Unless..." Char pondered, "You don't think Sinclair would have told her—no, never in a million years."

"My money is on Neil."

"Okay, make that call and then get right on the Jeep. Also, could you run a DMV on all owners of blue, two-door Jeeps in the parish? Extend the years from 1985 to the present. My friend in New Orleans said they have not changed the body style for years, so being certain of the exact year is exactly easy. Once we have the names, we will go through them to see if any known name pops up."

"I'm on it, Char."

My first order of business was to text Neil. I was rather hoping to find out that he had indeed dropped off his invoice, unsealed and available for all eyes. Warning him about keeping our project quiet had never occurred to me. If he had, it would clear things up, and I would gladly take the blame for this little faux pas. I sent my text and proceeded with my day's assignments.

I logged onto my office computer and wrote out an official search request to the DMV for all owners of blue, two-door Jeep Wranglers, 1985 to the present, registered within Terrebonne Parish. Once that request was faxed, I began making a list of every tire store in the parish. We only needed to go back two weeks because as of the second body drop, we knew the old mismatched tires were still on the vehicle.

I felt fairly certain we had narrowed down our search by model, color, and time frame. But years of experience with chasing down these types of leads, I knew better than to simply place a phone call. Whenever you are asking hourly workers to take their precious time to look back through their computer records, you need to show a badge and present a strong presence of authority. I typed up an official search order and made about thirty copies. I knew it would take the better part of two days to cover all the tire stores—even if we were only requesting two weeks' worth of records—but we were desperate for a lead.

I had just picked up my pile of copies when my phone buzzed. I saw that Neil was texting me. "NOT YET DONE MY BILLING. YOU IN A HURRY?"

I texted back, "NO, JUST CHECKING." *We have a real problem.*

As I made my rounds to the list of tire stores in Houma, my mind kept going over everything I had said and done once we found out about Mobile. To my knowledge, four people knew about Mobile: Sinclair, Wilcomb, Char, and myself. One of us had slipped up, but who? After three hours of retracing my every move, I knew I was not the guilty party. By process of elimination, three people were left. I began listing facts I knew for certain.

- Char is as careful as I am.

- Calvin Wilcomb would only talk to Sinclair.

- Sinclair would not talk to anyone but Calvin.

- Our war room has no bugs, but could Calvin's office be bugged?

- Gertrude has keys to every office except ours, or so we think.

- Gertrude knows about Mobile, but we have no idea how.

- Could seventy-year-old Gertrude be involved or just used?

- Where does Mrs. Treadway fit into all of these machinations?

- Does she know about Sinclair's cheating on her daughter?

- How close are Treadway and Gertrude?

- Is one or both of these elderly women being used?

- If so, who is using these women, and why?

- Finding this leak will be our greatest lead.

I pulled into store number five of six, turned off my engine, locked the door, and headed in to see the manager. As with the other four, my request produced a contrary attitude. "You've got to be kidding, man. You think I can hit a few keys on this computer and find out all the dark-blue Jeeps we've serviced in the past two weeks? First of all, we do not record the vehicle's color. Secondly, I would have to print out every sale and look through each one to see the make of car. Our system will not allow us to search by make of car, but if you wanted to know what type of tires we sold, that we can do. So, do you know what kind of tires you are looking for?"

Knowing the Jeep owner we are looking for had three different kinds of tires on his vehicle means they have only purchased one tire at a time as needed. Knowing that means we are not looking for someone who would walk into this tire store and purchase super-expensive mud-terrain tires, rock-terrain tires, or even bother with all-terrain tires. We are looking for someone who would most likely purchase the low-end, all-around tires—the cheaper the better. This owner has never spent money on larger rims, so we are looking at standard 33-inch rims. "Mister, we are searching for 33-inch rims, economy pricing. That should narrow it down for you, right?

Finally, the manager began to yield. "Yeah, I can do that, but I won't be able to get that report for you until tomorrow. My wife does all the computer stuff. Are you willing to come back when I text you?"

Protecting our investigation, I agreed, "I sure am. Please do not give this report to anyone other than me. I will not send anyone else to pick it up and do not drop it off. I will come get it, you got that?"

19

An Almost Perfect Fit

I T WAS almost six when I left the last tire store. Knowing Jewel would be waiting for me, I called it a night and drove toward Char's apartment. Shifting gears, I needed to set aside everything case related and now focus only on Jewel and Clara. That shifting of gears is so easy to say but doing so has never been easy. Your mind is constantly grinding on facts and trying to piece them together, worrying all the time that some small piece of information might have been overlooked. You go over and over every comment, every subtle twitch that might be significant, hoping that every diverted thread of conversation might lead to something. The life of a detective is all-consuming, unless you manage it instead of it managing you. As I knocked on Char's apartment door, I took a deep breath and purposely exhaled, put a smile on my face, and relaxed my shoulders for the first time in hours. I mused to myself, *my profession can wait, my mission cannot. Jewel needs one hundred percent of me right now.*

I looked up as the door swung wide open and Jewel stood in front of me, dressed in a simple cotton dress that draped loosely over her slender body. She wore almost no makeup, but she didn't need any. Although not at all glamorous or alluring, her natural beauty, coupled with her childlike openness, made me want to protect her and take care of her. I was also warned that many men with evil intentions would feel the same way, and I quickly realized the heavy responsibility that has rested upon Char's shoulders for many years. One of my many missions was to share this burden with Char so she does not have to go it alone anymore. "Good evening, Jewel, are you ready for an awesome dinner? Ms. Clara is not the friendliest of women, especially when she is busy. That is, until she gets to know you, but she sure can cook!"

Jewel smiled and offered, "My boss, Mr. Leaner, was the same way. When a big order came into the laundry, you never wanted to talk too much, or he would bite your head off. It was best to keep quiet and do your work."

As Jewel locked the door behind her, I smiled and thought, *this is going to be a good fit.*

As we entered Clara's Café, I noticed that Cindi Sue was working her shift, and her husband Clifford was sitting at the counter. I suspected that neither of them wanted to miss seeing this new prospect; besides, Clara would not be able to spend time at our table checking out Jewel if she was the only person servicing her customers. Cindi Sue wasted no time greeting us and taking us to our table. I could tell she was a little concerned at Jewel's looks, but every pregnant woman who feels as big as a house, feels threatened by any young woman with a slight figure. I'm sure that at any other time, Cindi Sue would have done just about anything to sabotage this interview, but right now, Jewel is her only lifeline. She needs Jewel as much as Ms. Clara does. Handing us a menu, Cindi Sue said, "The house special tonight is Ms. Clara's favorite, chicken fricassee, as only Clara makes it. It comes with her corn puffs and a drink."

Jewel returned a bright smile and said, "I had her corn puffs last night, so I will have the special."

"I will too," I added as I handed Cindi Sue the menu. "I will have my usual sweet tea, and what will you being drinking tonight, Jewel?"

"I like sweet tea too."

Five minutes later, Clara herself brought out our dinner plates in order to get a closer look at Jewel. The fact that Jewel did not start chatting away at her impressed her. I was a little concerned, knowing that simply looking at Jewel doesn't present the full picture, but once Jewel starts talking, you quickly realize she is quite childlike. "Ms. Clara, I would like to introduce you to my new friend Jewel. She just moved here from New Orleans, and she loves your corn puffs, don't you, Jewel?"

"Yes, I ate four of them last night, and they didn't even need any butter." Jewel smiled up at Clara, but quickly lowered her gaze and stared at her plate.

Clara smiled over at me before addressing Jewel, "Well, you will have to tell me what you think of my chicken fricassee."

Jewel looked up with a puzzled look, "But I haven't tasted it yet. You just brought it."

Clara quickly picked up on Jewel's childish response, and I hoped she remembered I had said she was a little challenged. Unbefitting for Clara, she smiled at Jewel and said, "Oh, right, how silly of me. You just enjoy your dinner and don't worry about anything else."

I winked at Clara and placed my napkin on my lap before starting to eat. Clara's chicken fricassee is my absolute favorite because, unlike most chefs, as Clara is wont to say every time she sets it down in front of me, Clara caramelizes her meat and vegetables, rather than just braising them before adding white sauce. She also makes the most decadent white sauce I have ever had.

Jewel was quiet all through dinner. Not until she emptied her plate did a smile show on her face. "Mike, now Ms. Clara can come and ask me her question. Now I have something to say."

As I passed over the last corn puff, I asked, "Would you like the last puff, Jewel?"

Taking it with a huge smile, Jewel offered, "My momma is a terrible cook, Mike. When I was eleven, I had the hardest time getting the last baby teeth to let go so my grown-up teeth could come into my mouth. Momma and Jasmine tied a string to the tooth that sat right here." She pointed into her mouth on the left side. "They yanked so hard I was afraid all my teeth would fly right out of my mouth, and I started screaming, so they stopped. It took two days before that tooth stopped flopping back and forth in my mouth. My momma warned me to be careful not to swallow that tooth, but then she made her terrible corn muffins that night. They were nothing like Ms. Clara's puffs. Momma's muffins were so hard and stiff, you could use them to build a house. Charlemagne always warned me not to bite into them without soaking them in the sauce or gravy, but that night we didn't have either, and I was really hungry and forgot. I bit down and that floppy tooth got stuck in the muffin, and I couldn't keep biting down. I couldn't take it out of my mouth without it hurting more. Finally, I just pulled it hard and out came the tooth with the muffin." Smiling at Clara, who had come back to the table during this story, Jewel looked up at her and said, "I bet no one has ever lost a tooth on one of your puffs, Ms. Clara."

With a softness I had never seen, Ms. Clara replied, "Well, Jewel, I don't rightly believe anyone ever has. Would you like some dessert now that you have polished off your dinner?"

"Sure, I like pie and cake," came Jewel's response, "but my favorite is chocolate ice cream."

Ms. Clara picked up our dirty dishes and offered, "I think we have some chocolate ice cream in the freezer." Then turning to me, "How about you, Mike?"

"Just coffee, Ms. Clara. I have added five pounds in five weeks eating your food."

"You hide it well, Mike," Clara said as she walked off. Five friendly comments in a row was a first for Clara. I lifted my fresh hot cup of coffee and took a sip. *Five pounds for five friendly comments; that is one pound per comment. I see some serious clothes shopping in my future.*

Clara placed the bowl of ice cream in front of Jewel and took a seat across from her as she asked, "So you grew up in New Orleans—a Louisiana girl. What did you do for a job?"

Jewel waited until her mouth was empty before answering, "I worked in a laundry. It was my job to move heavy tubs of wet linens from the washers to the dryers, and then I folded them and stacked them by size, so the hotels didn't have to unfold them to see if they were standard, queen, or king size. I liked my job, and I did it for twelve years, but my boss never made up for the months we were out of work after Hurricane Katrina. Besides, he was old and tired out. He just wanted to sell his building now that new people are moving into town and are willing to pay lots of money for a building in the French Quarter. The trouble is they don't want to do laundry anymore, so I lost my job."

Clara smiled and asked, "Are you looking for a new job?"

"Yes," responded Jewel rather quickly. "Do you know a laundry around here that needs a folder?"

Clara sat back in her seat, being careful how she approached Jewel with her response. "No, but I might need someone to help me here in my café."

Jewel stopped eating and placed her spoon on the table. "But I don't know how to cook anything. I work in a laundry."

"I am not looking for a cook, Jewel. I need someone who can pick up the dirty dishes and stack them in the kitchen for me. If you could lift those heavy loads of wet linens, a stack of dirty dishes would be no problem for you. And if you could separate the sheets and fold them by size for the hotels, you could separate my dishes and stack them before they go into the washer, and then take them out of the dryer tray and stack them in my kitchen, so I can plate all my delicious food for my customers." Leaning forward, Clara smiled at Jewel and added, "It is sort of the same kind of work you have been doing for twelve years, Jewel."

"But what if I drop some and they break? I wouldn't do it on purpose, but sometimes my fingers don't do what I want them to do."

"That's funny, Jewel, neither do mine. Just tonight I dropped a plate. It happens sometimes." Clara leaned back again and let Jewel think for a moment.

"Would I have to take orders?" Jewel asked, but quickly added, "I mean from customers—not from you. I liked taking orders from my boss. He was nice, but I never worked out front because I would get things all messed up. I'm not good at that."

"See that girl over there, Jewel? Her name is Cindi Sue, and she is good at greeting my customers and taking their dinner orders—just like she took your order tonight. She and I take turns doing that, but I need someone who would be good at cleaning off dirty dishes, wiping down the tables, washing the dishes and stacking the clean ones in my kitchen. I don't even want you to talk to my customers. Do you think you could do that?"

"I think I could do that, but I would have to ask Char if she thinks I can." Jewel picked up her spoon and returned to eating her ice cream. Clara and I looked at each other and smiled. Jewel was finished with this conversation. She knew better than to decide before talking with Char—a habit that had probably been in place since Char was a young girl. Jewel trusted Char implicitly. As far as Jewel was concerned, Char would make the decision, and that was that.

Clara excused herself, and Jewel kept eating her ice cream, while I reviewed all the questions Jewel was not considering, but questions I knew that Char would ask:

- ▶ How would Jewel get to work?
- ▶ If Char could drop her off, who would pick her up?
- ▶ Is there a bus line Jewel could learn to take?
- ▶ I can help out, but I too have a job to do. Many times, both Char and I have to be out of town at the same time. What happens to Jewel then?
- ▶ How will we protect Jewel with a killer driving around town in a Jeep we cannot even find?

As I paid the bill I suggested, "Clara, do you think Jewel would work out for you?"

"Oh, sure, she is a sweet little thing. I can see she is not the brightest bulb on the Christmas tree, but I am not looking for brains. I need dependable, steady, hardworking, and quiet. Jewel would be perfect. Do you think her sister will say yes?"

I smiled as she handed me my change, "After Char and I work out a few bugs, I believe it is doable, but I just don't know quite how yet. Can you be patient for a day or two?"

"Sure can," Clara confirmed. "Will I see you tomorrow?"

"Not for breakfast. I have an early morning meeting, but I will be here for dinner. Count on it."

With the meeting concluded, Jewel and I left the job interview without Jewel's even realizing she'd had one. Twenty minutes later we were entering Char's apartment, and I figured Jewel would tell Char all about the job offer, but no, all she wanted to talk about was the food and how nice Ms. Clara was. I watched how patient Char was with Jewel, listening without prodding her to get to the important items. I was watching years of experience being played out between these polar-opposite sisters. Jewel meanders through her thoughts as they come to her, whereas Char always seems to effortlessly arrange her thoughts in order and wastes no time with unimportant details; but when dealing with her sister, Char shows no sign of impatience—only love and support.

Char took a seat on the sofa and asked, "So you like Ms. Clara, Jewel?"

Joining her on the sofa, Jewel sparkled as she said, "Oh, yes, she is a nice lady, and boy, can she cook good stuff, Char." I thought she was going to stop there, so I took the seat across from the sofa, wondering how long this next rabbit trail was going to take, when Jewel said, "Oh, Char, Ms. Clara wants me to wash her dishes. Do you think that would be okay? You don't have to worry about me breaking dishes and getting hit for it like Momma does. Ms. Clara said she broke a plate herself just tonight, and she wasn't even mad. She said I wouldn't have to talk to people. You know how much I hate talking to people when I work. They talk fast, and I get all confused and then I stop because I get lost. Then they get mad like Momma does, and I just start crying. Ms. Clara said she doesn't even want me to talk to her customers! Isn't that a good thing, Char?"

Char put her arm around her sister and drew her close. "That sounds like a perfect job for you, Jewel. Do you think you would like to work at Ms. Clara's Café?"

Jewel started laughing and said, "Char, that's what it's called, Ms. Clara's Café. I will—if she promises not to yell at me when I get messed up, and if she promises not to hit me." Pulling away from her sister, Jewel looked straight in her sister's eyes and said, "I don't like getting hit, Char, especially across the face like Momma does. Do you think you could talk to Ms. Clara and make her promise never to hit me on the face?"

"I can do that, Jewel. Now that you live here with me, no one will ever hit you again. Why don't you go take a shower while I walk Mike out to his car. When I get back, I will make up your bed for you."

"Jewel got up and started toward the bedroom, but stopped and turned back, "Oh, Char, Mike does not have a car. He has an S.U.V., don't you, Mike? It is as big as a truck, but it is not a truck. Isn't that right, Mike?"

I stood up to leave and said, "You are exactly right, Jewel, and you spelled it just right."

"Good night, Mike. Thank you for dinner."

Char and I were quiet as we walked down the walkway to the parking lot. I wanted to quickly go through the list of hurdles that I knew needed fixing before Char could say yes to this job, but one look at Char, and I knew the hurdles needed to wait. I took charge by saying, "Char, it's been a long day for me. Do you think we could table everything until tomorrow?"

Relief washed over Char's face as the day's tension lifted just a little. "Bright and early. Remember, we have a working breakfast meeting. I ordered breakfast be delivered right at 8:00 sharp, so I will get there at 7:15, have the war room unlocked, and everything ready for our meeting. No reason for you to be there much before 7:45 a.m." As I closed the door behind me, I lowered my window just as Char added, "And Mike, thank you for tonight."

"My pleasure, Char."

Leaning in close, Char put her hand on my shoulder and said, "No,

Mike, I really mean it. Thank you for what you did for both Jewel and me tonight. You have no idea how huge it is."

I smiled as I put my Yukon in reverse and backed out of my parking spot. I had an idea. Listening to the sisters talking, I realized these almost seven weeks of Char's living here while Jewel was home with their momma must have been a huge burden for Char. I know having a challenged child is difficult, but taking out your frustration on such a defenseless innocent and striking her across the face is unforgiveable. As I drove back to my place, all I could think about was all the hard work we had accomplished while all that time Char knew what Jewel was most likely going through back in New Orleans. As I pulled into my parking space, it occurred to me that my place would be a much better fit for Char and Jewel. Although only a one bedroom, I have an alcove where I put my computer that could easily be turned into a small second bedroom for Jewel. The greatest benefit of where I live is Ms. Clara's Café is only one block away—within walking distance for Jewel. Would Char be willing to swap apartments?

As I put my key in the door, I could hear Tilly saying her favorite quote: "Don't be afraid to ask God for a miracle, Mike, but when it comes, be sure to give Him the credit."

I smiled and said, "I know, Tilly, and never tell God what that miracle should be because His are always better than the ones we come up with." I stood at the window of my bedroom, looking up into the brilliant night sky and prayed, "Lord, I know You love these girls more than I ever could, but I also know You sent me here because You have some amazing plan for them, and You are allowing me to be just a part of it. Guide my feet and stop me from taking over with my big ideas. God, make Your plan so evident that none of us can miss it. These two sweet girls need to know just how much You love them."

20

Tipping Our Hand

WAS up and showered extra-early. I was not going to Clara's for breakfast because we had a working breakfast scheduled. Driving down Lauder Lane, my mind kept going over different ways I could approach Char with the idea of trading apartments. I had worked out almost every hurdle and had gone over exactly how I would present them to Char when a car backed out of a driveway, and I had to slam on my brakes to avoid hitting the car.

As I was about to blast my horn in frustration, I caught a glimpse of the man behind the wheel. My hand stopped in mid-flight to my horn. An embarrassed Dr. Harvey sheepishly waved a "sorry about that," as he pulled up to the curb and lowered his window. I pulled up next to him and lowered my passenger's side window. "Good morning, Dr. Harvey. I didn't know you lived on this side of town. I never take Lauder Lane, but today the city is working on sewer pipes on Mission Boulevard, so I decided to take Lauder."

"I know, Mike, I have been hearing the heavy equipment racket since six this morning. The city officials are saying we will have to put up with this noise and dust for about two weeks."

"Well, nice *almost* running into you this morning, Dr. Harvey, but I have a business breakfast I must attend." As I put my Yukon back in gear, I thought about how lonely Dr. Harvey has been since losing his wife. I knew I should offer to take him out to dinner, but my schedule with these three murders was absolutely killing me. Add the conundrum with Char and Jewel, and I just cannot spare the time right now. Just as this excuse crossed my mind, one of Tilly's admonitions came to mind: "Mike, always take time to pay attention to the lonely, the lost, and the hurting because doing so is the purest form of love. Mike, when you give your time this way, God somehow stretches your time and rewards your efforts because God will never allow us to out-give Him." I smiled to myself, looked across at my new friend and offered, "Hey, Doc, how about you and I getting dinner together one night this week, my treat?"

"I'd like that, Mike," he replied as a warm smile washed over his face. "I'm getting really tired of fast-food and TV dinners."

I checked my watch and said, "I'll call you later today, and we can set the time and place then. If I don't leave now, I will be late for my meeting." With that promise, I waved a quick goodbye and headed down the street. Within a block I was back to my planning the perfect solution to all of Char's hurdles when I remembered my prayer from the night before. "But God, what if these ideas are coming from YOU?" That thought lasted about a second before I felt my face start to flush with embarrassment. "I know, I know. I always think my plans are perfect, don't I?"

As I parked and started into the building, I humbly prayed, "God, I know my plans are usually quite good, but I am asking for a miracle—not just good. Show Char just how much You love her by showing her a perfect plan—not just a good plan."

The smell of fresh hot coffee greeted me as I entered our war room.

Char poured me a cup and handed it to me just as the delivery boy arrived with our breakfast. We quickly plated our bagels and cream cheese, cut melon, strawberries, and yogurt cups before starting our working breakfast conversation. As usual, I wanted to talk about Jewel and what was going to happen next, but Char was now all business, and so we went with her agenda, not mine. "So, Mike, any results from the tire search?"

I sighed in exasperation. "That was a complete waste of time—not one good lead in any of them. At the very least we can feel somewhat confident that this dark-blue Jeep is parked somewhere with those mismatched tires still on it. I'm not sure why this person hasn't changed those tires. That person is the only one who would have bothered to destroy the tire impressions and leave the tires unchanged, and that, Char, does not make sense."

Char starting chuckling and again quoted her professor. "When your leads seem to conflict with reason, take heart. Criminals don't always do the smart thing, so follow the unreasonable links because they will tell you more about the criminal than one hundred smart moves. If criminals always did the smart thing, we would seldom catch them."

It was now Char's turn to share. "As you know, while you were tracking down tire sales, I had demanded and received copies of all the legal documents pertaining to the Wilcomb family. I was not going to take Sinclair's word for anything. I spent almost twenty hours poring over wills, corporate charters, ownership records, and dozens of addendums, each one more convoluted then the last. Mike, Sinclair truly is a web spinner. He has used his position to make sure his son is set for life. The courts do not care about bloodlines; they care about legal status. Calvin was born and given the Wilcomb name, which makes him a Wilcomb. He has been named in the will, making him heir to the Wilcomb fortune. Only Maximillion would care about the bloodline, but now, in his condition, if proven true, I suspect he might be too far gone to follow the DNA, and he might be too far gone for any court to allow him to make any significant changes now."

I nodded in agreement and asked, "Do we have that Wilcomb meeting date yet? You gave Sinclair until the day after tomorrow to set it up. Has he given you a date and time?"

"Not yet. I suspect he will make it at the eleventh hour, so to speak. I'm sure he does not trust us not to spill the beans. I did demand copies of all the medical records from the doctor in Memphis and a legally notarized authorization to speak with the doctor himself. I don't trust anyone to tell the truth. Too many people have too much to hide, and they have too much money not to assume they have not bought off other people's silence."

Switching subjects yet again, I asked, "Have you heard back from Investigator Lennord about the cruiser? His lab has had it for three days now."

Char smiled as she picked up her phone and said, "Just a short text saying, 'ALL SAMPLES HAVE BEEN SUBMITTED FOR TESTING. DON'T EXPECT ANY RESULTS FOR SEVERAL WEEKS. THIS IS NOT *CSI*. LOL.'"

Shrugging in frustration, I answered, "At least Dwight is keeping his sense of humor in all of this." I waited another moment before suggesting, "Char, since the tire stores provided no leads, I think we need to consider putting out a widespread BOLO, asking that every dark-blue Jeep between 1980 and forward be pulled over and inspected. If the vehicle has old, weather-beaten stickers, ignore it because old and weather-beaten cannot be manufactured. Ignore the Jeep if it has old matching tires; original, light-colored upholstery because we know it has dark upholstery, mismatched tires, and no stickers. They should get the registration, the driver's license, and run the plates. If anything does not match up, haul in the driver for questioning."

Char spun around and studied my face. "That will be tipping our hand, Mike."

I just sat quietly while Char grappled with my suggestion. I did not want to argue the wisdom of such a move. I needed Char to come to the same conclusion I had. Given a moment to weigh the alternative, I knew she would.

Char finally stood and nodded as she picked up the office phone. Issuing a BOLO required using a landline that showed up on the police system as confirmation of being legit. Char warned the officer taking the call, "This will be a very detailed BOLO, Officer, and it must go out exactly as I say. We do not need every Jeep owner in the parish to be hauled in for questioning." Then, without missing a beat, Char repeated every single point I had made. "Now, read that back to me, Officer." Char affirmed each one as repeated and ended with, "Okay, for the record, here is my name, title, and I.D. badge number. Run it!"

Turning back to me, Char smiled and said, "Well, the fat is in the fire now."

I stood and locked the deadbolt. "And you and I have to increase our safety protocol. The unsub has known about the tire impressions for almost three months, and he has not changed those tires. Why?"

"Right," Char agreed. "He must already know we are looking for a vehicle with mismatched tires but doesn't know that we are now looking for a dark-blue Jeep until now. I think we need to contact every autobody shop in the area and ask them to notify us if anyone brings in a Jeep for painting."

Char returned to her seat and moaned, "Mike, have you noticed just how many Jeeps are on the streets of Houma? I don't know if it is just because I am now sensitive to Jeeps, but it feels like every other car is a Jeep."

"It sure feels that way," I assured her. "It is like when you decide you want to buy a certain new car, and that is all you see. Let's hope this BOLO works the same way for the police."

Char circled a date on her calendar. "I'm going to give this BOLO one week to work. After that, since we have already tipped our hand, I will go on local TV and ask the public to watch for the Jeep. Anyone knowing of a Jeep matching our description sitting in a neighbor's garage, or backyard, should call in a tip. I want this guy to feel the squeeze and know we are onto him."

"So, Char, what do we do for the next seven days? We have run every lead to ground."

Char gave me a determined look—a look I knew well every time I looked in the mirror while on a frustrating case. "Mike, we keep the pressure on. I will call Sinclair and demand to see Mr. Maximillion Wilcomb today. We are no longer going to use kid gloves. Since we don't know who to trust here, Dwight Lennord offered to come and help us with interviews, but only if I thought we needed it. So far, you and I have been able to keep this investigation going, but as soon as potential leads start coming in you and I could easily get overwhelmed with details that must be followed, so I asked him to stand at the ready." Char dialed Sinclair's number and gave him three hours to get his clients ready for their interviews. She did not ask; she instructed and hung up. Turning to me, she inhaled and said, "Now we wait."

21

The Fortress of Privilege

A T THREE o'clock sharp Char and I pulled into the huge cobble-stone entry that was well defined as "Private Property." We had turned off LA 311, otherwise known as Little Bayou Black Drive, and continued on a dirt road for about two full miles before reaching the entrance framed by ornate wrought iron, with the name, Wilcomb, beautifully scripted in the same wrought iron. As we pulled up to these two huge gates that tell everyone, *"You are not welcome here,"* we saw that most visitors have to press a button and tell a guard what business they had there. Today the gates were already open, so we simply drove in.

This cobblestone drive lined with aged oak trees with many years of Spanish moss draping almost to the ground gave the visitor a perfect impression of privilege. The main house was positioned about ten feet higher than everything around it on a pronounced, obviously man-made knoll since everything in Terrebonne Parish was naturally flat marsh land. This location also added to the visual impression of privilege, since the grandeur and massive size of the house could not help but set a tone that few could ignore.

As I drove my Yukon along the circular drive in front of the massive steps leading to the Wilcomb's front door, Char chuckled. "Mike, this setting reminds me of a famous lawyer who came to speak to our third-year class. He was funny, entertaining, and quite full of himself. One line he repeated three times that has remained with me ever since is, "Buy yourself the biggest, most obnoxiously intimidating desk you can find to set the tone for everyone who ever comes to your office. Without saying a word, that desk will tell everyone that you are 'The Big Kahuna.' Just your sitting behind it while they sit in slightly lower-than-normal chairs puts the clients in their place, and they will feel too intimidated to argue with you." Looking at me as I turned off the engine, Char chuckled again. "So, Mike, I guess this is the biggest, baddest, Kahuna house I have ever seen, but we will refuse to sit in a low chair, right?"

"Right you are, Ms. Char, but you cannot argue with the results. It is intimidating." I pulled my key out of the ignition and stared at everything around us. "Char, those affects go both ways. Joseph and Maximillion built a fortress of privilege to put others in their place, but Char, can you imagine what growing up on the inside of all of this and being reared as one of the privileged ones did to young Calvin? In a quick or surface look, people tend only to see the benefits, the opulence, and the advantages, but imagine how much this privilege warps the child's impression of himself. The old man, Joseph Wilcomb, was hungry for position and status. He thought these intangibles could be purchased, but all I see as I look around is a fortress of isolation, secrets, and a desperate need for outrageous protection. After all, the very things they accumulated to prove their status are now the very things that hold them prisoners."

Before Char opened her door, she whispered, "And can you even begin to imagine what all of that intrenched thinking will do to Calvin if Sinclair's secret comes out? Calvin, the golden boy of privilege, simply because he has Wilcomb blood is neither! He may still inherit all of this but imagine being reared to believe you are a "chosen one, a rightful heir, privileged by birth," and have all of that swept away. Imagine learning that you are just like everyone else, except you have money in the bank. I do not think the money will ever compensate for the cataclysmic fall from grace Calvin will feel."

I smiled at Char as I opened my car door. "Isn't it interesting that you and I, having looked behind the mask of the "fortress of privilege," are getting ready to walk in and interview these people with a tinge of pity in our hearts—scarcely what they will be expecting."

Seeing Char's questioning look, I explained. "Char, as with you, I grew up with nothing, but I worked hard and made a place for myself in this world. The two things I most value in life these Wilcomb men have no idea of their value and will probably never understand their importance. The Wilcomb men have treated their wives as discardable possessions, and Stephen Sinclair traded the love of his life for position and power. I had the love a good woman who supported me, challenged me, was my equal in every way. She made me a better man for having shared her life with me."

Char pulled her car door closed again and asked, "Mike, you said two things, one is your Tilly, and I fully agree, but what is the second? Is it your boys?"

I closed my car door and turned to look directly at Char. I have only worked with this talented young woman for six short weeks, and I have been both respectful of her position as my boss, and I have also respected her right to not be preached at by me. Preaching never worked on me, so I assume it will not work on her; but there are moments when the pure beauty and honesty of faith should be shared, and this is one of those moments. "No, Char. I combine my two boys with their mother because I could not have had them without her. The second thing I was referring to is my relationship with God." Seeing the discomfort come across her face by my daring to talk about religion, I quickly explained. "You see, Char, the Wilcomb family is not so exceedingly different than anyone else; they have only lived life on a much grander scale, that is all. When people try to validate their self-worth by their accomplishments—be it their education, their profession, their possessions, or their social ranking—it can all evaporate like a puff of smoke. I am not saying any of those accomplishments are a waste of time or that we were foolish to go out and prepare for our profession. However, depending upon these achievements as the measurement of who you are is hollow because everything can be swept away in the twinkling of an eye. I can lose it all, and although it would be difficult, I will still be who I am—a man who loves God because He first loved me.

"I know that His love for me is not in any way dependent upon what I have achieved because the Bible says, *'That while I was yet a sinner, Christ died for me.'* He loved me long before I returned His love. I read somewhere this very comforting saying:

God loves you, period. He cannot love you any more than He does right now, and He cannot love you any less than He does right now.

"Char, that means His love is not dependent upon me but on Him. I did not earn His love; it was a gift He gave to me. I cannot ever lose His love because it never depended upon who I was but on who He is. In that respect, the Wilcomb men have nothing I would ever want more than what I already have; therefore, I can walk into this 'fortress of privilege' without any jealousy of what they have and without caving into their pretense that I am somehow less than they are."

Just as I said this, Stephen Sinclair opened the front door to greet us. I quickly opened my car door and said, "Char, if you are ever interested in hearing about why I believe this, I'm always here for you. Right now, let's go in there and get these interviews done."

"Thank you for telling me that, Mike. I am not at all sure I am ready to talk religion with anyone right now, but if I ever am, I'd ask you. I appreciate that you respect me enough to let me decide if and when I am ready, but I like knowing you believe what you just said."

I winked at Char, knowing I had said enough. *Now down to business.* As Char and I walked into the Wilcomb foyer, I had the distinct impression of a staged and professionally manicured mausoleum as opposed to the entry to someone's home. Completely devoid of anything personal, no would have any indication of this family's personality—except to say that from all appearances this is not a home—but rather a corporate office. Although this foyer lacks personality, it speaks volumes for this 'fortress of privilege' is not a home but a corporate financial resume on display.

My mind flies back to walking into our home after a long hard day at work and immediately seeing something my Tilly had recently displayed, showing anyone entering our home that ours was a home where our children are loved, appreciated, and encouraged. I used to tell my Tilly, "These speak more about you as a mother than it does about our boys. Every time our Joseph and Benjamin walk into their home, they are reminded how very much they are loved."

I look around this room and see or feel no love at all. As we are escorted into the expansive living room, eighty-three-year-old Maximillion Wilcomb is sitting in a chair that reminds me of a throne. I must admit that although the 'throne' does lose some of its grandeur with Max sitting there in a light-gray velour jumpsuit, house slippers, and a walker barely an arm's reach away. On closer inspection, Max is well-groomed, clean, and recently shaven; his hair is washed and styled although he needs a haircut. He notices us walk in, but beyond that brief attention, there seems to be no reaction. His eyes quickly glaze over, and he began fussing with a lap rug that seemed to be irritating him at the moment.

A highly attractive and well-dressed woman of seventy-three quickly steps over and removes the lap rug to distract the elderly man's attention from the rug—to no avail. Maximillion grabbed it back, demanding she put it back. Slapping his gnarly knees with equally gnarled hands, I could not help but flinch at how hard the old man hit his knees, knowing he had to be hurting himself. Char and I were watching Maximillion Wilcomb throw a tantrum, and he would not be quieted. I thought, *this is not an act. No one stricken with arthritis as badly as this elderly man would ever intentionally hit those knees with those hands just for show.*

Looking at the woman, I suspected she was Charisse, his second trophy wife, rather than a caregiver. Her clothing, jewelry, and make-up reeked of a woman who has been well-pampered all her life. Her uncomfortable demeanor as she attempted to calm Max indicated she had not often stepped into this caregiving role. I looked around for the caregiver who surely must be only steps away, but for some reason known only to them, this family is trying to give the impression that they alone are caring for this old man. Why, I had no clue. At this point in Max's condition, why try to give off this obviously uncomfortable false impression—other than pretending has probably been their lifelong habit.

Char took a seat next to Papa Max, having read all of the Memphis doctor's reports as well as reading literature on conducting interviews with dementia patients. While Char asked Max questions, I stood back and observed the actions of the others. Calvin was obviously concerned for his grandfather, whereas Mitchell paid little attention to anyone in the room. Mitchell was wearing clothes that appeared to have seen many-a-day's wear. Having read the medical reports, Mitchell's *quirks*, as the family still refers to them, include an aversion to tight-fitting clothes or having his hair washed or cut. The report indicated that Mitchell feels acute pain when his hair is cut; however, he finds facial hair so unnerving, he has been known to shave three or four times a day if not distracted.

As I observed Papa Max's son, Mitchell pulled his shoulder-length hair back into a ponytail with a ribbon because using a rubber band would send him into a rage. The report also indicated that Mitchell refuses to use soap or shampoo, believing they are poison he cannot wash away. This lack of care was also quite evident, and the months of this behavior was not something one could fake for an interview.

Once convinced that Max and Mitchell were beyond suspicion, we turned to the women of the family. Char had already dismissed Mitchell's mother, Sarah, Maximillion's first wife. She had moved to Europe, and according to reports, never reentered the United States and had died in 1971. So, we have Charisse, Max's trophy wife, now seventy-three, and Mitchell's wife, Catherine, who is fifty-two and Calvin's mother—not to mention Sinclair's lover. Calvin's wife, Jacqueline, a no-show thus far.

Char turned to Calvin and queried, "Where is your wife, Calvin? The order was that every member of the household was to be here."

"Oh, she is here," Calvin mocked, "Jacqueline Westbourough Wilcomb just intends to make her presence known in her own way and on her own schedule. My wife considers herself the embodiment of Scarlett O'Hara. You think my family takes their breeding seriously; we have nothing on the Westbourough clan. Jacqueline's debutante ball would put the Confederate charity ball on *Gone with the Wind* to shame. She has pictures of herself in antebellum attire that would start another war. She struts around believing she actually deserves to be pampered like Scarlett. When she has decided to enter, just watch and see how she struts into this room, and you will be reminded of how Loretta Young used to enter a room. No one tells my wife what to do. Ms. Smalls, you will find my wife to be the most selfish, self-centered, and most inconsiderate individual you will ever meet. She is twenty-eight years old and is so self-involved she refuses to have a child for fear of losing her perfect figure." Then, with a sarcasm that ran very deep, Calvin added, "Papa Max would never have pushed her on me if he had known she would refuse to continue the bloodline; but for now, I am stuck."

Within an hour Char and I had interviewed all three of these pathetic women and had determined that none of them were realistic suspects. Their level of pampering would indicate not one of them would do the deed themselves—for fear of breaking a nail or ruffling their clothes. They might have hired someone, but we wrote off that lead, considering they would have to sell some of their jewelry or other belongings to come up with that much money. Their every penny was doled out by credit cards and not cash. Beyond all of that, these women are exactly the kind of women the Wilcomb men would choose—pampered, selfish, and shallow. *This unsub is smarter than all of them combined.*

Driving away from the Wilcomb residence, Char groaned, "That was a complete waste of time."

"No, Char, we now know of seven people who are not the unsub. What has been a complete waste of time is all the time it took us to write them off as killers. This family with all of their lies, their ambitions, and their sense of privilege cost at least two women their lives, and two little girls lost their mother. None of these people care one little bit. Now, *that* is the real waste."

Char nodded in agreement before adding, "But I still believe the Wilcomb family is the key to solving these murders. Someone hates this family and is trying to expose them for who they are, and that person is willing to kill young women to do it; we must keep digging."

22

God Delivers a Perfect Plan

s I drove back to town, my heart wanted a diversion from thinking about anything Wilcomb related. I wanted to drive out the disgusting taste in my mouth and thought a good way to do so would be to bring up my idea of switching apartments and listing all of the hurdles this plan would solve. I was about to say something when that quiet little voice in my head warned, *Are you doing this for Char and Jewel, or do you want to bring this up simply because you want something else to think about? Study your motives, Mike, before you go jumping into someone else's life and offering suggestions.* Then I remembered the prayer I had said, "God, keep me from pushing my ideas and getting in the way of Your plans," and I decided to remain quiet because I knew my personal need had motivated my desire to bring up that subject—not Char's need for a better plan.

Once I was able to set aside my own agenda, my heart could see what my mind was too busy to see. I looked at Char and really studied her face and, I believe God rewarded my humility by helping me understand this strong, yet fragile woman who was so like me in so many ways. Char was busy filtering through every little detail about the Wilcombs, committing them to memory. I remembered how Char had said she has always organized her little world while the world around her was in chaos, how she carefully set about deciding a proper place for everything, and once it had its place, it always went there. I realized I was watching Char's method of keeping her chaos in order. Not only does she do it with the physical things in her world, but she also does it with every detail that might need to be recalled at a later date. Char was assigning every minute detail its own place in her mind, assigning them an address, if you will, so they will be there whenever she needs to recall them.

In this area Char and I are *not* alike. I am not quite sure what my method is, but I do know mine is not as organized as Char's. If we are going to be a successful team, I must remember to give Char the quiet time she needs to store away her thoughts. If I had not stopped myself, or more to the point, if God had not stopped me, I would have flooded Char with her "other life" details without any thought of what that would have done to her process.

It was quarter to six when I dropped off Char at her apartment and left to meet Dr. Harvey at his favorite restaurant, The Rusty Pelican. I was a little miffed that Char and I had no time to talk that entire day. Ms. Clara would not be patient for long, and the hurdles had to be addressed, but as I opened the door to The Rusty Pelican, I took a deep breath and said, "I know, Tilly. I'm to give this evening to Dr. Harvey, a lonely widower, and leave the miracle planning to God." I put a smile on my face and joined Dr. Harvey at his favorite booth.

"I'm glad you could make it, Mike. I know you and ADA Smalls have undue pressure on you to solve these murders, but a person must eat, right?" I noticed an almost pleading tone in Dr. Harvey's voice.

"Mike, might I recommend their Louisiana grilled bass? It comes with the most wonderfully tangy lemon butter sauce."

I smiled and thought of Ms. Clara's butter sauce and felt somewhat homesick as I said, "I love a well-prepared grilled bass, Dr. Harvey. Having never eaten here, I appreciate the recommendation."

Dr. Harvey smiled, but I noticed he had a different look in his eyes—a distant stare that told me Dr. Harvey had stepped away for a moment, so I waited. In a moment he was back and rather embarrassed.

"Oh, Mike, I am sorry, I've developed this terrible habit of going inside myself and having these strange conversations—the result of too many meals sitting all alone, I believe." But as he perked up, he apologized again and said, "But tonight I am not alone, am I? I was just thinking how very odd my life has turned out. You see, before my wife died, I would have never ever recommended a dinner choice to anyone. The thought would never have occurred to me because my wife was the culinary expert in our family. In that area, I gladly deferred to her recommendations, and she was always spot-on." With another bittersweet smile, he added, "Learning a new normal after fifty-one years has been hard."

Knowing exactly how he felt, I chimed in, "I found it almost paralyzing, Dr. Harvey. I stopped going to "our" restaurants because I felt Tilly's absence too keenly there. I found myself sitting there all alone, remembering conversations we'd had. Although I loved the memories, they were not always good for learning a 'new normal,' is it, Dr. Harvey?"

"Mike, I know it is not healthy to constantly live in the past, but the past with my wife is the only place I feel whole again. I'm afraid I give into it more often than is healthy for me. Having my work helps, but my daughter is married and moving on with her life. She is a pediatrician in California with a crazy schedule due to a full practice, a husband who is a lawyer, and two middle-schoolers. She calls me every Thursday evening at exactly eight o'clock.

"I am grateful that she calls and checks up on me, but I also feel like she is checking off her "to-do" list each week so she can go on with living her life. Please don't misunderstand me; I am so grateful for her contacting me. I just miss the spontaneity of life that is moving forward. Becoming a 'scheduled soul' has such a feeling of final days to me."

"Dr. Harvey, you stated your thoughts so well. You have described exactly how I felt after my wife died. My boys did the same. Factually, I knew they 'set their check-in date and time,' out of love because they didn't want to get busy and forget to call me. But like you said, it became 'our routine,' and I too started to feel 'checked-off.' I knew the way I was feeling wasn't their fault or their responsibility to fix. I had to make a change in my life so I could start living again. For that reason, I accepted this job and moved here."

"But I can't do that, Mike. I am ten years your senior. A seventy-two-year-old medical examiner can't simply start over, but I hear what you are saying. I have to make some changes in my life if I want to keep living in the present." Then Dr. Harvey started to chuckle, and said, "Is it wicked of me to want to be so busy living that my daughter has to leave a message?"

"No, it isn't, Dr. Harvey, and I suspect your daughter loves you so much, she will be pleased to leave that message."

For two hours we talked of our wives, the things we missed most, and explored how a person goes about building a 'new normal'—without running out and marrying the first woman who would look at us twice. So many of our friends had already made that huge mistake and found themselves embroiled in her family baggage. Being married to a lesser woman than our wives would feel unbearable at any age, but at our age, that mistake would bury us; or at least we would wish it would bury us. We both laughed at that comment.

Toward the end of the evening, I started telling Dr. Harvey how I have been keeping busy helping Char care for her sister, Jewel. I shared my concerns, as well as my victories, my plans, and my concerns of overstepping my boundaries. I'm not quite sure why I felt okay saying all of this to him, but I did, and we both had an enjoyable evening together.

As I said my goodbye to Dr. Harvey, I walked to my Yukon, feeling strangely satisfied. This dinner was my first in over six-weeks when I was not working an angle, plotting how to accomplish my next lead, or schmoozing Ms. Clara for more leads. Sure, I was there because Dr. Harvey was lonely, and I understood his loneliness all too well. I found I actually rather enjoyed being able to talk with another man who understood what I was feeling. I went to bed feeling thankful.

The next morning, I stopped by the police department on my way into work. Every morning we had a new list of Jeeps that had been pulled over, and a list of names of those that matched our description. That morning we only had three leads, and none of the names rang a bell. Just as I was walking up the hallway to meet with Char, a smiling Dr. Harvey left our war room. Before I could begin to theorize why he was there, Dr. Harvey grabbed my hand and started shaking it vigorously. "Mike, I hope I have not stolen all of your thunder, but I couldn't sleep at all last night, thinking about what you said about finding something to live for again."

Having no idea why he was apologizing, I replied, "I'm sorry you lost a night's sleep over it, Dr. Harvey, but from the look on your face, you must have settled something. In the seven weeks that I have known you, I have not seen you look so alive."

"Well, Mike, just you remember that when ADA Smalls makes up her mind, just know that you were the one who gave me the idea." Dr. Harvey turned and continued walking down the hallway of City Hall with a rather light kick to his steps.

I walked into our war room completely puzzled as to what Dr. Harvey had thanked me for, and Char's greeting only continued the puzzle. "Good morning, Mike. I believe you are the one responsible for giving Dr. Harvey that amazingly perfect idea."

I stood, looking thunderstruck. *Twice now, I am being credited for something I have no inkling of doing.* "Well, Char, would you mind telling me what it is that I am accused of having done?"

"You're kidding, right?" Char turned and looked at me rather perplexed. "Mike, Dr. Harvey said that you and he had dinner together last evening." I nodded my head in agreement before she continued. "He said he told you all about how lonely he is rattling around in that big house of his, but that the financial downturn of 2007 makes it not a wise time to downsize."

"Yes, I remember we talked about that. I rented my house in Miami rather than selling it for that very reason. I am hoping the market might turn around."

Char came around the conference table with a huge smile on her face. "Mike, Dr. Harvey is not ready to pack up all of his wife's things just yet and say goodbye to all their memories, so he just offered to let Jewel and me move in with him. He said he had already moved into the guest quarters in the basement they had built for his mother-in-law. He said he just couldn't stay upstairs in their master bedroom. He offered Jewels and me the whole upstairs, as long as a few nights a week he is invited upstairs to have dinner with us.

"Mike, do you see how very perfect this is for me? First, Jewels will be within walking distance to Ms. Clara's Café, we will each have our own bedroom and bathroom, I do not have to spend money I do not have to furnish a bigger place, and Dr. Harvey will always be home before Jewel and is willing to drive over and pick her up so she does not have to walk home in the dark. And Dr. Harvey won't feel all alone in that big house, so everybody wins! This is all because of you, Mike."

I continued standing and looking at my boss thunderstruck yet again. I was thankful for being given some of the credit, but I knew the One who had really orchestrated this plan. I thought of a saying I'd once heard: "It is amazing just how much God can accomplish in your life—when you don't care who gets the credit." I corrected Char, saying, "Char, I just need you to know that I have been praying about your situation, and I had come up with a few ideas about how to make you and Jewel feel more safe and more comfortable that would allow Jewel to work for Ms. Clara. But Char, my idea was nothing compared to this solution that I believe did not come from either me or Dr. Harvey. I believe God worked out this arrangement for you. I have been asking Him to provide you with a perfect plan—one that would show you exactly how much He cares about you and Jewel. I believe He came through for you big time."

Char didn't reply for a moment. "Okay, Mike, I'm not quite sure what to say here. Maybe you don't feel comfortable accepting credit. Maybe your God does listen to you, and He does do things for you in a big way. Either way, I am grateful, and I do want to say even though I don't pray, it feels good to know that you, my friend, are praying for me and for my sister, Jewel. You have no idea how knowing that makes me feel. Thank you, Mike."

Then quickly switching subjects, Char added, "Since I am on a month-to-month basis, and the apartment came furnished, all Jewel and I have to do is pack up our personals and move right in with Dr. Harvey. He said he only needed a day or two to clean out his wife's clothes, and we can move in over the weekend. Now, about Jewels, would Ms. Clara like Jewel to start this next Monday?"

I nodded my head and affirmed, "I think Ms. Clara would love that, Char."

"Okay then, let's get down to business. We need to start digging up anyone and everyone who holds a grudge against the Wilcomb family. I feel certain this will be the key to everything."

23

Char Connects the Dots

O N TUESDAY, Char and Jewel moved in with Dr. Harvey. The following Monday, Jewel would start her new job with Ms. Clara, and life could return to normal for Char; but until then, she decided it was best for her to work from home. I was knee-deep in research at the DMV, looking for any names associated with a Jeep, but I was regrettably coming up with nothing. About every two hours, I would receive a text from Char, informing me of her progress. We had no one else to interview; we had exhausted all of our leads. We knew the criminal lab techs were being thorough and any DNA tests would take time. The only thing we could do was the hard work of going over every note, making sure nothing had been overlooked.

I noticed that by midday on Thursday, Char's texts had become somewhat testy, and she sounded short-tempered, but I said nothing. On Friday morning I had agreed to load the last five or six boxes in my Yukon so Char could clean the apartment and turn in her keys. She agreed to meet me at her apartment around 8:00 a.m. As I entered the apartment, I could see Char was feeling incredibly pressured. She tried to hide her anxiety, but we both knew she was at the point of exhaustion and tears. I waited for a moment before asking, "So, Char, what has brought you to this point?"

Char collapsed on the sofa. "Mike, Jewel is driving me crazy with her nervous chatter. I cannot pull all of our notes together with Jewel interrupting my train of thought twenty times an hour. If I go into my bedroom and lock the door, she stands outside my door and knocks. Jewel has gotten herself in a dither, and the more I ignore her, the worse she gets."

I thought about how much Ms. Clara said she does not like a Chatty Cathy, and I wondered if Clara could hold out when Jewels first started working and give her time to calm down some. I could tell that Char needed quiet, undisturbed time to pull all of her notes together and put them in order, and she could not do it with Jewel in the house. "Char, can Jewel be trusted at home alone? I mean, will she do something dangerous? If not, why don't you stay here today?"

"I can't because Jewel will drive Dr. Harvey crazy with her incessant chatter, and I don't want him to regret inviting us to move in with him."

"But Char, Dr. Harvey is at the morgue, and he will be there most of the day. He has three bodies from a car accident late last evening, didn't you know?"

Great relief washed over Char's face. "No, I didn't know. I locked myself in my room last night, and I left really early this morning. That means I can just stay here and work uninterrupted."

"Yes, and how about if I were to run over to Clara's and pick up a large hot coffee and several of her puffs for you?"

Char was not used to being the one cared for, and those tears of frustration that had been right at the surface turned into tears of gratitude. "That would be wonderful, Mike."

In less than thirty minutes, I again knocked on the door of Char's apartment and waited for her to answer. Then I waited until she swallowed some of the hot coffee and one or two puffs before I shared my conversation with Ms. Clara. I doubt that I could have brought any news more wonderful to Char's ears than the comfort of knowing that Ms. Clara would definitely not hurt Jewel's feelings on the very first day of work. As I shared all that Ms. Clara had said when I mentioned Jewel's being nervous and chatty about her new job, Clara understood and said, "I have a cousin like Jewel, and what was stressful for her was not so much the actual change because she was a great rule follower. The anticipation and the waiting was what was hard. You tell Char not to worry; Jewel will be fine."

I smiled at Char sitting on the sofa, as she realized that Ms. Clara did indeed understand. She could trust her sister's future work to Ms. Clara. At the same time, she also knew that telling Jewel would not alleviate her fears or calm her, but the knowing was calming to Char. *My mission has been accomplished.* When I felt that Char had calmed down sufficiently, I suggested, "Char, Ms. Clara mentioned that Jewel could start today—that we not wait until Monday. That way, she doesn't have three more days to dread her first day. If you'd like, I could go by the house and take her over to Ms. Clara's Café. That way Jewel will get into the swing of things, you can stay here and do your research, and I am free to follow any overlooked leads we might have missed."

I excused myself and left Char to work in peace and quiet, but as I reached her door, Char warned, "Mike, be watching for my texts. If I find a loose end, I'll have you follow it up."

I couldn't imagine why she would warn me about texting me—until my phone started vibrating. I had no idea how many texts I would be receiving that day. Char began digging deep, and by her texts, I could actually see how her brain worked. Although she would send a blizzard of texts, her logic proved fascinating. Char started with the people she felt were "short-fuse" types before moving on to what she referred to as "long-term grudge" holders. I needed to refer back to texts and reread some before I could see the orderliness of the pattern developing. I created a folder for the texts, naming it "Char's order."

I went right over to Dr. Harvey's home and told Jewel that Ms. Clara wished her to start today.

Jewel was surprisingly relieved to know that she would be starting work today. She quickly went into her bedroom and put on the uniform Ms. Clara had for her. She slipped her feet into the white shoes that would make standing on her feet for the long shifts a little easier and then pinned the small white cap on her freshly washed head.

When Jewel walked into the living room, she looked every bit the part of a dinner attendee, and she knew it. The nervousness was gone, and in its place was excitement, so I drove her over to Ms. Clara's, who was standing at the door, ready to greet her new employee. I watched Jewel confidently enter the café and knew this day would be a good one for Jewel.

But no sooner had I thought that than my phone buzzed yet again. Char's conclusions were more intuitive than factual—completely different from the training I had learned, but I could see how these connections could prove to be on target. My job would be to find the facts to support Char's intuition. Thankfully, our courts demand fact in order to convict someone, and to be honest, we were still *grasping at straws.*

All day long, my phone kept vibrating, warning me that a text was forthcoming from Char.

9:00 — POSSIBLE "SHORT-FUSE" PEOPLE TO LOOK INTO

10:05 — FOCUS ON THE WILCOMB FAMILY BUSINESS

10:10 — CHECK WITH SINCLAIR FOR NAMES TO FOLLOW UP ON THIS ONE

10:15 — SOMEONE HARMED BY OR ANGRY AT THE WILCOMB FAMILY FOR SOME UNKNOWN REASON

10:20 — NOW, SHORT TERM GRUDGES!

10:22 — MAX. AFTER HURRICANE KATRINA HIT IN '05, MAX WAS NO LONGER THE BUSINESSMAN'S GO-TO GUY—LIKE HIS FATHER WAS. HE HAD CHANGED YEARS OF THE WILCOMB HABITS.

10:25 — MAX WAS 79 AND POURED 5 MILLION DOLLARS INTO CALVIN'S POLITICAL CAREER.

10:26 — FIND OUT WHO COULD BE HURT BY THIS. SOURCE IS SINCLAIR. WE NEED TO CHECK THAT OUT.

10:29 — *Mike, looking over my notes, I cannot help but think of my professor who said, "Pay attention to the anomalies—the things that don't fit."*

Between 10:40 and 10:45 came a rapid-fire succession of texts, one right after the other.

▶ WHAT DOES NOT MAKE SENSE?

▶ ANY RATIONAL PERSON WOULD HAVE CHANGED THE TIRES; ESPECIALLY ONCE THE OWNER KNEW WE WERE LOOKING FOR THE THREE MISMATCHED TIRES.

▶ HOW DO WE KNOW THIS? WHY ELSE WOULD ANYONE DESTROY THE MOLDS?

▶ WHAT ARE THE TIRES TELLING US THAT WE ARE NOT SEEING?

Then, without a hiccup, Char shifted gears yet again, texting "ENTI-TLED-BORN."

11:05 — WE KNOW THAT MAX FATHERED TWO CHILDREN DUR-ING COLLEGE.

11:05 — *I see this as a long shot but a valuable lead; therefore, we need to pursue this link. Mike, remember the first day we were in Houma? You said Clara explained about NON-LA, LAT, AND LAW?*

I texted back Ms. Clara's explanation:

1] "LA" refers to those who are Louisiana born, but not Ca-juns and not blacks.

2] "Non-LA" indicates anyone, no matter how long they have lived here, are separated by the fact that they were not born in Louisiana.

3] "LAT" refers to those who were born in Louisiana, but specifically those who were born in Terrebonne Parish.

4] "LAW" alludes to those who are the most esteemed of all—those privileged few who were born into the Wil-comb family in Terrebonne Parish, Louisiana. Papa Joe himself created the label of "LAW" behind Max's birth announcement in the paper to differentiate his son from every other "LAT" son born in 1929, by adding an unofficial courtesy title like "Esq." at the end of his name. I know that "Esq." refers to a person of letters, specifically a lawyer.

At 11:25, Char began texting again.

I find it interesting that "LAW" was what Papa Joe chose.

"LA" stands for Louisiana born, and LAT stands for Louisiana born in Terrebonne Parish. Even though his son was a true "LAT," Papa Joe dropped the "T" and replaced that "T" with a "W" for "Wilcomb"—the most elite and prestigious label—the top of the top at least here in Terrebonne Parish. Surely sounds to me like Joe wanted to be royalty.

Another text soon followed that revealed Char was finally relaxing and getting her sense of humor back.

11:35 — CONSIDER PAPA JOE'S EGO: "BIG FISH IN A SMALL POND. GO FIGURE HE'D OWN A FISH CANNERY." LOL!

Char does not miss a thing with her remarkable mind. If a comment was made or if Char read it, she remembered it and automatically filed it with like-minded items. The only way I can describe her mind is like a steel trap.

11:45 — *I read that Papa Joe spent a bundle to have his son's birth announcement plastered on the front page, but Maximillion was born on 25 October 1929, and Joe was miffed that the Wall Street Crash bumped his son's birth from the headlines. Papa Joe and the LAW has programmed this parish since as early as the 1920s to be exclusively separate. I find it classic that the ones who titled his son the LAW in this parish are the wealthy and the privileged. That the lowest born of this parish hold him in such esteem and continue to perpetuate this myth even today—long after Papa Joe is gone.*

I was about to text "Can we meet somewhere and talk? I am getting a headache with all these texts…" when a final text marked urgent came from Char:

1:50 — LENNORD JUST TEXTED ME. DNA RESULTS ARE IN! WILL CALL IN 30 MINUTES. MEET ME IN THE WAR ROOM ASAP!

Even though her message had been relayed through a minimum of two towers to reach its destination, her excitement was palpable. I really didn't like the idea of brainstorming in the war room because I have never felt safe there. But the meeting place is her call, and I head to City Hall because she is the boss. At 1:55 I texted back quickly, "I'LL BE RIGHT OVER."

Just as I walked into the war room, Char's cell phone began ringing, and I heard her say, "Hello, Inspector Lennord! I surely hope your lab has found something useful because we are grasping at straws on this end."

Char grabbed a pad of paper and wrote some notes just as a knock came on the outer door. Before answering, Char quickly looked around the war room. When she was satisfied that all of her notes were either hidden or turned up-side down, she carefully opened the door and was surprised to see Dr. Harvey.

"Ms. Char, may I speak to you about your sister Jewel? I just received a telephone message that makes no sense to me, and I thought I should run it by you."

Char stopped him and said, "I'm sorry, Dr. Harvey, I'm on an important phone call with Baton Rouge. Can you wait until I finish?"

Dr. Harvey looked at her strangely. "Okay…but make it quick."

Char returned to her cell phone and said, "Sorry for the interruption. You were saying, Investigator Lennord?"

Suddenly Char's face turned ashen-gray, and she quickly took her seat. "You have got to be kidding me! How long?" She began writing a message on her pad of paper.

I was busy sweeping for bugs and wasn't paying attention to Char's conversation, but thankfully, Dr. Harvey was. He came up next to her and read—out loud—what she had jotted on the pad. "WE ARE BE-ING BUGGED—NOW!"

I turned around and said, "Dr. Harvey, that's impossible. I just swept the room for bugs."

Char stood up and signaled for us both to be quiet before returning to her phone call.

"Dwight, based on what you just told me, I believe it is too late! I will have to call you back. We need to do some damage control here, and we can lay all of this damage right at the Houma City Council's feet. They wanted to hide their failure and save face, but now, they have blood on their hands."

Char started to end the conversation, but Inspector Lennord had not finished. I heard Char say, "Okay, but make it quick" as she grabbed her notes out of Dr. Harvey's hands and whispered in his ear, "WE ARE BEING BUGGED; DON'T SAY ANOTHER WORD!"

I argued. "Char," I whispered, "I just swept the room for bugs…."

"Excuse me, Investigator Lennord, I must explain what is happen-ing to Dr. Harvey and Mike. Can the DNA results wait? I promise I will call you back when we are in a safe place to talk."

Char hung up the phone and put her finger to her lips, "Don't say a word! We are not safe here."

Dr. Harvey whispered, "Want to go to my lab?"

"Bugged too!" Char quickly responded. "The *entire* building!"

Dr. Harvey then whispered, "Even in the morgue? Are you sure?"

Char wrote in big letters, "**Let's go to Mike's car—ASAP!**"

We were barely seated in my car when Char blurted out, "Inspec-tor Lennord told me that everything—EVERYTHING—we have ever said, in that entire building, has been listened to! That means someone has heard Dr. Harvey's confession, Sinclair's confession, Calvin's con-fession—everything!"

She continued to explain, "Inspector Lennord's boss, who was called in to supervise a security breach here twenty-three-years-ago, told him *a story the City Council of Houma wanted kept quiet* to protect the fact that they had been duped. Because of that breach, two criminals walked free, and one potential killer's case was so compromised that the DA was ordered not to pursue it. Once Investigator Lennord mentioned our privacy issues, his boss told him the following story:

"In 1980 to 1982, a low-level receptionist working here in Houma accidently came across a glitch in the phone system and began using that malfunction to her advantage. Apparently, the most expensive phone system the parish has ever purchased and wired in City Hall has a major flaw. The parish was already upset at the extravagant purchase and they decided not to let the parish know about this news....

"Lennord said she happened on a way to hit the "telephone-conferencing" button, and anyone could overhear what was being said in that office via the telephone system—regardless of whether or not the phone was still on the cradle. The loudspeaker remained open until the telephone operator deliberately hit the conferencing button again. Lennord said any conversation in any of the offices in this building can be overheard anywhere the person wished to use the telephone conferencing button inside the building. Thankfully, this glitch cannot be used outside of the building."

"If that is so," I surmised, "the listener is definitely working in that building. Maybe that listener is the killer or knows who the killer is. Perhaps the listener is merely helping the killer—just like in the first case. Bug sweeps do not detect this listening device because it is not a bug; hard-wired phones do not transmit a signal. So, all of my bug sweeps were useless in our war room."

Char continued, "Lennord said his boss told him that this receptionist helped two criminals get off because she overheard the DA discussing the flaws in his case with his assistant, in what he thought was the safety of his office. The receptionist who overheard this private conversation promptly went to the criminal's lawyer, who just happened to be her boyfriend's lawyer at the time and told him all about the DA's weaknesses in his case. The lawyer used this information to convince the judge to toss out his case.

"That lawyer used the secret of this telephone system glitch to stay two steps ahead of the DA for each of his clients. One year later, she gave her boyfriend's attorney information regarding the suspicious handling of evidence she overheard the DA share with the Houma police chief. Her boyfriend's attorney walked right into court and presented the question of the chain of evidence before the judge. The DA and his team were rather confused by this unprecedented move because that particular piece of evidence had already been ruled out as the murder weapon. What this move did was expose the glitch because the DA knew he had been overheard. What the lawyer's action did was, it ultimately force the City Council to order the DA not to press charges, for fear of exposing the glitch. Apparently, the DA struck a bargain with the City Council, that as long as he avoided any mention of the murders, the DA was free to take the man to trial. They served a search warrant, and found three rifles and two handguns; a violation of his parole, plus, when they entered his house, the police found his girlfriend, the receptionist, beaten so badly, they were not sure that would not become a murder charge. They believed he blamed her for exposing the secret. In the end, the DA got the girl to testify against her boyfriend, and the jury gave him fifteen to twenty years, with eight years added for the prior parole violation."

Char continued, "Inspector Lennord just checked and that inmate is still in Angola Prison, but he is due for release in ten months."

Char suddenly remembered she had promised Dwight that she

would call him back. She pulled her out cell phone and hit speed dial. I suggested, "Char, why don't you put it on speaker so we all can hear him?"

Dwight answered on the first right ring with, "Hello, Char."

But before he went any further, Char warned him, "I have you on speaker phone, Dwight. That way Mike can hear you, and I don't have to write every word you say."

"Char, guess who that man was who got that tire iron made inadmissible and got the first-degree murder charges dropped? I just looked him up. None other than Sammy Snow." I looked at Char with a puzzled look because she appeared to know that name. "Mike, wasn't his one of the names on your DMV list of Jeep owners? Remember, you said we could cross him off our unsub list because he is serving a sentence at Angola Penitentiary and could not have been our unsub."

"Char, do you ever forget anything?" I smiled in embarrassment. "Sorry, Char, there were so many names; it just didn't click right away."

"It's okay, Mike, I just read your notes yesterday, that is why I remember the name. Those council members decided it was better to let that dangerous man go free, then to expose their blunder. If nothing else, I'd love to drag this man into court just so I could expose these men. The treachery in this parish is unbelievable.

Dr. Harvey, who had remained silent, spoke up, "I would suspect that all of those council members have died, so what would be the point?"

"You are probably right, Dr. Harvey. We cannot prove it all these years later, but Terrebonne Parish has had lots of secrets for lots of years." Then, with a satisfying look of justice, Char added, "It would teach this parish to look more closely at those they put in charge. Maybe, someday, we can change this parish, and make it a trustworthy place to live."

"Char, as I said earlier, the city council learned that this girl got two criminals off because she overheard the DA go over his case with his assistant in his office and mentioned how his case is flawed. Now, no one asked the hard question, "Why? Why go to that much trouble, risking so much?" I believe they didn't want to look too deep. The city council was trying to save face. I believe the police chief was ordered to take the stand and fall on his sword, so to speak, to blame that detective in question, for the careless **chain of evidence and got the judge to toss it out.** Guess who that man was? And guess who I just learned is related to Sammy Snow? He's *Gertrude Sander's* brother-in-law by her first husband, of course."

Char turned around and said, "That is *our link!* Gertrude Sanders is the one listening in on our conversations, and she had access to Sammy Snow's Jeep. We need to get a search warrant and check out Sammy's house. I feel sure that Jeep is parked in his garage. She knows about the glitch in the phone system, which the Houma City Council, was assured had been fixed!"

Char turned to me and said, "**Mike, everything we have ever said in that building was compromised!**"

I instantly felt sick as I went over everything. "Char, they know about Dr. Harvey's confession, Calvin Wilcomb's confession, and Mr. Sinclair's confession—all of it."

Then the real issue hit me, and I said, "Char, they know **where you live! They know where Jewels works and what her schedule is! They** know **how challenged Jewel is!**"

Dr. Harvey cried out, "That's what I been trying to tell you, Char. Something is wrong with Jewels!" He then went on to explain, "Because I cannot miss a single phone call warning me that a body is coming to my morgue, about ten years ago, I added a telephone messaging system that texts my cell phone whenever someone leaves a phone message at my home number. Well, I got a text telling me I had a message, and I called my house to retrieve it. Apparently, Jewel had called the house from the café saying that she was sad to hear that I was sick. She then said, 'I'm bringing you the hot soup you ordered.'" As emphatically as he could, Dr. Harvey added, "Char, I am not sick, and I did not order hot soup!"

Char grabbed her cell phone and called Clara, "Hello, Char here. Can I speak to Jewels, Clara?"

Char went white and said, "Clara, he isn't sick! He is sitting right here. How long has she been gone, Clara?"

Clara responded, "But Char, his assistant made it very clear that Dr. Harvey was on his way home with the stomach flu. She thought he might like some hot soup, so Jewel took it to him. It's only a two-block walk from here."

Char turned to me and cried out, "Mike, the murderer is going after Jewel—because of me!!"

I started my engine, calculating how long it would take me if I ran every light. "If I can make it there quickly, maybe I can stop Jewel! Buckle up because I am running every red light!"

I was already turning south on Main, just ten long blocks away. My heart was pulsing so hard, I tried to pay attention to my driving, but my thoughts were envisioning what she had done to the two other girls, and my mind cried out to God, "Protect her, God. She is too naive to distrust an old lady. God, she needs Your help because I can't get there in time. She needs Your help NOW!"

I pleaded, "Let me get there in time! Time for what? I could not say for I could not go there! Not sweet, little naive, Jewel!

I cried out a prayer, "Guide me, God!" The plumbing workers were still blocking the main road to Clara's. I knew it would take too long to get there. I hung a right turn to get off Main Street and decided to take

Launderale Drive, but right as I turned off Main Street, Char pointed to a dark-blue Jeep crossing the intersection right in front of me, heading south on Launderale Drive at a high rate of speed.

"Mike, follow that Jeep! "Char cried out, "Oh, God, she has Jewel, doesn't she?"

I hung a right turn and speeded up to the Jeep. I glanced toward the Jeep, but I could not see any sign of Jewel in the car.

"Mike, keep following her!" Char urged.

I did as I was told but responded, "Char, who is SHE?"

Char answered with absolute certainly, "It has to be Gertrude! She is the only one who fits."

"This is no coincidence here; Gertrude or not, I am not letting this Jeep out of my sight—Jewel or no Jewel," I assured her. Suddenly I have visions of Jewel sprawled inside Dr. Harvey's house and thought, *should I go directly to Dr. Harvey's residence? Oh, God, please direct me! Should I not have listened to Char? Oh, God, could I have saved Jewel if I had not turned and followed the Jeep?*

I accelerated and overtook the Jeep. I looked in the vehicle, desperately wanting to see Jewel tied up and shoved down on the back floor, but I didn't see her. What I did see was Gertrude Sanders driving Sammy Snow's Jeep, so I warned, "Brace yourself, I'm going to force her to the curb." I was out before my Yukon came to a complete stop. I ran around my car, to the Jeep, but Char was already out of my car, screaming at Gertrude, "What have you done with Jewel?"

Years of training suddenly kicked in; I grabbed Char and spun her around, placing my body between her and Gertrude. "Char, you didn't even check to see if she had a weapon before you began screaming questions. And you know you are never to ask a single question of an unsub before you mirandize the person. You know the rules, Char."

Right then, I spotted Clara's soup container on the floor, tipped over with the soup spilled out, so I knew Jewel had been near this car today. In my mind I was screaming nonstop, "Gertrude, what have you done with Jewels? What have you done with Jewel?" But years of practice at keeping my emotions under control kicked in. First, I made sure she was not armed, then I calmly read her Miranda rights and received an audible response—not just a nod of her head.

Always be aware of killers being tramped and spilling out their guts before you get the chance to read them their Miranda Rights is the first lesson for all detectives because we don't want what the person says tossed out of court. *I am going to nail Gertrude for three murders… and whatever she has done to Jewel.*

I wanted so badly to smack the face of the last person Jewel had seen; instead, I quickly checked her out, and somewhat relieved, said to Char, "There is no blood on her anywhere, and she did not have time to clean up."

I turned to our detainee and snapped, "Gertrude, where is Jewels?"

24

Motives Make Obscure Clues Clear

Taking a quick look at my right front tire, I could see that the collision had bent my rim. I was not going to be driving my car anywhere today. Not being sure that Gertrude was acting alone, I was certainly not going to leave this Jeep sitting here unattended, so I made a quick decision to drive the Jeep back to Dr. Harvey's house in hopes of finding Jewel. I pulled Gertrude out of the driver's seat, and as I handcuffed her, Gertrude winced with pain, and I noticed it was freshly burned and blistered. I felt no sympathy for this woman, as I pulled her around to the other side of the car, I called out, "Char and Dr. Harvey, climb into the back seat of this Jeep. We cannot drive my car." I pushed Gertrude down into the front seat, removed the handcuff from her burned hand and then cuffed her to the grab bar built into the dashboard. With Gertrude secured, I hurried back to the driver's side and climbed in.

I backed the Jeep up to free it from my Yukon, made a tight U-turn and headed back to Dr. Harvey's home, not really knowing what we would find. I found it rather disconcerting to hear Char calmly filling in the doctor on what we had learned. She started with the known, irrefutable facts that can be built upon. "Dr. Harvey, this morning the Baton Rouge Lab reported finding DNA that matches Maximillion Wilcomb."

At first Dr. Harvey sat speechless and then finally said, "I thought Dwight said they found the DNA was female? Now you are saying it matches Maximillion Wilcomb? In his condition? You couldn't possibly expect to sell a jury on this finding?"

"No, Dr. Harvey, they are not saying it is Max's DNA; rather it is a match to him—a blood relative who happens to be a daughter."

"But, Char," Dr. Harvey protested, "Max does not have a daughter!"

I thought, *And right there, in one sentence was going to be the problem for the whole parish—convincing them that they don't really know the whole of the Wilcomb family history.*

Char started quoting from those old articles, laying out how Papa Joe had bribed the girls who got into "trouble," rather than having his son marry one of them. "After all, the whole parish was aware of Papa Joe's plans, right?"

Dr. Harvey quickly nodded his head in agreement. Anyone who knew Papa Joe would understand to what lengths he would have gone. Yes, it was believable. As I listened to her talk, I felt as if Char was testing out exactly how she would have to present her case to the jury. "Well, Dr. Harvey, Max's daughter has been here living among you for thirty-seven years. May I be the first to introduce you to Maximillion Wilcomb's daughter, Maxine Gertrude Johnson Saunders." Char sat quietly, allowing the truth to settle in.

Then came a voice that had been quiet since we got into that Jeep. Gertrude herself broke the silence. "You have no idea how long I have waited to hear that truth come from someone other than my mother."

Char returned a cold stare. "So much that you murdered three women? Was it really worth it, Gertrude?"

Char quickly and succinctly explained the facts as we knew them to Dr. Harvey, then carefully wove in facts that she only surmised but could not yet prove. I suspected that Char was hoping Gertrude would correct her because her motives have been immensely important to her. This is also the first time she can tell her own story. Most assuredly, she does not want it to be told wrong; not now. She will not allow errors to stand uncorrected; after all, her whole life has been a comedy of errors.

"I never meant to become a killer. Killing was never my intention, but I overheard Calvin and his lawyer, Mr. Sinclair, that wretched snake-in-the-grass, talking about this girl who was threatening to expose Calvin. She had no qualms about ruining five years of careful planning and five million dollars of prep work to get Calvin into Louisiana politics. Sinclair was the man who continually stonewalled my every petition to perform DNA tests to prove that I am Max's daughter, so I thought if I took her out while Calvin wasn't even in the state, no one would look at Calvin. I would finally become the hero of the Wilcomb family."

Char and I watched as years of frustration showed on Gertrude's face, and her voice became hard and determined. "Then I heard how they were going to pay her off—just like they had my mother, stealing from me my birthright. They think money solves everything."

Char leaned forward and asked, "Why now? Gertrude, you have waited your whole life for this moment. Why now?"

Gertrude turned to Char and answered—as if we should have clearly understood her why. "Because I overheard them talking about Max's dementia, and I knew I didn't have much time."

Char wanted more clarity, "Much time for what?"

"For my father to remember me. You see, it's not about my being a Wilcomb; I've never cared about the money. I wanted my daddy to recognize me and to call me his daughter, and for him to remember my mother, like I always promised her, so he could remember me. I was running out of time."

Char responded, "And you thought murdering three girls was worth it?"

I held my breath, hoping Gertrude would not correct *that number!* To my relief, she said, "You don't know what it's like, not knowing who you are or where you come from. Having old women snickering behind your back and insulting your momma is brutal."

Char merely offered a pathetic, knowing stare and said, "Gertrude, many have lived with that hurt, and they did not become murderers. What a pathetic excuse for what you've done. You took a mother from her two little girls just so you could have YOUR dream come true, and you have now sent those little girls into a nightmare."

The coldness of Gertrude's response gave me chills. She turned to Char and said, "We've all had our nightmares, right, Char?" I could see no sense of guilt for what she had done.

I knew that childhood trauma marks a person, but it does not give them a pass for evil. However, knowing that childhood trauma was involved does help to understand the motives behind why they do the things they do. Looking over at Char, so cool and factual as she laid out these facts bothered me more than little bit. But then, knowing how Charlemagne Smalls is wired to handle drama, I realize this is exactly what she would do. Stay with the facts and avoid the hysterical drama of what might be coming is how Char, as a small child, learned how to defend herself against all the drama that was her young life. She had learned to stay calm and deal with all her unknowns only as they came in her life.

But I was fast approaching what might be a *watershed moment* for Char. *What did Gertrude do to Jewel?* You can only hide in facts for so long before those facts will bury you as I buried Tilly. As I reached the 1400 block of Lauderdale, I could see Ms. Clara quickly walking up the sidewalk, obviously coming from her café, and I pulled into the driveway at 1425 Lauderdale Lane.

As soon as I stopped and turned off the engine, Dr. Harvey's long-time next door neighbor, a woman in her eighties, all of one hundred pounds dripping wet, came out the back door of her house and started screaming and swinging around her much used rolling pin as if she was quite experienced at defending herself, shouting, "I dare you to get out of that car. You are not going to lay a hand on our sweet little Jewel again." She obviously had not looked in the back seat where Dr. Harvey was sitting. Then looking past this crazy old woman, my eyes settled on Jewel, panicked, but safe, saying, "Don't hurt him, Ms. Carlyle, that is my Mike Majors, and he is my friend."

I wanted to climb out of the Jeep and hug Jewel for being safe and alive, but I still wasn't sure Ms. Carlyle wouldn't hit me over the head as soon as I stepped out of the Jeep. But just as I thought that, Ms. Clara ran past my window and grabbed Jewel and started crying, "Oh Jewel, I thought you were injured for certain. I am so thankful you are all right."

Jewel laughed and said, "Char warned me about getting in a car with strangers, especially a blue Jeep, but that woman grabbed me so hard and tried to drag me into that car, but you saved me Ms. Clara."

Clara cried out, "How did *I* save you?"

Jewel laughed as she said, "Because you make your soup so hot. When I could not pull away from her, I poured your hot soup all over her hand, and then she let go. Then I just tossed the container in her car and started running. See?" She held up her arm, now bandaged by Ms. Carlyle. "All I got was a little burn."

I looked over at Char as she stood three feet away from her mentally challenged older sister. Her eyes filled with tears, and a sense of gratitude filled her smile. Stepping up to Jewel, Char wrapped her arms around her sister and said, "Jewel, just like that night with the fire, you came up with the best solution to protect yourself. You thought of pouring that hot soup all over Gertrude's hand so she would let go of you. I am so proud of you, Jewel. You really are the smart one!"

Jewel puffed out her chest, reminding me of a male peacock, standing there, getting ready to fan her tail-feathers in pride. I guess hearing praise from someone you admire is the best praise of all.

With Jewel standing right by her sister, Char pulled her cell phone out of her pocket and dialed the Houma Police Department. "Hello, ADA Charlemagne Smalls here. Please send a police car and a police tow truck to 1425 Lauderdale Lane. We have the Jeep we have been looking for, and we have the suspected killer of the three women as well. We need to have the police escort her to the jail where I will swear out a warrant for her arrest and book her into custody." Char was grinning from ear to ear as she asked, "How long will that take, Officer? Thank you, we will be here waiting for them."

Char turned to me and said, "Mike, as much as I would love to go inside, we need to stay with the Jeep until the police tow it back to the police impound yard. I am going to ask Investigator Lennord if he will send his team to pick it up on Monday. I don't want one little thing to be overlooked on this car. Too much is at stake."

Ms. Clara, Gertrude's oldest friend in the parish, had not said a word this entire time. She stood listening, adding up things, and absorbing the facts, and no one paid any attention. She waited until the police had come to arrest Gertrude and place her in the back of the squad car. After the police tow truck pulled away, she finally turned to Char and said, "Might I come in and ask you a few questions?"

Char returned a grateful smile to Clara, but said, "I'm sorry, but can it wait? I need to ride in with Gertrude so I can formally arrest her. I have a ton of paperwork to do so nothing gets overlooked. I should be back in about three hours. Can you stay away from the café that long?"

Clara leaned over and hugged Char. "I can stay for as long as it takes. I've been waiting for 23 years; three more hours is fine with me."

I noticed a strange look come over Char's face, one that I had seen often. It came whenever Char heard, read, or saw something that made a connection, and I thought, *twenty-three years? Where have I heard that?*

It was almost six o'clock before Char returned. I had tried several times to get Clara to talk but she wouldn't budge—not without Char. She did, however, call her husband, Michael Brown, and invite him to come to Dr. Harvey's house. I overheard her saying, "Mike, I really do need you here, and you do not want to miss this."

But I didn't know what *this* was. Clara was obviously nervous, unable to sit for more than a few minutes, she kept pacing back and forth. Her unusual behavior and having no idea what Clara was going to ask Char was making me uncomfortable—not to mention she was not talking.

When Char returned, she came in with her very professional attitude and called everyone to the table because she said she had something to tell us. I looked at Clara, who had waited so patiently to ask or to tell Char something, but she simply took a seat next to Jewel.

Char began, "Every professor drummed into us to look for anomalies as well as for patterns or similarities, and the three tires always bothered me. While I was waiting for the police to fingerprint and take Gertrude's photo, I called Investigator Lennord and asked for more information about that tire iron from that case 23 years ago. I have been bothered greatly ever since hearing that it was a tire iron that Sammy Snow had his lawyer get tossed out. I don't like similarities, and I have been trained to watch for links that might go together."

Char proceeded to tell everyone sitting at the table about the lengths Sammy and his lawyer went to in order to have the tire iron tossed out, and she continued, "Since that tire iron had already been excluded as the murder weapon, I was bothered by the lawyer going to the trouble of having it precluded from the evidence. I could only believe that he had a very good reason why he did not want a detective to look a little more closely at that tire iron. So, of course, I looked closer. I am not in any way suggesting that detective wasn't doing his job. Monday morning quarterbacking is always perfect. We had a car with three different tires! He had three dead women, and if he looked closely, he had a man with a car with three mismatched tires. I know this is easier for me because I have been looking for a dark-blue Jeep with three mismatched tires. But, he did not. When Sammy was arrested at his home, his Jeep was parked in the garage and never was taken into custody, and even that was due to his laziness. But to be fair, it wasn't in his face as it was in mine. That much we know. Not knowing about Sammy Snow, what we had to ask was *why three mismatched tires?* At first, we thought the car was owned by someone who didn't have enough money to buy a whole set of tires at once. Makes sense, right? But now, you add the fact that this lawyer risked losing his license for using illegally gained information to have a tire iron tossed—one that could not hurt his client—so I looked even deeper. Three mismatched tires and a tire iron just bothered me."

Char continued, "Then earlier today, Investigator Lennord said three girls were killed in the summer of 1982, and looking directly at

Ms. Clara, she added, "That was 23 long years ago, wasn't it, Clara?" The police couldn't prove they were murdered by the same man, and the murders in those cases were never solved. Now my brain was ringing. Three murders, three tires, and a tire iron had to be more than a coincidence. But then Investigator Lennord told me the name of the first victim."

25

Time Does Not Heal Old Wounds

URNING TO Clara, Char said, "Would you like to tell everyone the name of one of the victims, or should I say, the only victim who could have and should have been linked directly to that man, Clara?"

We all turned toward Clara, who was now struggling to control her emotions. "She was my daughter, Mikala. She was a senior in high school. I named her after her father, Mike Brown, and she was murdered by Sammy Snow 23 years ago."

Ms. Clara Tells Her Story

Turning to me, Clara explained, "Mike, that day you came into my café was a hard day for me. For twenty-three long years we had waited for someone to look into the murders of our local girls, but no matter how much we complained, the DA wasn't interested. What we didn't know then was, he knew about the privacy breach. I only learned about that today, but he knew about it and didn't want to re-open the case that he had botched. We were sure that Sammy was the one who had killed our daughter. She had driven her car, a 1979 Chrysler LeBaron out Long Turkey Road to pick up her girlfriend, but she never made it that far. A person who lived on Long Turkey Road told the police that when he was driving home about 5:30, he said he saw a *good Samaritan* changing a tire on a Chrysler of some sort, though he couldn't remember the color or the model and he didn't recognize the person changing the tire because his back was to him. He remembered his car was pulled up behind the car with the flat, his headlights were on, and he never saw a young girl in either car or standing around. But he remembered seeing a late model, dark-blue Jeep, pulled up behind the LeBaron with the headlights on. Then, later that night he came back down Long Turkey Road and the Chrysler was still parked there. No flat tire, no driver, no note, so he called the police. That was when we got the call. The police had Mikala's car, and she was missing.

"What that witness saw was *why* Sammy was arrested. He drove a dark-blue Jeep, and the police were well aware of how dangerous Sammy was and that he was on parole for a similar crime. When they arrested him, the tire iron from Mikala's car was tossed on the sofa, and the only reason the police even gathered it as evidence was because they thought he had used it to beat his girlfriend half-to-death. That was two days after Mikala went missing and four days before they found her beaten body about two miles off of Long Turkey Road. But the ME ruled out the tire iron, saying she was beaten by a piece of wood, as was the girlfriend, most likely a baseball bat.

"Because Sammy was on parole for a vicious beating in 1971, and because they found several guns in his possession, the DA refused to charge him with Mikala's death. No matter how loud we protested, he kept saying, 'We have no evidence to charge him with your daughter's murder.' He got Sammy on the beating of his girlfriend, plus he had to serve for his parole violation, he was looking at twenty years in Angola Prison. Everyone in the parish was just glad he wasn't still walking the streets, but our Mikala's murder was not solved, and no one cared but us."

Mike Brown, who had remained silent this whole time, finally spoke. "And all that DA was interested in was locking away Sammy. I bought that car for Mikala's senior present. I wanted her to have a reliable car when she was going out at night. The funny thing is the police kept the car, but right after Sammy went to prison, they returned the tire iron—I guess because it was not used in the trial."

Turning to me, he asked, "What did I need with that tire iron? I didn't have the car and wouldn't have driven it if they could have returned it. That vehicle was Mikala's pride and joy. Do you think I could have driven it around town after that?"

Then Clara added, "We didn't even know about the other two murders until months later. I don't know why the police thought it was the same man, but slowly, word got out that they thought it was the work of one man, but they would not explain."

Then turning to me, Clara explained, "Mike, we have not talked about our daughter for twenty years because the memory was too painful, but one week before you showed up in my café, our son found out he was going to be a father, and he had come to us, saying that if it was a girl, he intended to name her after his big sister, Mikala." Stopping to wipe away the tears, Clara continued, "Mike, of all the eating places you could have picked, you came walking into mine. I so wanted to be a grandmother, but I was afraid of loving another Mikala. What if something happened to her? I just could not go through that again."

As Clara said this, I remembered how rude she had been, and I finally understood her pain. But then she added, "Mike, I hated you before I met you. Do you understand how hard we fought with that

DA to find Mikala's killer? He was lazy and, as we now know, he was ordered not to pursue charges against him. He only went after charges he could prove. We wanted them to hire an investigator—someone like you, but we were told the parish couldn't afford one. Then all these year later, three more girls died, and they not only replaced Calvin and hired a new, hotshot ADA, but then they hired a thirty-plus year decorated detective from Miami. You came in here with that fancy suit of yours, and I could hardly talk to you that day. But no matter how rude I was to you, you were always nice in return, and you slowly won me over."

I smiled and said, "Well, it only took adding thirteen pounds to do it, and I can't even fit into that fancy suit you mentioned." The laughter around the table was tension-releasing, but I dared not confess how much weight I had really added. The thirteen pounds was just a low estimate, but to change the subject, I asked, "Mike, how did they know that tire iron belonged to Mikala's car?"

"Well," he said in his Louisiana drawl, "you see, I bought her that Chrysler LeBaron because Chrysler was having a hard time selling them and put them on sale. The factory that built the LeBaron M model was in Saint Louis, but lots of the parts were bought by Chrysler from companies down in Mexico in order to save money. In '78 Chrysler announced plans to retool that factory in '81 and begin building the K-Car. To differentiate between the jacks, the plants in Mexico painted the jack kits a bright red to distinguish the parts for the M-Car from the newer products for the K-Car, which they painted a green color.

"I had identified her iron by a mark I had made on it. You see, that tire iron came with three different lug nut sizes, and when I taught Mikala how to change her own tire, I found the right lug nut that fit her tire and made a mark on it so she could quickly change her own tire. So, you see, Mikala didn't need a *good Samaritan* to change her tire; I had already taught her." When the police called me in to look at the tire iron, I pointed out the double scratches that I marked on hers, thereby linking Sammy with Mikala, but that lazy DA said it only proved that Sammy was the *good Samaritan.*"

I studied this man for some time, before asking, "Mike, do you do that often? I mean, do you mark things?"

He smiled rather shyly before answering. "Well, yes, sometimes. Like when I took her car in for service, I scratched the oil filter, just so I'd quickly know that the mechanics installed a new one. You know, Mike, things were tough back then, and everyone was looking for ways to save a penny."

Things were coming together in my head, but I did not want to tell them where I was going with my questions. "Mike, let's say you were going to have the tires on Mikala's car rotated, would you have scratched them too?"

"Yeah, sure, I did that."

"Mike, do you remember how you scratched them? You couldn't just scratch one of them, right?"

"NO! I marked them all. Starting with the left front tire, I put one scratch right next to the air pressure valve. Then the right front tire got two scratches, then the back right got three scratches, and lastly, the left rear tire got four scratches."

"Now, Mike, think hard. Did that witness say which of Mikala's tires he was changing?"

Clara didn't wait for Mike to answer; she responded, "He said it was the left front tire."

"Are you sure of that, Clara?"

"Yes, why?"

"Clara, I just had a thought. Let me run it by Char before I say anything else."

Char was on her feet as soon as I said that. "Let's go into the living room and talk."

Before I could say a word, Char whispered, "Mike, I know what you are thinking, and it is brilliant. You intend to connect one of those three tires on the Jeep to Mikala's car; therefore, connecting it to Sammy Snow, aren't you?"

"Char, I don't think Mike or Clara realize exactly how close they are to solving their own daughter's murder of twenty-three years ago, and we cannot tip our hand. We already have a chain of evidence issue since the Jeep has been in Gertrude's hands for the entire time that Sammy has been in Angola Prison."

"First off," Char conferred, "we need to record Mike's testimony about how and why he marked the tires *before* he sees the Jeep. That way we do not have a slick attorney saying that he saw the scratch and made up the story."

Then Char suggested, "I think we should have everyone who was sitting at the table fill out a comparative statement of what Mike said to you before we tell them what we think and how we shall go about proving it in a court of law. Mike, say as little as possible to get them to write their statement. Do not lead them in any way. Do not mention the tires and the scratches. I want to put them on the stand and ask them how they were instructed to write what they wrote, and hopefully they will remember Mike's story of why he scratched the tires and can now be trusted to look at the four tires on Sammy Snow's Jeep and identify one of them as Mikala's tire.

I believe Sammy was such a smug, sick person, he took great pleasure in driving around town on top of *"his trophies."* That is the real reason Gertrude dared not buy all new tires; she knew how much all three of those tires represented the three girls he killed in the summer of '86. We might not be able to link the other two, but now that we know why there were three killings and his Jeep had three mismatched tires, we know what we are looking for. I just hope the other girl's cars are still in police custody. It's been a long time."

"Char," I pleaded, "you are the lawyer, and you will be the one who questions them in court. I'd feel much better if you instructed them. I do not want to say one word out of order here."

Char walked back into the dining room and said nothing as she placed several pieces of paper in front of everyone. "Without talking to each other and without looking at what your neighbor is writing, I want you to use the paper in front of you to write everything Mike Brown just said. Be as specific and detailed as your memory will allow. Be sure to identify who said what to whom, and when you are done, I want you to sign this paper, stating that it is true and that you have not been coached by me or Mike Majors in any way."

Char stood there to make sure no one asked a question or gave any advice until all the papers had been collected. Then Char asked, "Mrs. Carlyle, would you mind being a witness by signing each of these papers right below where they stopped writing. That way no one can accuse me of adding anything to these witness statements."

"Of course, my dear Char, I'd be happy to." So, by Char's instruction, as each person held up his hand when the affidavit was finished, she signed her name and dated it, right below each person's signature. Once everyone was done and the papers had been collected, Char explained why she had done this.

"For the past twenty-three years, Mike Brown, the father of Mikala Brown, has had no contact with Sammy Snow or his Jeep. We will have trouble proving that Mike Brown did not do this after the fact; all a good lawyer needs to do is link Gertrude and Clara, and the jury will toss out this evidence. We need to find another independent source to make this stick. Today, the Police Tow had already hauled away the

Jeep before Mike Brown arrived on Dr. Harvey's property. Did anyone mention this fact on their witness statement?"

Two hands went up: Mrs. Carlyle and Ms. Clara. "Good," replied Char, "two of you mentioned that important detail."

"Now, how many of you mentioned how Mike Brown said he marked parts on his daughter's car?" Everyone's hand went up. Again, Char was thrilled.

"Lastly, how many of you indicated that Mike Brown had scratched each of her four tires, and detailed what tire and how many scratches?" Again, all hands went up.

Turning to Mike Brown, Char stated, "Mike, I believe, you have solved your own daughter's murder, and if this proves to be what I think it is, you and you alone are responsible for putting her killer back in prison—where he belongs for the rest of his unnatural life. He is one month away from being released, and I suspect one of the first things he wants to do is drive all over Houma on top of his trophies. I believe he was taking off one of her tires when that witness saw him. I believe your Mikala was already dead, and her tire was his keepsake, or trophy, of the killing. If we can match the other two mismatched tires with the other two killings, even better. But I'll take this one. We do not want Sammy Snow walking or driving around this town ever again. The level of treachery in this parish was deep and profound, but I think we have finally reached the bottom of it."

Then, because Charlemagne Smalls is absolutely thorough in every respect, she simply could not hold back, "It is too bad that the real perpetrators of all of this treachery will never stand trial. The city council that hid the truth in order to save face were responsible for letting the murderer of three young girls go free. Then, because they wanted to keep the breach quiet, they are responsible for our three murders. They must have suspected, and yet they said nothing. Sinclair, desperately wanting to keep his secret, stonewalled Gertrude's honest attempt at getting her DNA because it might expose his sin, then he kept quiet when the killings continued. He knew that Gertrude must have held a grudge and still he kept quiet. And finally, there is Maximillion, who thought so little of his children that he allowed his father to bribe their mother and send them on their way—never even thinking about the children he created. To him, his trysts were a fun afternoon of pleasure and that is all, but to Gertrude, it was her whole life. All she ever wanted was for him to acknowledge her as his daughter, and she was driven to kill for it. None of these people set out to be accomplices to murder, but when we set out to deceive, we spin a web that not only entraps our enemy, it will snare us in the very web we spin for others."

Char stood up and finally said, "This following Monday morning, I will escort Mike Brown to the police impound where we will be attended by two police officers to inspect all four tires on the Jeep."

On that Monday, I was not going to be left behind, so I accompanied them. I could tell that Mike was nervous about seeing his daughter's tire on Sammy's Jeep, but he walked right up to it and pointed out exactly where the scratch was with a shaky voice. "That was Mikala's front left tire, Char. See, it has one scratch, indicating the right front tire." Char pulled out one of the witness statements, and asked, "Officer Benson, would you please swear that Mike Brown did not put that scratch on that tire today, that he only pointed to it, and that it is just as the witness statement says it is?"

"Also, would you mind taking a photo of this tire with the date stamped upon it and deliver it to my office by the end of today? The Baton Rouge crime lab will be coming to collect and inspect this car, so would you please cover the tires and lock the doors before they take possession?"

26

Justice Delayed Is Still Justice

Eighteen Months Later

FTER MANY months of painstaking legwork, there was no paperwork left on the other two murders that summer. My research showed that the first girl had been a member of a well-known parish family. Word had it that the younger brother had taken the car out to California, San Diego, to be specific, and had sold it before joining the Navy there. No one remembers the second girl's family, but old newspaper articles mention the father was deceased by the time the girl was ten years old, and that the mother was battling cancer when her daughter was murdered. No leads there at all.

Char was disappointed by the lack of leads that would have proven Sammy's pattern of collecting trophies but proceeded to build an airtight case over the next few months. She drove to Angola Prison, some 142 miles from Houma, on two different occasions to interview

Sammy Snow. Char had hoped that he would shed some light on Gertrude because the guards had mentioned that he was really angry that because of her, his tires were gone. But Char knew that Mike's testimony would not sell the jury on his guilt. It had too many gaps, and a good lawyer would plant too many questions in it, but having an unrelated case, with the same evidence, would have clinched it. Therefore, she and I continued building our case.

One day I was so nervous about how a jury could be persuaded, I decided to go through every single car stored in the evidence garage, matching up the paperwork with the actual car; just in case. It took me three long weeks of effort, but one day, I found what I was looking for. Behind a tow-truck, parking behind a Cadillac, I saw the bumper of a 1954 Plymouth Hi-Drive and climbed up on the tow truck to take a better look. There sat the two-toned, blue-and-white car I had been searching out for almost three weeks. I wrote down the license plate number and jumped on my computer to confirm it was the car that had gone missing twenty-three years ago from the impound records. Without touching it, I spotted one spare tire. It took two days to get the impound garage to move the Cadillac and the tow truck, but when they did, I had Inspector Lennord's team there waiting to take possession. That was a good day!! But then it got even better!!

After the Baton Rouge lab boys loaded the Plymouth onto the flatbed truck and signed for the evidence, I decided to take in my Yukon for service and watched the techs through the service bay window. One after another, I watched as the tire expert, whose bay was right in front of me, rotated the tires, or pulled a spare out of the trunk. Suddenly the tech's procedure caught my eye. I watched him pull out yet another spare, and I grabbed my cell phone and captured a photo of exactly how he lifted it out.

The answer was right in front of me as time after time, the tech

slipped his fingers into the round hub of the tire as he lifted it out of the trunk. I shot a message right to Lennord and instructed him to remove the spare tire off of Mikala's car—the car that had sat in police custody since the day Mikala was
killed. "Turn over the spare and fingerprint the inside center hub. Then do the same on the Plymouth as soon as it reaches your lab."

Two hours later we had our evidence—evidence no one could talk away. Three remarkably preserved prints of Sammy Snow on two cars had been protected by time and by the Houma Police Department. They were the proof that linked two murders. Then it hit me; if it worked for the spare, it could work for the Jeep. If Sammy lifted the tire like I saw the technician lift the tires on my Yukon, so must have Michael Brown. *If we can fingerprint the tires of the Jeep, we just might find his prints which would prove that these tires were trophies—not just tires. That Char can sell to any jury.*

Char was now satisfied that all our hard work was going to ensure that Sammy Snow would never be released from prison.

Once she had the proof that one of the mismatched tires on Sammy's Jeep could be positively identified by Michael Brown and once the Baton Rouge lab found his prints on two different cars, Sammy fate was sealed. Who would have thought to remove the lug nuts and remove the tires, but anyone who ever changed a tire knows that you don't pick up the tire by the rubber; instead, you reach into the center of the hub to lift it out. A lab technician fingerprinted the back side of that hole and found three clear fingerprints, protected all these years by being bolted where Sammy Snow had placed it.

Bringing Sammy Snow to trial required eleven long months. In

Louisiana, justice was not swift; however, it was going to be thorough, if we had any say in it. Because this trial would be Char's first of her career, she was determined to do it correctly. She leaned heavily upon her law professor for directions to prevent newbie mistakes, and she spent endless hours with Gertrude gaining insight into how she best might present her case. Once Gertrude realized that the evidence was splashed all over the local newspaper, she could no longer pretend that the Wilcomb family did not know about her, and still Max did not come to see her. She could no longer blame an overbearing father; Gertrude was running out of people to blame, and that deep hurt was hurtful to watch. Sitting in the Houma Jail not twenty minutes from his home, her father could not say traveling to see his only daughter was too far. After months of sending several petitions by mail, the family would not bring him to see her.

Only after her last ray of hope had faded and the truth of a face-to-face meeting with her father would not happen did Gertrude begin to talk to Char. I remember Char coming home quite upset after one of their long meetings. Gertrude was very aware that Charlemagne Smalls was looking to put her in prison, but once all her hope was gone; she no longer cared. That lack of caring upset Char.

"Mike," she said, "watching a person devoid of all hope is terrible, especially one who went to the great lengths that Gertrude did to achieve it. Now all she wants is for this to be over, to be found guilty, to serve her time and do her penance for what she has done. She says she simply wants to forget what she did and eventually forget her father as he has forgotten her."

"Mike, you won't believe it, but Gertrude turned around today and looked me straight in the eye and said, 'Char, it's the dementia; I waited too long. She is still lying to herself. She is blaming the family and the dementia for why he isn't coming—not on his lack of character. So, I guess there is a little thread of hope still alive, but not good hope. Why do people do that? Wouldn't it be easier to face the truth and accept it?"

I remember treading very carefully on that question, knowing that Char was asking a deeply profound question, and I didn't want to trample down on her. After all I am not a psychologist, but I am an expert of the human condition and spending all this time with Gertrude was causing Char to question her own path out of the same bitter childhood. Char questioned how blind she had been to all the lies she had told herself. I knew that Char was questioning her own blindness as she watched Gertrude work so hard to avoid the truth that was staring her in the face. Hers was a question I had NO right to answer; it was Char's. I would always be there to support her until Charlemagne Smalls found her answers.

I was so proud of Char that day. She was finally looking at herself and asking, "Why?" I knew God was going to answer an honest why question and lovingly connect those dots between herself and Gertrude. The answer did not happen overnight, but I heard Char's answer. It was the day the jury came in with a guilty plea on Gertrude. As everyone congratulated Char for her brilliant work in solving five murder cases in six weeks and getting two convictions after only being an ADA for less than two years, she hushed everyone seated around Dr. Harvey's table. And Char opened with a confession of her own.

"I really appreciate all the accolades, I really do, but I've been doing some deep soul searching since I've witnessed how Gertrude's past motivated her killing. She and I have deeply similar wounds of being unwanted, discardable children, and the lengths she went to in order to force society to recognize her worth are frightening. Once I said those words, I remembered thinking, *that was how I felt my whole childhood.*

I could not argue the other children out of the insults because they were all true; they knew it, and I knew it.

"Then I read the book *Evidence That Demands a Verdict* that your Tilly gave to you, Mike. It was all about proving that Jesus was not a liar, for society to recognize who Jesus is and what He did for us.

"The evidence is so powerful even I could take it into court and prove that He did raise from the dead. But then, just as with this case, the key to breaking it wide open was the motive—not the clues because the clues made no sense until you understood what fears were driving the killer.

"Then it made perfect sense—not sane sense—because murder is never sane, but once you understand the fear behind that motive, it makes sense, at least to the perpetrator. So, I started looking at why I had resisted God's love so many times and why I had resisted what Jesus had done for me. I looked into my motives and my fear behind it.

"Looking honestly at your fear takes courage because there is where all your secrets lie or have been hidden. But looking at Gertrude, I finally wanted to stop being blind to mine as she was and sadly still is to hers. So, I started with my birth. I know that I am a product of a New Orleans streetwalker's profession. I will never fully know who I am. I have known this since I was in the first grade. Mine is a wound not too dissimilar to Gertrude's. But I took another path—a healthier one than Gertrude did—but just as unsatisfying. I set out to prove society was wrong about me. I spent my youth studying, earning top grades, garnering awards, scholarships—anything that I could do to force society to acknowledge my worth.

"But the reward is unsatisfying because regardless of how hard I worked, I could not shake the feeling that I still believed I was unworthy. No amount of rewards could shake that inner feeling. Being only one year out of law school and solving five big murders might impress others, but it cannot shake loose who I know I am deep down inside. That is where I needed to start.

"And I started where that book suggested: *If Jesus is who He said He is and if He rose from the dead with enough eyewitnesses that it could be proven in court, why wouldn't I trust Him?* Then I read *The Purpose Driven Life* by Rick Warren because I knew I wanted to find purpose in my life; all I ever wanted was to know that I had a purpose for being born. Spending so much time with Gertrude and watching how she so needed validation from others, I knew I needed to look at myself. Oh, I didn't kill people, but seeing that hunger in her eyes was a look I have often seen in my own—my needing validation and purpose are what I have strived for since I was a little child.

"Being humiliated by everyone, not knowing who my father was, being the daughter of the town's streetwalker was bad enough, but the other children being told to stay away from me, just like Gertrude strived to prove she was a Wilcomb, made me strive to prove my worth. I started proving my value by earning good grade, becoming the top of my class, and winning scholarships. Unfortunately, none of that satisfied me; the hollow praise lasted for a moment and then vanished. Mike, I don't mind working hard, but it has to be for a right purpose. When I read the title *Purpose Driven Life*, just like *Evidence that Demands a Verdict*, I felt these books you loaned me were written just for me.

"So, Mike, I prayed the prayer at the back of that book and asked Jesus into my heart to save me and to make me one of His children— something none of my hard-working effort and awards could grant to me or qualify me to become.

"I know God has a purpose for my being born, even if my earthly father was simply pleasuring himself and could have cared less about the child he was creating. But the Bible says that He purposed us from the foundation of the world, that we are knit together in our mother's womb, that we are not a mistake—an illegitimate nobody—God loves us, and He wants a relationship with me."

Finally, I sensed it was my turn to confess something. "And Char," I added, "it takes a purposeful God to have put us two together. I needed to find purpose in my life after I lost my Tilly, and you needed to know that your life wasn't just a mistake. I believe God purposefully sent me to Terrebonne Parish to share His love with you, to finally close the wounds for Mike and Clara, and to finally shelter Jewel from harm. God made that happen by sending me here.

"Char, I didn't do it. I am not that intelligent, but God is. I could never have known how much He was offering me when that strange job offer came in—without even an interview required. You don't know how close I came to tossing it out. That night back in Miami, the thought of moving to Terrebonne Parish—especially for someone who hates fishing—looked dismal for sure. I am sure glad that my Tilly said, 'Mike, when you ask God for direction, walk through any door that opens; you never know what He has for you.' Not only would I have missed this wonderful adventure here in Terrebonne Parish, but I would have missed seeing God work so wonderfully in so many lives.

Epilogue

My Final Do-Over Begins

I T IS now 2020, and I just finished writing about my experiences in Terrebonne Parish. I moved to Terrebonne Parish in 2009; that was eleven years ago, and new doors continue to open for me. Once Char had established herself as a successful ADA, securing five solid convictions and sending Sammy Snow to prison for the rest of his natural life, that next year, Charlemagne Smalls became the DA of Terrebonne Parish, and no longer needed me. Jewel was happy and secure working at Clara's café, and it thrilled my heart to see both Clara and Mrs. Carlyle mothering Jewel and giving Char a break from years of watchful responsibility for her sister. Char could finally consider her own future, and soon a young man joined our close little group who both Dr. Harvey and I believed was right for Char. Believe me, that was a hard sell!

I was glad to see that my purpose in Terrebonne Parish was coming to a happy end, but in 2014, at sixty-seven years of age, and although I felt free to leave, I was not ready to hang up my skills and retire. Six wonderful years had now passed, and being six years older, I was certain another Terrebonne Parish would not be looking for a 67-year-old sleuth still capable of ferreting out clues, unmasking lies, and connecting the obscure dots. But that is what almost forty years of being a detective has created.

So, again I followed Tilly's suggestion and asked God to open a door for me. And guess who He sent? None other than my old friend Inspector Dwight Lennord, now facing the harsh reality I was facing six years earlier. He called and asked, "Mike, are you was free for dinner?"

Over that dinner, he explained that Baton Rouge was looking for "young blood," and as was true of most police departments; the problem was no one equated "young blood" with "inexperienced blood." So Dwight had been dabbling with the idea of going independent, hanging a shingle, and offering help to those who had been caught up in a corrupt, biased, and lazy system.

He had experienced the famous "Innocence Project," who had come into Baton Rouge in the winter of 2013. They were lawyers, but they needed skilled detectives who had our unique same skillsets to do the legwork the others had ignored, and then covered up by fast-talking DAs, looking for a fast and easy conviction. The citizens wanted someone held responsible and didn't question the speed of justice.

One thing I know for sure, Lady Justice, to be right, does not move quickly. It takes time to prove a man innocent, but if you are simply looking for someone to sit in prison, that can be done fast and dirty—without any justice. When police are pressured to "find" someone, anyone will do. Ignoring leads that take too long to follow are buried in the minutia of a blizzard of paperwork, hoping no one will spend the hours of digging through them to find the trust. Lazy DAs think as long as they have their man, who cares? All they want is a fast guilty from a jury who sadly believes the police have done a thorough job. Once the criminal is walked into the courtroom in police handcuffs, they already believe he is probably guilty. But as Dwight reminds me, that person is seldom from the upper classes because they can afford to hire the help they need. We need to focus on these most vulnerable that the lazy system most abuses. By the end of dinner, I knew this job had my name written all over it. I went home that night and decided to list my home in Miami for sale. I told God, "If You don't want me to do this, don't let it sell. If You do, then sell it quickly and give me some kind of sign that this is what You want me to do."

The people we want to help will not be able to pay for our services. I intend to use the money from the sale of my home to bankroll the opening of our detective agency. We are not lawyers, but we know how the system works, and we both know how to ferret out leads that could have and should have proven a man innocent. Hence began:

THE MIKE MAJORS DETECTIVE AGENCY
Where it is as important to prove one man is innocent
as it is to find a dozen ones guilty.

In the last six years, Dwight and I have been responsible for unmasking coverups by lazy DAs, biased police, and a system that no longer believes you are innocent until proven guilty. We have assisted three men to prove their innocence and escape an inevitable prison sentence. You might think that saving only three men from prison isn't such great deal, but they would be if you were the one being railroaded and sitting in a Louisiana prison. And I can honestly tell you that I sleep well at night, knowing my days are purposeful, and righteous, and I know my Tilly would approve.

Who knows, maybe one of these days, my skills might be called upon by someone you love—not because of the lifestyle that loved one had lived, but simply because he or she was in the wrong place at the wrong time. You might need someone willing to spend the long dog days of tracking down the leads that others ignored. But then again, let's hope you never need my services; but if you do, just look up **The Mike Majors Detective Agency**; remember that name. Maybe I will write another book about my experiences and expose some of these stories—when I finally retire and have the time to write about them. After all, what else can I do with my retirement years? Remember? I hate fishing! Maybe I'll call it a *Mike Majors Mystery.*

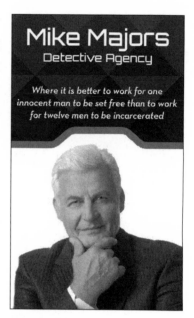

Mike Majors
Detective Agency

Where it is better to work for one innocent man to be set free than to work for twelve men to be incarcerated

About the Author

DOREY WHITTAKER has spent the past twenty-five years polishing her gift of storytelling with this, her sixth, novel. This is an amazing accomplishment considering the fact that Dorey was deaf until age thirteen and illiterate until the age of seventeen. Her greatest accomplishment—learning how to read opened doors for her, taking her places she could never go and meeting people she could never meet. Reading opened new worlds for her that she could not even imagine. This fueled a hunger in her to study these authors and learn their secrets, that had changed her life for the better. Books became her teachers, her best friends, her schoolroom, and her invitations into an amazing life that she had never dared to dream; now she is that author.

She is the one who invites you to come sit, read, and meet friends who will make your life richer and fuller because you now know them.

Available on Amazon:

DEFEATING THE GIANTS SERIES
Book #1
Wall of Silence

Book #2
Hope Returns

Book #3
Treasure in a Tin Box

Book #4
The Attic on Sycamore Lane

Book #5
Stonehaven: The Shadow Dweller

Check out this first novel of the Stonehaven Saga
in Amazon's Audible Audiobooks
to hear Buzzard Bill tell this story
as only this humble, self-effacing man can.

Visit Dorey's website:
DoreyWhittakerbooks.com

Made in the USA
Columbia, SC
02 July 2020